THE YEAR OF
THE GUN

A WAPC LOTTIE ARMSTRONG MYSTERY

CHRIS NICKSON

THE YEAR OF THE GUN

The
Mystery
Press

First published 2017

The Mystery Press is an imprint of The History Press
The Mill, Brimscombe Port
Stroud, Gloucestershire, GL5 2QG
www.thehistorypress.co.uk

British Library Cataloguing in Publication Data.
A catalogue record for this book is available from the British Library.

ISBN 978 0 7509 6984 0

Typesetting and origination by The History Press
Printed and bound by CPI Group (UK) Ltd

PRAISE FOR

Modern Crimes: A WPC Lottie Armstrong Mystery

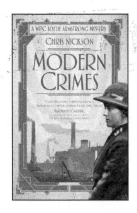

'This was masses of fun to read; with its incisive historical detail, colourful Leeds references and strong female characters. Lottie Armstrong is simply wonderful. I want to be Lottie. She is a force to be reckoned with.'
northerncrime.wordpress.com

'Nickson's rich, outstanding and complex characters and his attention to historical detail will keep you riveted to what is also a story strong on social comment and which brings to life the city itself.'
crimereview.co.uk

'No author has used the city of Leeds as a backdrop for crime stories so profoundly as Chris Nickson.'
crimefictionlover.com

CHAPTER ONE

Leeds, February 1944

'WHY are there suddenly so many Americans around?' Lottie asked as she parked the car on Albion Street. 'You can hardly turn a corner without running into one.'

'Are you sure that's not just your driving?' McMillan said.

She glanced in the mirror, seeing him sitting comfortably in the middle of the back seat, grinning.

'You could always walk, sir.' She kept her voice perfectly polite, a calm, sweet smile on her face. 'It might shift a few of those inches around your waist.'

He closed the buff folder on his lap and sighed. 'What did I do to deserve this?'

'As I recall, you came and requested that I join up and become your driver.'

'A moment of madness.' Detective Chief Superintendent McMillan grunted as he slid across the seat of the Humber and opened the door. 'I shan't be long.'

She turned off the engine, glanced at her reflection and smiled, straightening the dark blue cap on her head.

Three months back in uniform and it still felt strange to be a policewoman again after twenty years away from it. It was just the Women's Auxiliary Police Corps, not a proper copper, but still... after they'd pitched her out on her ear it tasted delicious. Every morning when she put on her jacket she had to touch the WAPC shoulder flash to assure herself it wasn't all a dream.

And it *was* perfectly true that McMillan had asked her. He'd turned up on her doorstep at the beginning of November, looking meek.

'I need a driver, Lottie. Someone with a brain.'

'That's why they got rid of me before,' she reminded him. 'Too independent, you remember?' McMillan had been a detective sergeant then: disobeying his order had put her before the disciplinary board, and she'd been dismissed from Leeds City Police. 'Anyway, I'm past conscription age. Not by much,' she added carefully, 'but even so…'

'Volunteer. I'll arrange everything,' he promised.

Hands on hips, she cocked her head and eyed him carefully. 'Why?' she asked suspiciously. 'And why now?'

She'd never really blamed him for what happened before. Both of them had been in impossible positions. They'd stayed in touch after she was bounced off the force – Christmas cards, an occasional luncheon in town – and he'd been thoughtful after her husband Geoff died. But none of that explained this request.

'Why now?' he repeated. 'Because I've just lost another driver. Pregnant. That's the second one in two years.'

Lottie raised an eyebrow.

'Oh, don't be daft,' he told her. He was in his middle fifties, mostly bald, growing fat, the dashing dark moustache now white and his cheeks turning to jowls. By rights he should have retired, but with so many away fighting for King and Country he'd agreed to stay on for the duration.

He was a senior officer, effectively running CID in Leeds, answerable to the assistant chief constable. Most of the detectives under him were older or medically unfit for service. Only two had invoked reserved occupation and stayed on the Home Front rather than put on a uniform.

But wartime hadn't slowed down crime. Far from it. The black market had become worse in the last few months, gangs, deserters, prostitution. More of it than ever. Robberies were becoming violent, rackets more deadly. Criminals had guns and they were using them.

And now Leeds had American troops all over the place.

'Back to Millgarth,' McMillan said when he returned, balancing a brown paper bag carefully in one hand. 'If nothing's come up while we've been gone, you can call it a day and get off home.'

Good, Lottie thought. The Co-op might have some tea left; she was almost out. She didn't hold out much hope for the butcher by this time of day, though. At least it had been a bountiful year in the garden: plenty of potatoes and carrots and a decent crop of peas and marrows. One thing about all this rationing, she hadn't gained any weight since it started. If anything she'd lost a little; clothes she'd worn ten years before still fitted.

She followed McMillan into the station and up the rickety wooden staircase, gas mask case banging gently against her hip. Why she bothered with one, she didn't know; most people had stopped carrying them. On the landing a poster read *Coughs and Sneezes Spread Diseases*, the words so faded they were almost invisible. His office was the second one along a corridor where the old linoleum curled at the edges and the paint flaked under the fingers.

'Quiet for once,' McMillan said as he inspected his desk. 'Close the door.'

'Sir?'

'Chop chop.'

She did as he ordered, then watched him reach into the paper bag and draw out two eggs. Real, fresh eggs. When was the last time she'd seen any of those?

'Go on, take them. They're for you. When I saw Timmy Houghton he gave me four. Or don't you want them?'

Lottie scooped them up carefully, swaddled them in a handkerchief and placed them in her handbag.

'Of course. Thank you.' She didn't know what to say. He had a habit of doing things like this. A little something here and there. A pair of stockings, some chocolate. Even a quarter-pound of best steak once that tasted like a feast. In the three months she'd been working for him she felt spoilt. It was his way of thanking her.

At the bus stop she cradled her bag close, miles away as she dreamed of the eggs, maybe with a sausage and some fried bread. The kind of breakfasts they had before the war. So many things had changed after Chamberlain spoke on the radio. Most of all, her life: two days later Geoff was dead from a sudden heart attack at work.

He'd left good provision for her. The man from the Pru came and explained it all. Insurance would pay off the mortgage on the house they'd bought in Chapel Allerton. There was an annuity as well as a pension from his job as an area manager at Dunlop. She'd never want for anything.

Her life was comfortable. Even Geoff's death, even the war, couldn't seem to shake her out of it. She was sheltered, numb. Lottie burrowed into it, hid in it. She was just too old to be called up for war work. Everything seemed easier that way. Until McMillan knocked on her door and turned her life upside down.

And she couldn't remember when she'd been so grateful.

CHAPTER TWO

'DON'T take your coat off,' he said as she walked into the office. Half-past seven, growing light, but with a bitter, miserable wind in the air. What she wanted was to sit for a few minutes and warm up. She wasn't going to have the chance.

Lottie gathered up the car keys and followed him out of the door.

'Kirkstall Abbey,' he said as she started the engine and felt the power of the Super Snipe's engine.

'Yes, sir.'

'We have a murder.'

The old monastery was only three miles from the city centre, standing by the River Aire. It was hard to believe this had once been the middle of nowhere, she thought. But that was what they'd taught her at school; she still remembered it. They drove past the loud thrum and activity of a dozen workshops along the road, all going round the clock to win the war. Traffic moved in a steady flow.

The abbey had been a ruin for centuries, a shell of what it used to be just as surely as if Hitler's bombs had landed on it. Lottie parked the Humber at the tail of a line of cars, close to the path that led down to the ruins.

A knot of men had gathered around one of the buildings, eight or ten of them together. She could pick out Detective Inspector Andrews with his stooped, crooked back, and

Detective Constable Smith following on his heels like a puppy, the way he always did. A few uniforms, and then two men in army khaki. What were they doing here?

Lottie looked sharply over her shoulder at McMillan. 'Who's dead?'

'An ATS girl,' he answered. 'You'd better come along.'

She walked at his side, hunched inside her greatcoat, looking around, taking it all in. She and Geoff had come out here regularly; he loved the history of the place. This was the first time since he'd died. For a second she half-expected to see his ghost wandering over the grass, rubbing the stones and staring up at the sky. But there was only the empty cold of winter.

'What do you have for me?' McMillan asked as they tried to shelter from the frigid wind.

'She's inside, sir,' Andrews said, 'as much as anywhere can be round here. In the chapter house, just off the cloister, through there.' He gestured vaguely. 'I thought you'd better see her before the coroner hauls the body away.'

'Who found her?'

'A woman walking her dog first thing. Scared the life out of her.'

McMillan nodded and rubbed his hands together against the chill. 'Do we know who she was yet?'

'Her name's Kate Patterson. ATS private. She's a kinetheodolite operator, whatever that is. Just twenty-three, poor girl. From Redcar. Stationed at Carlton barracks.'

The Chief Superintendent studied the ground. Too hard for any useful footprints. 'How was she killed?'

'Not so good, sir. A gun. Single shot. Up close, powder burns on her clothes. No other wounds that I can see, nothing on her arms, doesn't look as if she put up a fight…' Andrews shrugged helplessly. He was a man with too much on his plate already and dreading this.

A girl in the service, shot to death out here. That was as bad as it could be, Lottie thought.

'Right, I'd better take a look. Which way?'

'Follow me, sir,' Lottie told him, leading him through the old church, its roof long gone, and down a pair of steps to the cloister path around a square of scrubby grass, then to the arched opening of the chapter house.

Such a bleak, terrible place to die, she thought. So bare and barren. A stone floor, windows open to the bitter east wind. Kate Patterson had probably come here with a man, seeking a private place for a little companionship, a few minutes of loving, and he'd killed her. At least someone had put a blanket over the body to offer her some decency.

McMillan pulled the cover away. Grunting as he knelt and steadying himself with one hand on the ground, he peered closely at the corpse. Lottie watched, standing silent, notebook and pencil in hand in case he had any thoughts. He simply moved around like a crab, then stood, took a torch from his overcoat and shone the light on the floor.

Stone. Not much to see. A dark patch of blood under her where flies and God knew what swarmed, even in this cold. Empty eyes staring up at the stone ceiling. It was damp enough to chill the bones; Lottie shuddered.

'God,' McMillan said finally. 'Why?'

'Are you giving the case to Andrews?' she asked.

'No.' He shook his head. 'This is the first girl who's ever been shot to death in Leeds. She's in uniform, too. I'm going to look after this one myself. The brass will insist on it. Anyway,

Andrews already has enough to keep him busy until Doomsday.' He glanced around. 'Do you know this place?'

'A little. It's not as if it changes much.'

'Sarah and I came out years ago when the children were small. She's not one for history.'

His kids were grown now, one boy in the army in Burma, another air force ground crew, his daughter a WREN somewhere down south. He wore that nagging fear she saw on the face of all parents. She and Geoff hadn't been able to have children; sometimes it seemed for the best.

'Were you looking as we drove out here?' she asked.

McMillan gave her a curious glance. 'At what?'

'We passed one pub down the road, but it looks like a local, not the type of place you'd go for a pick-up. There's nothing bigger until much closer to town.'

'What are you trying to say?' He stared at her, eyes narrowed.

'Whoever brought that poor girl here didn't just stumble on the abbey by blind luck. There's nothing nearby. And he certainly wouldn't have found the chapter house without knowing the layout. No lights round here, never mind the blackout.'

'The perfect place,' he said quietly. 'Especially if he intended to kill her. Far enough away from all the houses that nobody would hear the shot.'

'That's true,' Lottie admitted. 'But think about it: unless they really were at that pub down the road, they made a special trip. That means they'll have taken the bus or a taxi.'

He shook his head in wonder. 'You've worked that out in ten minutes. My men have been here for two hours. I knew there was a reason I wanted you working for me.'

'It seems obvious, that's all.'

'Not to everyone, apparently. I'm going to need to talk to these Army and ATS people. Can you get whatever information Andrews has found? Tell him to send some of those bobbies who are milling around down to the pub and ask questions, and get others on a house-to-house round here. I want everyone working flat out on this.'

'Yes, sir.'

By the time he returned to the car she'd read through everything and placed it on the back seat. Only a few sheets, the basics. She saw the black coroner's van arrive and the men in their brown shop coats carry out the wrapped body, no expression on their faces.

'Where now?'

'You're the one with the bright ideas this morning. I'm sure you read the bumf.'

'For what it's worth.'

He paused for a fraction of a second. 'Did you see the body?'

'I tried not to look.' Lottie hadn't wanted to watch but she'd been unable to turn away. Now the image was burned in her mind.

'I don't blame you. Shooting her… I don't know what's happening to this country. Why on earth would anyone kill a girl like that?' In the mirror she could see him staring out of the window and chewing on the flesh around his thumbnail. 'You know, something did strike me. She was lying on her back. Her head was pointed towards the – what did you call it?'

'The cloister.'

'Yes. So whoever was with her was deeper inside that room.' He was silent again. 'Don't mind me, I'm just thinking out loud. I'll have the evidence boys go over that place with a

15

fine-tooth comb. With a little luck we can find the cartridge. The post-mortem should tell us something.' He glanced over his shoulder at the ruined stone tower of the abbey. 'Do you think there'd be anyone in a place like that at night?'

'I don't know.' Lottie answered, then thought. 'Could be a tramp, I suppose.'

'That's possible,' McMillan agreed. 'Once we're back at the station I'll start asking around. It's worth a shot. If a tramp was there he might have seen something.'

'The newspapers are going to play all this up,' she warned.

'No, they won't,' he told her. 'Not yet, anyway. You won't read anything about it. A quiet word and it'll be hushed up. Bad for morale.'

'I see,' Lottie said doubtfully.

'Don't you agree?'

'I'm not sure.' It was an honest answer. If you couldn't trust the papers, who could you believe? Surely people could handle the truth. 'Millgarth?'

'Soon as you can.' He stared out of the window as she drove along Kirkstall Road. Business and factories, and on the other side stood houses, rising up the hillside towards Burley. Nowhere to attract the young looking for some fun and games.

She'd learned to drive twelve years before, when Geoff sold the motorcycle and sidecar and bought a car. A Morris Minor first, then the Morris Eight once they started selling them. Lottie loved the freedom it brought. Lock up the house and go anywhere you want; it was perfect. But she'd never dreamt she'd become a driver. There'd been so much in the future she couldn't anticipate.

She heard the rustle as McMillan glanced through the papers.

'She was in a barracks in Headingley,' he said.

'Maybe her friends will know where she was going.'

'Let's hope so.' He sighed. 'We've got enough with the Jerries and the Japs trying to kill our troops. We don't need our own people doing it, too.'

On the way back into town she passed a pair of bombed-out buildings. Almost three years since the last raid and they hadn't been pulled down yet. Leeds had been lucky; not even a dozen visits from the Luftwaffe and very little damage. Not like the footage of London and Liverpool and Hull that she'd seen in the newsreels. Or the devastation that had once been Coventry. And she was grateful.

There were two other WAPCs in the canteen. Lottie carried her tea over to join them. Helen was a telephonist, handling the switchboard, while Margaret worked as a records clerk. Stuck in offices all day, they envied her the freedom of being a driver.

'At least it's never going to be boring,' Helen said. 'And you get to see what's happening.'

'All that fun out there in the cold and wet?' Lottie said. She wasn't going to mention the murder. They'd hear about it soon enough, anyway. 'The heater in that car hardly works and I've been trying for a fortnight to get the garage to put on new back tyres. No rubber, that's what they tell me.' She shook her head from side to side. 'Don't you know there's a war on?'

They began to giggle, ducking their heads together. Ten minutes later Lottie was sitting there alone as the others returned to work.

But they were right, it *was* a good job. She enjoyed working with McMillan, they had an easy relationship that had built over the years. For the most part the work was interesting. Her fifty-five hours a week passed quickly, almost before she realised it. And she was doing her bit. It was certainly more satisfying than the volunteering at the nutrition centre she'd done before.

But this was going to test her, she knew that. Kate Patterson's dead face came back into her mind.

'Tell DC Smith I want him to check all the taxi companies and see if they had a fare out to the abbey last night,' McMillan said when she returned to the office. 'If he can drag himself away from Inspector Andrews, that is.'

Lottie's mouth twitched into a smile. If Smith stuck any closer he'd be following the other man home at night.

'Yes, sir.'

'After he's done that he can talk to the conductresses on the Kirkstall Road buses. See if anyone remembers a young couple.'

'Will you be needing the car again today, sir?'

'Yes. I'm meeting Private Patterson's CO at the ATS head-quarters in an hour.' His voice was quiet, very sober. 'Then I'm going to talk to the girls she shared a room with in the barracks. I want you with me for all that.'

Standing back from Clay Pit Lane, Carlton Barracks looked cold and imposing, the Victorian brick black with years of soot. Lottie had never been inside; she'd never had a reason. It carried the air of an institution, everything regulated and ready to stamp out all traces of individuality. McMillan showed his warrant card to the sentry at the gate. Lottie eyed the rifle hanging from the soldier's shoulder, polished and menacing.

She trailed behind the superintendent, through an office where a harassed lance-corporal muttered to herself as she rummaged through a stack of paper. A door was open and beyond it, an officer. She was a smart, alert woman in her early forties, hair neat and short, her uniform tailored, eyes an unusual deep blue, intelligent and questioning.

'I'm Captain Hayes.' She stood and extended a hand. 'Private Patterson...'

'We're going to find whoever killed her,' McMillan said before she could continue. Not a trace of doubt in his voice.

The captain paced behind her desk. She wanted to understand, Lottie thought, to try to make sense of it all. To give it some order and reason. But how could you, when it was so senseless?

'I just don't see...' the woman began, then, simply: 'Why?'

'We don't know yet.' His voice softened. 'I've been doing this job for a long time and it's always bad when there's a woman involved. I'm sorry, I truly am. Have you told the other girls what happened?'

'Just that she was murdered. That was hard enough. I didn't tell them how.'

'Thank you. I need that to stay quiet. You understand.'

Hayes nodded. 'I've never lost any of my girls before, Superintendent. I didn't imagine I would, not up here. This is supposed to be a safe posting.' She gestured at the pen and paper on her desk. 'Now I have to write to her parents. I don't even know what to say.'

'It's hard, I know that,' he agreed. 'I served in the last war.'

Hayes nodded. 'Do you have any clues at all?'

'Not so far. We've just started. We will, though. And I'll make sure her killer hangs.'

'Thank you.' She tried to smile but there was nothing behind it. 'I prepared her file for you.' The woman hesitated. 'I hate to speak ill of her when she's barely dead, but I'd better tell you: Private Patterson wasn't exactly a model ATS girl. She's been up on charges several times: reporting back late to barracks, sometimes drunk.'

'I understand she was a kinetheodolite operator?' McMillan asked, and the woman nodded. 'What's that?'

'It's an instrument that lets us track the trajectory of shells,' she explained. 'Quite skilled work. Very specialised.'

'Was Patterson good at it?'

'Very. That's why I was willing to tolerate a lot from her. If her behaviour had been better she'd have been a corporal by now.'

'Do you have the girls from her barracks here?'

'I do. They're waiting in the canteen, the far side of the square.' She pushed the folder across the desk. 'This is a copy for you.'

'Interesting woman,' he said. They walked around the edge of the square as a sergeant-major with a voice that could reach across the Pennines was putting recruits through their drill.

'Sounded like she was trying to appear concerned when she didn't really have a good word to say about Kate,' Lottie said.

'She did make Patterson seem like a bit of a wild one, didn't she?'

'Maybe her friends can tell us more.'

They were gathered at the far end of the canteen, three young women, heads close as they talked, sadness in their eyes.

'You get the teas, I'll make a start,' McMillan said, and passed her a sixpence.

By the time she arrived he was already talking to them. The girls all had that pale, sober beauty that sorrow brought. Losing a man overseas was one thing; that was the risk of war. A friend murdered in the safety of home was entirely different. Too close, too real.

'She always got to know about parties and that,' a blonde woman with a Birmingham accent said. Her fingers twitched at a cigarette. 'If she was going somewhere you knew it was a fun place. Kate was like that.' She glanced at the other faces, receiving nods of confirmation. 'She didn't deserve anything like this.'

'Did she have someone special?' McMillan asked. He took out a packet of Four Square cigarettes and offered them round.

'No,' a brunette with a hard face told him. 'She didn't want none, neither. Lost her fiancé in North Africa a couple of years ago and decided she wasn't going to get tied down again. Not until it's all over, anyway.'

'Was she a popular girl?' Lottie wondered, and the eyes turned to her.

'How do you mean?' the blonde asked.

'With the other girls. With men.'

The three girls looked at each other and began to laugh.

'Blokes couldn't get enough of her,' the brunette said finally. 'She knew what she wanted, if you get what I mean.' She blushed slightly. 'I know she's dead and that, but it's the truth.'

'She liked to live up to her reputation, too,' the blonde added with a smirk.

'What did the other girls here think about that?'

A shrug as a response.

'She didn't care.' The last girl spoke slowly. She looked almost too young to be in uniform, still very thin, her skin smooth, features not yet fully formed. Her face was pale, as if she'd been crying. But her voice sounded older, wiser. 'That was the thing about Kate, you see: she didn't give a monkey's. She was good at her job, but as soon as it was over, she was out to enjoy herself. Whoever wanted could come along.'

'And did you?' Lottie watched them all. 'Go along, I mean.'

'Sometimes,' the brunette admitted. 'She'd be off on her own if no-one else was interested.'

'What about last night?' McMillan asked, looking at their faces. 'Did any of you go out with her then?'

'I took the bus into town with Kate.' The young one again. 'We both got off on the Headrow.' A long silence, then she spoke with a catch in her voice. 'That was the last I saw of her.'

'Did she say where she was going?'

'No. I don't think she knew. She just wanted to be out and doing something. Feeling alive.' She realised what she'd said and her face crumpled.

Feeling alive. Lottie let the words echo in her mind. Treasure the moment because who knew if there'd be another. Like so many these days. Who could blame them? It had been the same the last time around. Grasping those few minutes, knowing they couldn't last.

Even if the Allied landings in Italy had put the first scent of victory on the air, the end was still a long way off. Plenty more would die before any armistice.

'What about you?' Lottie asked. 'Where did you go?'

'I was meeting a chap. We went to the Odeon, saw *To Have And Have Not*. It's very steamy.' She reached into the breast pocket of her uniform. 'This was in Kate's locker. I thought it might be useful.'

An address book. It might be valuable. Lottie took it.

A few more questions but no more information they could use. A pair of detective constables would go through the rest of Patterson's belongings.

'Kate sounds like she was desperate to be the life and soul,' Lottie said as she drove cautiously out of the barracks.

'Or she was drowning her sorrows,' McMillan grunted.

CHAPTER THREE

I N the office she dropped Patterson's ATS file on the tottering pile of papers. That was the thing about a murder case: in just hours the paperwork grew like Topsy. But it was still too soon for the results of any searches or the post-mortem.

'I'll fetch us some tea,' Lottie offered and McMillan nodded absently as he started to glance through the reports.

'No, wait,' he said before she'd reached the door. 'We're going straight out again.'

'Him?' Lottie asked. 'He's got to be sixty-five if he's a day.'

'His name's George Chadwick,' McMillan told her. 'And I doubt there's anyone who knows this area better.'

She'd parked by the blue police box on Kirkstall Road. They could see the constable approaching. He looked sound enough, with a firm, easy gait, but the bushy white whiskers, thick moustache and the deep lines on his face gave away his age. McMillan rolled down the window.

'George. Over here.'

The bobby squinted, trying to make out who'd spoken, then his face broke into a wide grin.

'Mr McMillan. Not seen you in donkey's years, sir.'

'I heard you were back for the war.'

'Colin Selby joined up. I wasn't doing much and me missus wanted me out of the house more, so I became a Special Constable...' He shrugged and gave a hearty laugh before his face turned sombre. 'I hear you want to talk about tramps out this way.'

'I've got an ATS girl who was shot to death at the abbey. I wondered if anyone dossed down there who might have heard or seen anything.'

'I heard about her. That's...' He couldn't find the words, shrugged his shoulders and collected himself. 'There are two who spend time out there. I've been looking for them since I got the message but there's neither hide nor hair today.'

'Is that normal?' McMillan asked. He had his head cocked, listening attentively. Lottie was paying attention. The copper might be knocking on a bit for the beat, but he sounded sensible enough.

'They come and go,' Chadwick said. 'No telling really. There's Harry Giddins, he's scared of his own shadow. Took bad in the last war and never got himself right again. And Leslie Armistead, he's as gentle a soul as I ever met. If you want my opinion, sir, they've probably made themselves scarce, what with all the attention round there.'

'I'll still need to talk to them both. Find out if they saw anything.'

'Fair enough, sir.' The constable nodded. 'I'll try to track them down for you this afternoon. You might do better if I'm there when you question them, if you don't mind me saying so. They trust me.'

McMillan smiled. 'I can probably arrange that. Call in as soon as you find them.'

Lottie turned the car and began the drive back into Leeds.

'Back in 1912, George Chadwick took on a man armed with a knife,' McMillan began. 'Chased him for a mile then brought him down. Stabbed in the arm. Joined the Leeds Pals, survived the Somme. Wounded twice, decorated for gallantry. I've plenty of time for someone like that.'

'I'm sorry.' She felt chastened. 'I didn't know.'

'I trust his judgement.' He lit a cigarette and stared out of the window.

They passed a US Army lorry that was parked at the side of the road. Three men stood at the back, laughing and smoking. They all looked so... Lottie struggled to find the right word. Fresh. Clean. Scrubbed.

Happy.

That was it. They always seemed to be smiling, as if they didn't have a care in the world and nothing could touch them. So different from the British, ground down by the years of war, rationing, walking around with grim, grubby determination. Hanging on. There'd be time for joy after the job was done.

She was waiting. Only to be expected, she supposed, working for a senior officer, although she'd rather be doing something than sitting on her behind. Lottie had never been one to relax easily.

She'd learned to carry a book with her, something from the library. Along with the newspaper, it filled the time. A Peter Cheyney thriller, or maybe James Hadley Chase. Georgette Heyer if she was in the mood. And there was always Daphne du Maurier – she'd read *Rebecca* seven times since it was published. But McMillan always seemed to interrupt just as things were becoming interesting. As if he knew and wasn't going to let her become too comfortable.

'We're going to Headingley,' he announced as she slipped a bookmark between the pages. *The Power and the Glory* would have to wait.

'Whereabouts?' she asked as she nosed the car through the traffic on the Headrow. Blast walls protected the large glass doors of Lewis's, and the huge water containers of the National Fire Service still stood on the central island in case of air raids. They were empty now, rusting, unused; please God they'd never be needed to put out fires.

Lottie turned on to Woodhouse Lane, then out past the university and the moor. The sky was grey, the threat of sleet in the air. Past a rag and bone man, trundling along, the horse drawing his empty cart. But who threw things away any more? The government had taken everything worthwhile.

She turned on to Shire Oak Road and within a few yards she was in a different Leeds. Large, spreading trees. Big houses, expansive gardens. Room to breathe, it seemed, nothing cramped. The humps of Anderson shelters showed in a few places, disguised until all that was visible was mounds of sod.

'We're looking for a house called Woodmarsh,' McMillan told her. 'Strange name.'

She scanned the words carved into the stone gateposts. No iron gates now, of course; they'd long since been fashioned into Spitfires or Hurricanes. Finally she spotted it, at the far end of the street, set apart from all the other buildings, looking down the hill over Meanwood Valley.

The house looked abandoned, in need of attention. She counted four slates missing from the roof, the garden was overgrown, and weeds poked through in the drive.

'Park on the road,' he told her.

'But it looks empty.'

'I know.' He was smiling. 'Come on.'

The front door was unlocked, the wood warped. He pushed at it with his shoulder until it gave, swinging open. Inside, the rooms were bare boards and empty walls. Anything that could be carried away had long since gone.

The house smelt of decay. But there was more. An empty gin bottle that had rolled into a corner. A pair of knickers tossed on a windowsill, a torn handkerchief bunched up against the skirting board.

'What is this place?'

'Someone came here to enjoy themselves,' he answered wryly. 'Can't you tell?'

'It looks... miserable.' How could anyone find pleasure here? Lottie glanced around. A couple had found an empty house for a good time. 'I don't understand. What does any of this have to do with the Patterson case?'

'We had a telephone call from a neighbour this morning,' McMillan told her. 'He said he glanced out about midnight two nights ago and saw someone carrying a girl in his arms to a Jeep. She looked as if she was passed out. His words,' he added carefully. 'That's why we're here.'

'I still don't understand how that connects to Patterson. Was she wearing an ATS uniform?'

'He didn't see. I don't know, it's a hunch,' he said, as if that explained everything. 'As soon as I saw the message I got a feeling in my gut. I just wish he'd rung when he saw it happen, instead of thinking it over for so long.' McMillan rolled his eyes in frustration. 'The public.'

'There's not too much to see in here now.'

'Enough, though. We'll take a nosey around,' he insisted. 'I'll look in the bedrooms if you want to search here and out in the garden.'

The clean-up must have been quick, probably done in the darkness. A few items still remained. Not just the abandoned knickers, the handkerchief, and the empty bottle. Cigarette ends. She stirred them with her fingernail. Player's. Lucky Strikes. People had been here, they'd had sex. But it didn't look like the aftermath of a party. Outside there was nothing. A rusted spade, a fork, and an empty cup, all caked with dirt as if they'd sat there for months.

McMillan's tread was heavy on the stairs. At the bottom he turned and looked back up, as if he was assessing something.

'What is it?'

'Nothing much. All I really found was this.' He held out a crumpled note.

It was a man's handwriting; Lottie was certain of that. Small, cramped. An address on Lower Basinghall Street.

'At least we have somewhere to go,' she said. 'But I'm still not convinced. I haven't seen anything that says Kate Patterson was here.'

'It's just… call it copper's instinct.' He groped for the words to explain. 'Sometimes you *know*. I'm going to get the fingerprint and the evidence crews out here.'

Lottie glanced at the crumpled underwear.

'Was she wearing knickers when her body was found?' The uniform skirt had been in proper order; impossible to tell.

'No idea. It'll be in the pathologist's report. Put those in a bag and bring them along.'

She did as he ordered, picking them up with a pencil. Silk. Expensive. Not something you'd get at Woolworth's with clothing coupons. She took the handkerchief, too.

'I need to talk to the chap next door first,' McMillan said. 'See if I can get more from him.'

'He said the girl was put in a Jeep?' Lottie asked.

'Yes.'

'There are American cigarette ends on the floor. Lucky Strikes. British ones, too.'

'Then the Yanks were involved. And if I'm right and Kate Patterson was here, you'd better prepare for some hands across the water.'

The neighbour was waiting expectantly outside his front door. He looked close to eighty, comfortably plump even on the ration, a yellow waistcoat bulging over his belly. The type who didn't approve of a woman in uniform; she could see it in the glare he gave her.

That was fine. She could sit in the car, open her book, and spend a little time with Graham Greene and the whisky priest. As she sat, a tune popped into her head: *Imagination*. She'd heard it twice on the radio in the last week and now it wouldn't leave her alone. She didn't even particularly like it. She began to read, humming under her breath and wishing the song would go away.

It was impossible to park on Lower Basinghall Street without blocking the entire road. Even walking down it gave her the creeps. The buildings rose to block out all the light and warmth of the day; it felt like stepping down into a chilly cellar.

'Number seventeen,' McMillan said. Judging by the brass plates outside the main door, it was a warren of offices. Insurance, a commissioner for oaths, manufacturers' representatives, a jumble of mankind scraping a living.

'What name?' Lottie asked.

'It's not written down. Just the address.' He raised an eyebrow. 'Well?'

'Just a thought: maybe a cup of tea before we start. We can make a plan. We don't even know what we're looking for.'

He jingled the coins in his pocket and nodded, glancing again at the list of businesses.

'Probably a good idea,' he agreed.

At least the British Café in the crypt of the Town Hall did a decent cuppa. Strong enough for a spoon to stand up, plenty of sugar. A bunch of servicemen crowded round one of the tables, caps through the epaulettes, cradling the mugs lovingly as they talked. A woman walked by, her legs a curious brown colour, the stocking seam a suspiciously crooked line. Painted with diluted gravy browning, the seams marked in with eyebrow pencil. God, Lottie thought, that was vanity.

'How do you suggest we approach it?' McMillan asked. He lit a Four Square, holding it with fingers stained gold by nicotine.

'Maybe someone at Basinghall Street has the keys to the house.' She'd considered it as they walked. Something to do with business seemed the only feasible connection.

'That's possible,' he allowed.

'If it's someone young, they might have been at the party.'

'Good thought.' McMillan nodded. 'If there *was* a party. I'm not convinced it was as wild as that.'

'What did the old buffer next door have to tell you?'

'Evidently the chap who owned the house died a year ago. The will's in limbo for now. One of the heirs is dead, the other two are off fighting. I'll get someone to track down the solicitor and ask questions.'

Lottie ran her cup around the rim of the saucer. She knew what she wanted to say; finding the words was the hard part.

'This seems to be an awful lot of work just for a hunch.'

'We know someone was in that house,' he told her.

'Yes,' she agreed slowly. '*Someone*. A man and a woman, maybe more, we can't tell yet. And with a Jeep and the Lucky

Strikes, one of them could well be American. But that's *all* we know. Right now there's absolutely nothing that links it to the Patterson murder. No evidence. Only your hunch.'

She felt better for getting it off her chest. He was a detective, he had a good record, but nobody was right all the time. At least they'd known each other long enough for her to be candid. 'I'm sorry,' she added.

'No, you're right,' he agreed. He didn't look annoyed. If anything, there was relief on his face. 'See, this is why I'm glad I asked you to be my driver. You stop me getting carried away. You're right: the feeling is all I've got. But I can sense it.' He stubbed out his cigarette in the ashtray. 'The P-M and the other reports won't be in until late afternoon. I've nowhere to turn before them. And this feels right. That's why we're following it.' He stared until she nodded her agreement.

He started from the top floor while Lottie worked her way up from the ground. Office after office of old men who looked expectant and hopeful when she opened the door. Each time she disappointed them. No one knew anything about the address on Shire Oak Road.

The last door. Finally. A Commissioner for Oaths. She didn't even know what that was. Perhaps Ewart Hardy could tell her.

He was close to seventy but still with a twinkle in his eye, the *Times* spread across his desk. A clipped moustache, a good suit, old but cared for, a heavy beak of a nose.

'How might I help you, young lady?' An educated voice, crisp and clear. He looked like someone who'd retained an appetite for life and found it endlessly amusing.

'I'm WAPC Armstrong, sir. We're making a few enquiries in the building.'

He gestured at a chair. 'Make yourself comfortable and enquire away. It's a pleasure simply to have a visitor during the day. A lovely young lady is a bonus.'

Lottie smiled and sat, back straight. Who could turn down a compliment like that?

'Are you familiar with Shire Oak Road, sir?' The same question she'd already asked a dozen men. This time though, it brought a surprised gaze.

'I should hope so. I live there.'

She felt a shiver along her spine. Something. She had something.

'Whereabouts, sir? I know it's a fairly long street.'

'The cheap part, I'm afraid, down towards the shops on Otley Road,' he answered with a bewildered smile. 'Why, what's going on?'

'Do you know the empty house that looks out over the valley?'

'I do. It's funny, someone was asking me about it just last week.'

'Oh?' Lottie took out her notebook and pencil. 'Would you mind telling me about it, please?' she asked, trying to make it sounds like nothing.

'An American,' Hardy told her. 'I think he was an officer. It's so hard to tell with them, isn't it? There was something on his shoulder, anyway, and a hat, not a cap. I was walking past, going to take the dog down on Woodhouse Ridge. He was standing by the entrance to the house, with his hands on his hips.'

'What did he ask you?'

'Who owned it, how long it had been empty, if it was for rent.' He shrugged. 'The usual things, I suppose.'

'What did you tell him, sir?'

'Not a great deal. I didn't know much. It's been vacant a year or so. I wrote down the address here for him. Said if he came in I'd see what I could do. But he never turned up.' He paused, just a fraction of a second, then smiled. 'You found my address there.'

He'd already put it together, not that it took a genius.

'Can you remember anything about the man?'

'He was taller than me. Broader. But the Yanks are all like that, aren't they? Strapping.' He stroked his chin as he tried to recall. 'I didn't pay him much attention. We only talked for a minute or so. Oh,' he said suddenly, 'he had a mole on his right cheek. Bang in the middle. I do remember that, I thought it was a smudge of dirt at first.' He grinned and for a moment she could see the cheeky schoolboy who still lurked under the old skin.

'Was there a Jeep parked close by?'

Hardy frowned. 'Not that I recall, no. I'm sure I'd have noticed.'

'Which day was it? Do you remember?'

'Thursday. I'm positive about that. I'd closed at twelve, I had an appointment with the doctor. Went home and took the dog out before I went to the surgery.'

Last Thursday. Today was Wednesday. Six days. She wondered if that meant much.

'If anything else comes to mind, could you ring Detective Chief Superintendent McMillan at Millgarth?'

'Of course,' Hardy agreed easily. 'But I doubt there will be.'

At the door she turned. 'If you don't mind me asking one more thing, sir, what exactly does a commissioner for oaths do?'

'Very little these days, it seems.' He gave a rueful sigh. 'But the idea is we take affidavits and witness documents that have to be done under oath. Things like that.'

'Thank you.'

'Good work,' McMillan said when she told him. 'You haven't forgotten the job, at least.'

'If I read the instructions properly, I'm not supposed to be doing the job at all,' she reminded him. 'I'm just a driver.'

'Then you can drive us back to the station. And you're still better than most coppers on the force.'

'Do the Americans have a base round here?' Lottie asked as she nosed the car down Commercial Street, weaving around the vans and pedestrians.

'They must have, from all the numbers around. I know there are a few of them out at the old Masonic Hall.'

'What's that?' she asked, pushing hard on the brake to avoid an old woman who had strayed into the road.

'It's the HQ for this area. More high ranks and decorations than you can shake a stick at, all parading around and looking important. Not the best idea considering it's supposed to be hush-hush.'

Standing at the bottom of the stairs in Millgarth, for a fleeting moment she thought about Cathy Taylor. They'd been police-women together, two decades before. The only two on the force back then. On patrol together every day. They were friends after a fashion, but never that close; Lottie was always surprised that Cathy had resigned from the force after her dismissal. After that they met a few times for a cup of tea, exchanged Christmas cards for a while, then drifted apart. Where was she now? Doing war work? At home with children?

A long time ago. Truly another life.

Standing in the bathroom, Lottie caught sight of herself in the mirror. She desperately needed her hair styled; it had been over two months. There was too much grey in there, it made her look old. And feel it. Saturday afternoon, she decided; she'd make an appointment on the way home.

A banging on the door pulled her out of her thoughts.

'Are you hiding in there?' McMillan shouted.

'Just coming.' She rubbed a sleeve over the shiny WAPC badge on her cap and put it back on her head. 'Where now?' she asked as she emerged.

Lottie had to check the Leeds map she kept in the car. She'd never heard of Castle Grove Masonic Hall before. But there it was, in Far Headingley, no more than a stone's throw from the Cottage Road cinema.

The house was a grand pile of weathered stone, looking bleak and unloved in the winter light. It could have belonged to a family that had once been wealthy and lost most of its money. But the staff cars parked on the gravel and the sentries on the gate told the truth.

The warrant card got them inside. She glanced in the mirror. McMillan looked strained, heavy bags under his eyes. He ran a hand over his shiny scalp.

'Should I wait here?'

'You might as well come along,' he said. 'No one's going to notice another uniform. Maybe if you trail around behind me they'll think I'm someone important.'

But nobody had much time for a civilian. This was a fishing trip, she knew it as much as McMillan, but no worms were nibbling. After a quarter of an hour of being shuttled around they ended up with Master Sergeant Andersen, his close-cropped hair so blond it was almost invisible. Tall, broad-shouldered in his tailored olive drab uniform, impeccably polite and with the whitest teeth she'd ever seen, he listened patiently before shaking a cigarette from a green packet of Lucky Strikes and lighting it.

'We do have some troops in the area,' he admitted. 'But I'm not sure why you need to know, if you understand me, Chief Superintendent.'

'The incident I mentioned,' McMillan told him. 'From the description, the Jeep had an American insignia. We want to make sure the young lady who was carried out is fine.'

Andersen ran his tongue around the inside of his mouth. 'Has any girl been reported missing or injured?'

Would McMillan mention Kate Patterson, Lottie wondered? How public was he willing to be with his hunch?

'No.'

'Then you can appreciate I'm reluctant to say more. It sounds a bit like—' he flashed a brilliant smile '—a storm in a teacup. That's what you guys say, right?'

'Maybe it is,' McMillan agreed. 'I'm just trying to make sure the storm doesn't overflow on to the table.'

'I don't know anything about this house you've mentioned, OK?' Andersen waited for a nod. 'Something like that would be completely unacceptable if it's true. But right now it sounds like all you've got is rumour and conjecture.'

'We have an American officer with a mole on his cheek who was asking about the place.'

'Doesn't mean anything to me.'

'And there were cigarette ends,' Lottie pointed out. 'Lucky Strikes, like yours.'

'Standard PX issue.' He held one up. 'And plenty of GIs give them away or trade them for something.'

'Yes, we've all heard for what,' she said, surprised at how prudish she sounded. 'But we know there are Americans here.

I've seen plenty of them in town. That's hardly a secret. We'd just like to know *where* they're stationed. After all, Sergeant, we're the police.' He wouldn't know she wasn't really a copper.

'Ma'am,' he began, then: 'What the hell. You can probably find out through other channels if you want. We have a detachment of men out at an RAF base. Church Fenton.'

'That's not especially close to Leeds,' McMillan said.

'This is the nearest big city.' Andersen shrugged. 'If a guy's got some free time, that's where he'll go looking for fun. And to an American it's not that far.'

'Who should we talk to out there?'

'No one.' The sergeant's words had a hard finality. 'I've told you where the men are. Unless there's a pressing reason, you don't need to go there, do you?'

'I don't imagine we do.' McMillan rose, holding out his hand. The sergeant shook it warily. 'But if I get a sniff of something I'll be out there like a shot.' He tipped his hat. 'Thank you for your time.'

'Like getting blood from a stone,' Lottie complained as she drove back along Otley Road.

'That's the military for you.' He looked at his watch and sighed.

'You decided not to say anything about Private Patterson.'

'Not yet, anyway.' He smiled. 'We can always come back. Millgarth now, I think.'

She knew he'd be in the office long after her shift was over, going over reports, asking questions. There were all the other investigations to supervise. The black market goods that never seemed to run out, a glut of them in the last few months, the protection rackets. He'd told her once that these days the uniforms kept their eyes open for deserters and prostitutes; too many of them, and too few men in CID. He had to select what they looked into. Even then all the men had caseloads that never ended. And McMillan was responsible for it all.

'What time do you go home?' she asked not long after she'd started the job.

'Late,' he answered, rubbing his eyes with the heels of his hands. 'Sarah knows it's like this until it's over. Still, it could be worse. At least I'm in my own bed every night.' Not like his sons; he didn't need to say it. He'd served in the last war. He knew exactly what it was like.

'What are you going to do when peace comes?' Over the last few months she'd heard the words more often. They still seemed tentative, but each time they felt a little more solid. They'd go on and beat Hitler, then the Japs. Maybe it was the Americans who gave them heart. Maybe the Allies' progress in Italy. Whatever it was, the hope was taking shape.

'Retire,' he answered. No hesitation. 'I feel like I could sleep for a month. What about you?'

'Go back to my life, I suppose.' She hadn't given it much thought. She'd been too busy with everything going on now, juggling it all. 'There won't be much call for women my age to do things.'

'You might be surprised. Everything's going to change.'

'Is it?' She had her doubts. 'They said that the last time.'

'The politicians will have learned. And people have had enough. You can smell it. The mood's shifting.'

He wouldn't be drawn more than that. Lottie had raised it a couple of times, but he'd sidestepped the conversation.

A queue at the Co-op for sugar. She handed over the buff ration book, watching as the assistant cut out her coupons. No butter, of course, but at least they had some marge and a quarter of Bourn-vita. Then a dash to the hairdresser to wheedle an appointment from Denise for Saturday afternoon.

There was a little bacon in the larder and she still had one of the eggs McMillan had given her. Potatoes from the garden sitting in a dark box. She'd put up some beans at the end of the summer. For once she could spoil herself.

She was making her morning cuppa, re-using the leaves from last night, when she heard the sound. Tyres on the gravel along the road. Lottie peeked round the curtain and saw the squad car parked outside her house, a policeman unlatching her gate.

'This can't be good, Bert,' she said as she opened the door.

'Sorry, Lottie.' He managed an apologetic smile. 'The DCS wants you.'

She was a passenger for once, watching Leeds in a different way as they headed down Scott Hall Road. Crowds waiting for the buses and trams. Thursday morning.

'What is it?'

'They're not saying anything official yet, but it's a body. A girl. That's all I know. But the Chief Super's looking after it himself, he's not handed it off to one of the others, so it must be important.'

'I see.' A second girl? Bert must have it wrong; that was impossible. McMillan must have come up with something to tie Kate Patterson's body to the house on Shire Oak Road. Another five minutes and she'd find out.

'I'm sorry if I got you out of bed.'

'Already up and about. Bert Lancaster said there's another body. That can't be right, can it?'

'It is.' She'd never heard him sound so grim. 'A WAAF. On leave, which is why no one had reported her missing at first. Found just after first light. She was in the woods about a quarter of a mile from Kirkstall Abbey.' He paused to let that sink in. 'Looks as if she'd been dumped over the wall from the road.'

'But…' Lottie began, then realised she had nothing to say. Too many thoughts were swirling through her head. 'Two in two days? The same area?'

'It gets worse.' He ran a hand over his scalp. 'She was shot, same MO as Patterson. WAAF, in uniform. Still had her identification card, change and cigarettes in her pockets. Anne Goodman. Twenty-three years old.' He paused for a heartbeat. 'No knickers. The pathologist said Kate Patterson didn't have hers on, either.' He lit a cigarette. 'This is turning into a bloody mess.'

'Dear God.' It was all she could say. After a long silence she asked: 'Where was she stationed?'

'Linton, near York. She was here on leave, visiting her sister. Andrews is with her now, seeing what he can find out.'

'Had she..?'

'Very likely. The post-mortem will say for sure. I've put a rush on it. Meanwhile, we're going out to Linton-on-Ouse.'

She had the map with her, for all the help it offered. No signposts to guide them and out in the flat countryside everything looked the same, the sky grey, the fields brown and muddy.

Two wrong turnings, directions from a grumpy pub landlord, and she finally found the camp. Ten o'clock. Her hands ached from keeping a tight hold of the steering wheel and her eyes felt gritty.

At least they'd had time to talk on the way. The report on Kate Patterson's body confirmed that a single gunshot had killed her. She'd had sexual intercourse, almost certainly willingly, and there was alcohol in her bloodstream. No bruising or signs of violence on her body. They'd retrieved the bullet and passed it to the Leeds City Police ballistics man, Detective Sergeant Arthur Lawton. His qualification was that he'd taken a course with Robert Churchill in London.

The evidence crew had discovered the cartridge but little else. Now Lawton was trying to work out what weapon had fired the shot.

'The lab bods checked the hairs from the knickers from Shire Oak Road under the microscope with Patterson's,' McMillan told her. 'There's some way they can compare and see if they're from the same person. But they didn't match. And they can't be Goodman's; she hasn't been dead long enough.' He sounded as if he was carrying the weight of the world on his shoulders. And he was. Leeds rarely had two murders a year. Never two in as many days. And not women.

'If the knickers didn't belong to Patterson or Goodman...'

'I know. We might have another body somewhere. I've given orders for them to go over every inch of ground up and down the river from the abbey.'

The sentry had an accent that sounded American but his uniform was wrong.

'Royal Canadian Air Force,' he explained, looking hurt as he returned McMillan's warrant card. 'You guys mix us up all the time. We're the ones who like the king and don't chew gum.'

'Sorry,' the superintendent said. 'We need whoever's in charge of the WAAFs here.'

'In charge?' He looked confused. 'There's a Warrant Officer, I guess. But they're all sleeping. They were working until the squadron returned three hours ago.'

'I'm still going to need to talk to her. It's very important.'
Warrant Officer Jill Castleton prowled around the room, smoking. She'd looked barely awake at first, hair roughly brushed, her uniform mussed.

'I hope you have a very good reason for this,' she said. There were circles of dark skin under her eyes and she looked stretched with strain.

'I wouldn't be here if I didn't.' McMillan introduced himself. 'It's about Aircraftwoman Goodman.' Lottie saw Castleton's body stiffen.

'What? Has something happened to her?'

'I'm very sorry,' he said quietly. 'She's dead.' There was never an easy way to break it. 'Someone killed her.'

'But...' Castleton began and blinked in disbelief. 'She can't be. She went on leave to see her sister.'

'I'm afraid it's true,' McMillan said gently. 'There's no mistake.'

The woman dug into the pocket of her skirt for a handkerchief, swiping blindly at her eyes and blowing her nose. Castleton had to be used to death. She and the other WAAFS were plotters, following the squadron on the radio when they went on raids, advising them, mapping everything on the ops table. How many aircraft hadn't come back in the last few years? How many men lost? But this was different.

'How?' It came out as an accusation.

The superintendent gave Lottie a warning glance before he answered.

'The best we can tell, she must have met someone and he did it.'

'Someone?'

'A man.'

'Christ.' It wasn't a word often heard from a woman. But Castleton lived in a man's world where there was danger as soon as the engines turned over.

CHAPTER FOUR

'CHIEF Superintendent, I care about Anne. There are only eight girls here. We sleep in the same place, we see each other every day.'

Castleton looked as taut as a wire, caught between what she wanted to show and her rank. She understood that for now, duty had to be the winner.

'Of course,' McMillan said.

'I'm going to let the others sleep on,' she said. 'They need it. If the weather holds, the boys will be flying again tonight. I'll answer everything I can. If you want to talk to them you'll either have to wait or come back later.'

'We'll wait,' he said. It was better than using petrol for a second trip.

'You can find some breakfast in the canteen.' She gave a weak smile. 'At least the food's good. Plenty of it, too. Perk of having the Canadians around. Give me a few minutes to sort myself out and I'll join you.'

The mess was easy enough to find; the smell guided them. Bacon and sausages… it was like following a memory. Lottie half expected it to be a mirage: to arrive only to find runny powdered eggs and weak tea. But Castleton was right; there was plenty of food, so much it was as if rationing didn't exist. Lottie felt guilty as she mounded her plate. Her rumbling stomach reminded her she hadn't eaten since the night before. Apparently it wasn't just the Yanks who made sure their troops were well fed.

Off in the corner a radio was playing the American Forces Network. Dance bands: Benny Goodman, Tommy Dorsey, Glenn Miller. Funny, Lottie thought, she knew all of them; like everyone else, she'd taken in the music by osmosis.

They didn't speak as they ate. Words would have seemed like a travesty. It wasn't until she'd mopped up the last of the egg yolk with a slice of white toast that she said, 'You won't find that in Gert and Daisy's cook book.'

'I know.' McMillan had cleaned his plate, but sadness filled his voice. 'I just wish this wasn't all because of a dead WAAF.'

And now her pleasure tasted like cinders.

Castleton bustled in, stopping for a cup of coffee. She looked more composed, her uniform straight, tie in a smart knot, hair carefully brushed back into a serviceable Victory roll.

'I'm sorry,' she said. 'I needed a little while. After we've talked, I'll wake the others.' She bit her lip. 'They're going to be horrified. We're rather close-knit. You get to be that way out here.'

She had nothing but praise for Anne Goodman. The girl did her job with dedication, a fine record, no bad behaviour. But she enjoyed life too, going into York to dance and meet men. No different from any other aircraftwoman.

'Did she have a boyfriend?' McMillan asked.

Castleton pursed her lips. 'I hadn't heard of one. She'd been engaged, but her boyfriend died at Dunkirk. I think that's what made her join up.'

'There are plenty of men right here,' Lottie said. She'd watched some of the flyboys eating, the loud bonhomie of survival as they talked.

'Yes.' Castleton smiled. 'A bit too close to home, though. And the survival rate for aircrew isn't good.'

'How do the girls get into York?'

'Jeep or lorry if one's going that way,' the woman replied breezily. 'If not, hitchhike. It's easy enough in uniform.'

The women were in shock. Airmen dying at the hands of the Jerries, they were used to that; it happened almost every night. But Anne Goodman was one of them, a friend. It had occurred at home, in a city she knew, where she should have been in no danger. Plenty of tears, sentences that stumbled into nothing. One or two of them found their voices and said what they could. But it wasn't much.

Anne had had a three-day pass. A lorry was leaving and had taken her to York, where she was going to catch the train to Leeds and see her sister. Completely ordinary. She'd kept herself free of any great romance, just enjoyed short flings. The same as the rest of us, one girl said defiantly.

The voices could just as easily have belonged to the women who'd served with Kate Patterson. The same loss and bewilderment. And fear; it was there in their eyes even when their voices were steady. Lottie searched Goodman's locker. A photograph of Clark Gable, cut from a magazine and glued to the door. A faded bundle of letters, the last dated early May 1940. Some clothes – the rest would probably be at her sister's house. She found an address book and pocketed it.

She took the road through York. She and Geoff had visited the city often, first on the motorbike, then in the car. Just far enough from home that it seemed like a good run out. Back then the place always seemed scented with chocolate from the Rowntree's and Terry's factories. Now it just smelt of exhaust fumes and decay.

It was almost three when she parked behind Millgarth. McMillan had slept away much of the trip, head resting against the window. Twenty years before he'd still have been alert. But both of them were older now; grabbing sleep when you could was like gold.

Who had Anne Goodman met in Leeds, Lottie wondered. Where had she gone? DI Andrews had gone to interview the sister. The report would be waiting. Lottie turned in her seat and gently shook McMillan awake. He surfaced slowly, rubbing his face and letting out a long sigh.

'Back to the grindstone. You might as well come up to the office, I'm sure I'll be needing you soon enough.' He stifled a yawn then smiled hopefully at her. 'Maybe a couple of teas from the canteen on the way?'

He was working through a pile of papers when she nudged the door open. The heating wasn't working and he sat in his overcoat and gloves, tossing some papers aside, then scanning others. Finally one caught his full attention. He read it, then again, more slowly, before handing it to her.

'Lawton's checked the bullets. They're both from the same gun.'

'My God.' Lottie glanced at the report. The words meant little to her, other than the conclusion, and that they were both .45 calibre. Lawton had added that the standard US army sidearm was a Colt M1911, which used .45 calibre bullets. She looked up sharply at him. 'You saw the last part?'

McMillan nodded grimly. 'That just made solving this a lot more difficult,' he said.

How could they even start? They'd need the co-operation of the US Army brass. But surely they'd give that. Two murders… that could turn people against the Yanks.

'Let me make a few telephone calls,' McMillan said. He gestured at the papers on his desk. 'Do you think you could put those in order?'

'I'll try.'

In the office across the corridor she began to sort the correspondence into piles. So many different cases and the Chief Superintendent received copies of everything. But only two investigations really concerned her: the killings of Kate Patterson and Anne Goodman. She read through every word on them, taking her time over the search results from the house on Shire Oak Road. Plenty of fingerprints, from at least twelve different people. Two sets on the bottle, lipstick on the Player's cigarettes. However, none of the fingerprints matched the dead women. They didn't match anyone on file. And the knickers hadn't come from Patterson or Goodman. Maybe the party had been innocent, the girl just passed out drunk; McMillan's hunch could be wrong.

None of it was good news. Nothing to help them find a killer. She scrabbled through. The search out at Kirkstall hadn't found anything. No more bodies. No reports of missing women. Lottie sat back, trying to make sense of it all. But with so little information it was like grasping at smoke. She was still thinking when McMillan returned, a cigarette in his hand.

'The head of the American troops in the area will see us,' he said and paused for a moment. 'But not until tomorrow.'

'Why—' Lottie began.

'He's involved in operational matters, apparently. I said we had two women who might have been killed by an American serviceman, but his aide didn't seem to feel that was important enough.' His face flickered with disgust. 'Did you find much in the reports?'

'Not that you'd notice.' She gave him a sad smile. 'You should go home. There's nothing more we can do on this until tomorrow.'

'No rest for the wicked. I still have to keep an eye on all the other cases.' He looked at his watch. 'You might as well call it a day, though. Early start tomorrow; we're due there at oh-eight hundred.'

Lottie gathered up her coat and handbag. 'Don't work yourself too hard.'

It was a night for the pictures. Something to make her forget about the world for a while. *Stage Door Canteen* was showing at the Kingsway, just ten minutes' walk from home. Margie next door was at a loose end. They strolled down together, chattering and complaining about the ration, the quality of produce that Ken the greengrocer had in his shop. Anything but work.

Walking home later, the blackout thick around them, humming *Why Don't You Do Right?* from the film and listening for cars as she scuttled across the road, Lottie thought about the squadron from Linton-on-Ouse. They'd be on their way to Germany now. How many would return tonight? Who'd be mourning tomorrow?

Seven o'clock and Lottie sat in the canteen at Millgarth. Hot, weak tea and a plate of scrambled powdered eggs. It hardly compared to yesterday's breakfast, and barely seemed worth the effort of eating. Finally she pushed it aside and walked up to McMillan's office.

He was freshly shaved, a clean shirt, different tie, but he didn't look as if he'd slept much. A cigarette was burning in the ashtray. He stubbed it out.

'We might as well go,' he said. 'Get there bright and early.'

Even at this time there was plenty of activity around the old house on Castle Grove. British and American officers, clerks, civilian staff, all moving round with purposeful strides and intent faces.

Sergeant Andersen was at his desk, looking neat and groomed. He gave them coffee, but he couldn't let them see General Wheaton before eight.

'He's a busy man,' Andersen said apologetically.

'Generals often are,' McMillan said wryly. 'All that responsibility. I'm surprised you have a general in this place.'

Andersen glanced around cautiously before answering.

'He's a one-star general, sir. That's equivalent to brigadier in your army.'

'I see.'

They kept an awkward silence until the general's aide arrived, staring curiously at Lottie's uniform.

'Excuse me, ma'am, but you're a cop?' He was so young, and sounded so earnest that she almost laughed.

'She is,' McMillan interrupted. 'And she's my assistant.' He winked at her.

Wheaton's office looked out on the bare winter garden. He was sitting behind a large desk, neat creases along the sleeves of his shirt as if it had come straight from the laundry. He looked young for the rank, probably in his early forties, dark hair in the buzz-cut all the Americans seemed to favour.

'Detective Chief Superintendent.' He stood and held out a large hand to shake. 'Ma'am. Have a seat. Corporal, coffee here, please.' He waited until the door closed. 'I believe you feel we have a problem.'

'The biggest, General.' He started to explain, stopping when the aide returned with a tray and three cups. Once they were alone again, he continued. 'Both the bullets are from a Colt M1911. I'm sure you know what that means.'

'Of course.' He nodded, took a cigarette from the packet on the desk and lit it. 'What do you have besides that?'

'Nothing,' McMillan said. 'But those sidearms are issued to US troops, that's correct?'

'It is.'

'So you'll understand why I'm here.'

Wheaton took a long time to reply, smoking and running his tongue along his lips as he thought. Finally he said: 'I guess I'd better tell you. We had a crate of guns go missing. The quartermaster in charge of stores reported it a month ago. There were ten Colt M1911s in there. We've been hunting for it since then.'

McMillan leaned forward in his chair, his voice hard, disbelieving. 'A crate with ten weapons went missing a month ago and you didn't think to tell the police?'

'I reported it to our Provost Marshal and he has our own CID working on it.'

'What you're telling me is that those guns could be on the black market and nobody mentioned it to us?'

'It's possible,' Wheaton admitted reluctantly. 'We don't know.'

God, it couldn't be worse, Lottie thought. Finding an American with a gun would be hard enough. Knowing that anyone might have the weapon made their job almost impossible.

'I'll need to see your investigator,' McMillan said.

'I can arrange that.'

'I want him in my office at Millgarth at ten.'

'Yes, sir.' Wheaton nodded and McMillan stood.

'Thank you for your time.'

He marched to the car, long, fast strides that showed his anger. Sitting in the back seat, he smoked a Four Square as Lottie drove.

'Bloody Yanks,' he said finally. 'Maybe they'll win the war for us but they're an arrogant bunch. Act like they own the place.'

'What do we do now?' she asked.

McMillan sighed loudly. 'Honestly? I haven't a clue. Anyone could have the gun now. It could be in the river. We can talk to all the snouts but I don't think it'll do much good.' He slammed his palm down on the leather seat. 'I thought we were getting somewhere and it's thrown back in my face. Worse. If there's a bunch of guns floating around…'

'Maybe they'll find them.'

'You believe that as much as I do. Along with Father Christmas and the Tooth Fairy. If we hadn't gone there I'd never have even heard they were missing. I can guarantee you that.'

They both knew the stories about items vanishing from the service stores, only to appear for sale a few days later. Not just American; British, too. The black market was where the country shopped, whether they admitted it or not. More goods than ever, Inspector Andrews had said, a glut of them that seemed impossible to stop. On top of that, a pair of detectives was investigating a break-in at a government office where thieves had stolen over a thousand ration books. Forged coupons were everywhere. Whatever you wanted was available – for a price. But pistols… she didn't even want to imagine.

CHAPTER FIVE

RIGHT on the dot of ten Helen rang through from the switchboard.

'There's an American here to see your boss. A Captain Ellison.'

'Send him up, will you?' Lottie said.

'He's on his way.' She lowered her voice to a whisper. 'He's very good looking. I could eat him for my tea.'

'Get away with you,' Lottie laughed. Never mind; she'd find out for herself in a moment.

Good looking, she wondered as he entered the room, cap under his arm and a diffident grin on his face. Maybe. At least he didn't have that terrible cropped hair like the other Americans. His had a little style to it, dark, parted at the side, and his smile showed strong white teeth.

'Hi. I'm Cliff Ellison, US Army CID. Looking for Detective Chief Superintendent McMillan?' It came out as a question. Helen was right; there was something endearing about him, she decided. Lines around his eyes and mouth that showed he'd lived, but no real brashness to his manner.

'I'm WAPC Armstrong. I'll show you through.'

A knock on the door and she entered. 'It's Captain Ellison, sir.' Her mouth twitched into a smile. 'Here just as you requested.'

'Could you find three cups of tea, please, then join us?'

'Yes, sir.'

By the time she returned the men were talking earnestly. Any frostiness in the air had already vanished.

'It's not a trickle, Chief Superintendent, it's a flood,' Ellison said as he stubbed out a cigarette. 'We're never going to admit that officially, but it's the truth. And before you say anything, it's the same in your services. I've talked to those guys in the Special Investigation Branch and they say it's pretty much impossible to stop. You arrest one thief and two more take his place.'

'The only thing that concerns me right now is these handguns,' McMillan said. 'One in particular and what it's done.' He pushed a file across the desk. 'Take a look for yourself.'

He drank his tea and glanced at Lottie as Ellison skimmed the pages.

'Two common factors,' the captain said when he'd finished. 'Both in the service, both shot.'

'Three. Both the bodies were at Kirkstall Abbey. It's a ruin,' he explained, 'an old monastery. One was killed there, the other dumped in the grounds.'

'Is that important, do you think?' Ellison asked sharply.

'I have no idea,' McMillan told him.

'Look, I was a cop before I joined the army. Back in Seattle. A lieutenant, detective.' He gave a sad smile. 'I've seen murders before.'

'Anything like this?'

'No, sir.'

He was trying, Lottie thought. And there was something about him; he seemed like an inherently decent man.

'I have someone running round killing girls. Two of them in two days. The murderer could be anyone – British, American. I've got nothing to go on. Nothing at all.' McMillan cocked his head. 'You say you were a copper. What would you do?'

'Well…' Ellison stroked his chin. 'I'd be using my informers. And I guess I'd try and get someone on the American side to follow things from there.'

'I have people talking to the snouts. Grasses, informers,' he explained when the other man looked confused.

'I can try to help from our end,' Ellison said.

'I'll take anything I can get at this stage.'

'What would make sense is a co-ordinated operation, Chief Superintendent.'

'John. I never liked being called by my rank.'

'John.' Ellison nodded and smiled. 'I'm Cliff.'

Cliff, Lottie thought. Clifford. Why did Americans have such strange names? Bing. Clark. It sounded like they made them up on the spot.

'If you can help me catch my killer, I'll be grateful.'

'No promises, but I'll do what I can.' He gestured at the file. 'Is there any chance I can get a copy of that?'

'I'll have one typed up and sent to you.'

'I saw something about a house in there. Where is it?'

'My evidence people have gone over it.' McMillan hesitated a moment. 'I thought it had something to do with the murders, but it seems I was wrong.'

'Hunch?' He nodded. 'We all have them. I'd still like to take a look at the place. It says in there that an American was looking at the place and there was one of our Jeeps.'

'OK. Lottie can drive you. It's easier than giving directions.'

She was taken by surprise. He'd never offered her services to anyone before; Ellison was honoured and he didn't even know it.

'Of course, sir,' she said.

'Lottie?' Ellison asked as she weaved through traffic on the Headrow, past the Town Hall steps where she'd heard Mr Churchill speak a couple of years before. 'Is that short for something?'

'Charlotte, sir.'

'And WAPC?' He read the letters off her shoulder flash. 'What's that?'

'Women's Auxiliary Police Corps.' She glanced in the mirror and smiled. 'Not a proper copper.'

'So you're his driver?'

'And dogsbody. Conscience, too, if he needs one. We've actually known each other for years. It's a bit of a long story.' One she wasn't about to spill to a complete stranger. 'You said you're from Seattle. Where's that?'

'Kind of the top left hand corner of the country.' Ellison gazed out at the clouds and the green of Woodhouse Moor. 'The climate's pretty much like England.'

'Is it really all cowboys out there?'

He began to laugh so hard Lottie thought she'd need to park and thump him on the back. Finally he stopped, pulling out a handkerchief and wiping his eyes.

'Sorry, but you Brits…' He took a breath. 'That's all history. Seattle's a big city.' He looked out of the car window. 'More modern than this. Newer.'

'We have history,' she said defensively. 'A lot of it.'

By the time she parked at the end of Shire Oak Road she'd learned that he was forty-three, had a degree in history and he'd spent eighteen years in the police. Divorced with a pair of children. Americans were always so open about themselves; she'd noticed that before. She glanced at him again in the mirror; she'd never met a divorced man before.

'Have you been inside this house?'

'With the superintendent. We did the first search.'

He looked at her more carefully. 'You're more than just an auxiliary, aren't you?'

'Not really.' She smiled. 'I was a real policewoman once. That's all.'

Ellison gave her a curious look. 'OK. So show me round.'

There really was nothing to see. Everything had been taken for examination, fingerprint dust over most of the surfaces. He listened attentively as she pointed out where things had been, then she left him to poke around the place. Maybe he'd spot something they'd missed.

'The old guy next door?' Ellison asked when he'd finished.

'You'll need to talk to the Chief Super about him.' She repeated the man's claim.

'Definitely an American star on the Jeep?'

'That's what he said.'

'Hmm.' He looked at his watch. 'It's nearly lunchtime. Is there somewhere we can eat?'

'I think we can find a place,' Lottie told him with a grin. 'Come with me.'

Charlie Brett's had been on North Lane for years, so long that the grease must have soaked into the walls. Fish and chips, about the only food that wasn't rationed these days. And they did them well here. She and Geoff used to cycle to Headingley to eat. Lean against the wall outside, enjoy the meal with a bottle of Tizer while they watched people go past.

'You know,' Ellison said as she led him along the path to the old cottage that housed Brett's, 'I've been here six months and I've never eaten this stuff. We had a place back home selling fish and chips for a while but it closed down. Ivar's.'

'Then it's time you found out what the real thing is like.'

'That's not too bad.' He sounded surprised. At least he'd been chivalrous enough to pay.

'Well, if you want to understand the English, you'd better enjoy it,' she said. 'This is more or less our national dish. With lots of salt and vinegar.'

'I can't see it going over big in our canteen, but it's tasty,' Ellison said. 'What's your take on these killings?'

'Me?' Lottie was astonished he wanted her opinion.

'Yes, you.' He grinned, showing those white teeth again. 'Come on, you're more than a driver, you've said that. You must have an opinion.'

She allowed herself a smile for a second, then her face turned serious.

'Honestly, I don't know.' Lottie sighed. 'And I've no idea if the Shire Oak Road house is even involved in anything. The boss thinks it is but there's no real evidence.'

'Hunches are important to cops.'

'But they're not infallible.'

'No,' he agreed. 'But if he feels it that strongly…'

'We'll see.' This conversation would just take them in a circle. Time to change the subject. 'What's Seattle like?'

'Pretty,' he told her after a moment. 'There's water on one side and mountains on the other.' He scrambled in his pocket, brought out a wallet and dug through for photographs. 'That's my house.'

She'd never known anyone who carried a picture of his house. It seemed such a strange thing to do. People, events, pets. But never a house. Still, he was far from home, divorced. Maybe it gave him a kind of anchor. It looked to be a pleasant enough place, a wooden bungalow, a large car sitting next to it in the drive.

'I don't live in Seattle itself,' he explained. 'I'm across Elliott Bay in West Seattle. Long drive round, but it's nice and peaceful.'

But Lottie was looking at two other photos that had come out.

'Are those your children?'

He laid them out on the table and his voice softened. 'Yeah. Jimmy's in eighth grade. I'm just hoping all this is over before he's old enough to be drafted.'

'It will be,' she said with certainty. 'What's your daughter's name?'

'Karen. After my mom. She's in sixth grade. I get letters from them but it's not the same. How about you, you have kids?'

'No. My husband was wounded in the last war. We couldn't.'

'I'm sorry.' He narrowed his eyes a little. 'What does he do?'

'He died five years ago. Heart attack.' It didn't feel so painful to say these days. Not when so many others had lost family to much worse.

'That's terrible.'

'It happens.' She pushed the empty plate away and drank the rest of her tea. 'Come on, I'd better get back or he'll have me up before the firing squad.'

'You took your time,' McMillan said as she walked into the office.

'He was hungry so I took him to Charlie Brett's. I'm fostering co-operation with our allies.'

He raised an eyebrow. 'Is that what they're calling it these days?'

Lottie snorted. 'Do you have to go somewhere?'

He sat back, putting his hands behind his head. 'I wish I did. At least I'd feel we were making some progress. Everyone's talking to their narks, the bobbies are putting the pressure on all the small-time crooks. Anything that can get us a lead on that gun.'

'Nothing so far?'

'Not a dicky bird.' He played with his fountain pen, idly moving it between his fingers. 'Got more patrols out at night, but that doesn't help too much.' The telephone rang. 'Who knows?' McMillan said to her. 'Maybe that's our change of luck.' He picked up the receiver and listened for half a minute, then said, 'Good work, George. We'll be there in a little while.'

'George Chadwick?' she asked. 'The Special on the beat?'

'He's found one of the tramps.' McMillan was grinning. 'Maybe it really is a little bit of a break. Let's find out.'

CHAPTER SIX

T HEY drove in silence. McMillan's face was set, tense, every strain visible. Lottie moved through the gears, thinking over the conversation with Ellison.

As they'd headed back to the station, he'd said, 'I know this probably sounds crazy, but would you like to have dinner sometime?'

'What?' Her hands had jerked on the wheel; she almost hit the kerb.

'You heard.' He put out a hand to steady himself against the dashboard.

'But… why?' She was a widow in her forties. Hardly glamorous, hardly anything really. What did he think, she'd be easy prey? He was divorced. Pleasant enough, but… divorced.

'I enjoy talking to you,' he told her. 'We're about the same age. I get sick of being around young guys all the time.'

She glanced at his face. He sounded sincere enough. Maybe he simply needed some company; she couldn't blame him for that. It had been a pleasure talking to him, too, learning how different America really was from the films. But…

'I work long hours,' Lottie said.

'So do I. Crime never stops, even in the service.'

She parked in the yard behind Millgarth and turned off the engine.

'What do you say?' Ellison asked. 'Yes or no?'

'Yes,' she answered after a few seconds. She was going to make sure she put conditions on it. 'But friends only. Understand?'

'Yes, ma'am.' He grinned. 'When?'

'Tomorrow at seven? Will you be on duty?'

'I can swing it. Where do you want to meet? I can pick you up if you'd like.'

'Let's meet outside the station here.' She wasn't allowing him anywhere near her house.

'I look forward to it.'

She wasn't going to tell McMillan about her date; he'd never let her live it down, and come Monday he'd be asking all sorts of questions. Better to keep it quiet, thank you very much. Besides, she told herself, it was simply two friends going out for a meal. Nothing more complicated than that.

Lottie parked the Humber near the abbey.

'Down by the weir, George said. He'll be waiting down there to make sure his man doesn't do a flit.'

The ground was hard and rutted. Easy to turn an ankle, she thought as she made her way carefully along, then on a trail between brambles that snatched at her uniform. She looked up the hill towards the houses, the faded paint of a Bile's Beans advertisement on a gable end.

'Over here, sir.' Chadwick's voice called loudly from ten yards away.

The tramp had built himself a bivouac between some trees, a few feet from the River Aire. It was well hidden. She'd have walked right past it if the big old copper hadn't been standing there. Next to him was a small, thin man in baggy, torn clothes, everything topped with a thick overcoat that reached to his ankles, a flat cap covering long, unruly grey hair.

'This is Harry Giddins, sir.' Chadwick was smiling. 'Found him a little while ago by his campfire.' He nodded at the small blaze on the ground.

'I'm Detective Chief Superintendent McMillan. We're hoping you can help us.'

Giddins looked around. He gazed everywhere except at her, Lottie noticed, and she stepped back from his line of vision. Perhaps that would make him more comfortable.

'I told him what you're looking for, sir,' Chadwick said. 'Didn't I, Harry?'

'Yes.' Giddins nodded. He was a reluctant witness; everything had to be teased out of him. But at least he seemed honest. He'd been at the abbey the night Kate Patterson was killed. He'd heard the shot and knew what it was.

'Heard enough guns before, haven't I?'

'What did you do?' McMillan asked.

'Went over there, careful like. So no one would know I was around.'

'And what did you see?'

'Her. There were enough of a moon. She was dead. Saw enough like that at Passchendaele.' Another survivor, Lottie thought, and glanced at him again from the corner of her eye. He looked older than that. Rough living, she supposed.

'Did you take anything?'

Giddins shook his head. 'I couldn't do nothing to help her.' His boot kicked nervously at the ground. 'Thought I'd better make myself scarce or you lot would be thinking I'd done it.'

'I know you didn't, Mr Giddins. Did you see anyone leaving? Hear anything?'

'Someone running.' He pointed to the open area of grass and shrugged. 'Just a figure, that's all.'

'I need you to think,' McMillan said softly. 'Was it a man?'

'Yes.' No hesitation in the answer. 'Could see from how he ran. There was enough moon for that.'

'How was he dressed? Were you able to see?'

'Not really.' His face brightened. 'But he did have a cap on, like officers wear.'

'Are you certain about that?' McMillan stared at him.

'Course I am.' He turned his head, hawked and spat.

'What else? Could you make out any kind of uniform?'

'Don't know. Too dark.'

Worth the attempt, though. Something occurred to her. 'Did you hear anything else that night, Mr Giddins? Sound carries in the dark.'

He looked sharply towards her, then away again. There had to be a reason, Lottie thought, a woman in his past, perhaps.

'No. Not until the shot.' He paused. 'Oh, there was something. A little while before. A car door.'

'After the man ran off did you hear a car starting up?' She held her breath.

'Don't know.' Giddins looked from face to face. 'I don't,' he insisted.

Better the truth than a lie that had them chasing ghosts.

McMillan gave him a shilling as they left. Worth that, she thought. Chadwick strode off with them.

'What do you think, sir?' he asked.

'A little something. You're right, he had nothing to do with it. Any luck finding the other tramp yet?'

'Leslie?' The constable shook his head. 'No, nobody's seen him. He'll turn up when he's ready and I'll have a word.'

'Let me know, George. And good job.'

Chadwick beamed. 'Thank you, sir.'

'An officer's cap,' Lottie said as she drove. 'Do you think it helps?'

'It narrows things down. If Giddins is right,' he added.

'He seemed convinced.'

'By something he saw for a moment in a little bit of moonlight,' McMillan said dismissively. 'For now I'll take it with a grain of salt. That question about voices and sounds was good, though.'

'The car door could have been a taxi.'

'We've tried all the companies. None of them dropped anyone off here that night.'

'Could be a lone operator.'

'He wouldn't get the petrol coupons.'

'They're easy enough to buy on the black market,' she reminded him.

'I know,' he admitted with a sigh. 'I'll get someone asking. The papers have been sniffing around; someone must have got word. The Chief Constable and the Home Office have had to slap them down.'

'You can't blame them,' Lottie told him. 'It's their job.'

'And I've got mine. It'll be easier without them looking over my shoulder. What do you think – will Ellison help us?'

'Yes,' she said. 'He was already looking into the guns vanishing. Now he has a bigger reason. He seems thorough.'

She glanced in the mirror, seeing McMillan watching her. Lottie could feel the pinpoints of heat on her cheeks starting to grow.

'Good luncheon, was it?' His mouth twitched into a smile.

'Very pleasant. He told me about Seattle. Did you know Frances Farmer comes from there?'

'Who?'

'The film actress. You must have seen *Calamity Jane*.'

He snorted. 'I don't think I've had chance to go to the pictures since 1941. Sarah goes with her friends.'

'You need time at home, too.'

'You ought to try telling the criminals round here that. On top of everything, now I have this. And I can't even trust my gut any more, it seems. I was certain that house on Shire Oak Road was involved. I'm getting old, Lottie.'

'We all are.'

As soon as she was through the door, Lottie padded around in the darkness closing the blackouts. Maybe it was a ridiculous ritual now, as silly as carrying a gas mask, but it was the law and she didn't want a summons from the warden.

Nothing in the post. But there rarely was, other than bills. In the bedroom she took off her uniform and eyed herself in the mirror above the dressing table. Not too bad, she decided. The girdle helped, the slip was flattering, and she weighed what she had twenty years before. Maybe she'd have the hairdresser put a little colour in her hair…

Don't be so daft.

A housedress, light the fire in the lounge and see what was in the larder for tea. Once the war was over she'd sell the house. It was far too big for one person. She'd be more comfortable in a flat.

The smell of distemper had still been fresh on the walls when they moved in nine years before. It had been too big for just the pair of them even then, but Geoff was doing well at work. A new semi was a sign of success. And there was a big garden where they could plant. Over time, the things they owned gradually expanded to fill the spare rooms. She'd thrown most of it away after Geoff died but there was still too much.

He'd enjoyed making furniture for the house, working from the plans in *Practical Handyman*. A bookcase, an occasional table, stands on either side of the bed. He was good with his hands, always tinkering, enjoying making things take shape.

Yes, after peace arrived she'd sell up. She'd miss the neighbours – Dr Smith at number nine, Margie Kennedy at number five – but it wasn't difficult to keep in touch.

Corned beef hash for her supper, and she felt lucky to have a tin of corned beef. The radio played in the dining room, Tommy Handley and the others in ITMA. Sometimes in the evening Lottie believed she could still sense Geoff here; sometimes she thought she caught a glimpse of him out of the corner of her eye. Less in the last couple of years. And rarely since she'd started the job; that had given back something of herself, a purpose.

As she ate, Lottie's thoughts strayed back to the case. The two dead women… she didn't see how they could find anything without a huge stroke of luck. What clues they had didn't seem to lead anywhere yet.

She sighed as she washed up. Maybe the Americans really would help. That brought her back to Captain Ellison. Enough, she told herself. Quite enough. He's divorced.

Frost during the night, lingering to make her cautious as she drove. She'd had to scrape at the bedroom window to peer out into the darkness.

As they left the city centre there were still patches of black ice on the road. They passed one car that had spun off into a bank on Selby Road. By the time they reached Whitkirk, though, the sun was peeping out. No warmth in it, but at least it made her feel hopeful.

'Turn right here,' McMillan told her as she passed the old church. A few houses and then it felt like a country lane with tall hedges on either side. 'Along there.' He pointed to a track between two stone posts.

It must have been a farmhouse once, a dour-faced building of dark stone. But she couldn't see any ploughs or tractors. Lottie turned in her seat.

'Have we come out here for more fresh eggs?'

McMillan gave her a wry smile. 'A copper does a good job and rises through the ranks, he might be able to afford a place in Horsforth. A black marketeer can put down the cash on somewhere like this.'

She looked at the building again. 'Crime pays.'

'If you get away with it,' he agreed. 'Harry Park has.'

'Not enough evidence to arrest?'

'Not since he got smart, and that was long before the war.' He opened the door. 'Come on, let's see how public-spirited he's feeling.'

The ground was so hard and sharp that crossing the dirt to the front door felt dangerous. Inside, though, a fire was roaring in the dining room. They waited until Park's wife had bustled around with tea and slices of Dundee cake. When she closed the door behind her, the man pulled out his pipe and lit it. Time for business.

Harry Park was a bony man with a full head of white hair and a long, pale scar down his left cheek. Fifty, at least, a thick cardigan under his suit jacket. He didn't look like a criminal. But most crooks didn't; she'd learned that her first time around with the police.

'You haven't come all the way out here to pass the time of day, Chief Superintendent.' Park smiled. He had a resonant, cultured voice. 'And you're not here to arrest me; you're not smiling.'

'Guns,' McMillan said.

The other man shook his head quickly. 'You know me better than that.'

'Times are changing, Harry. Leeds is getting to be like the Wild West.'

'Going to be worse after the war, Mr McMillan.'

'I daresay. But I'll be gone by then, thank God. I'm thinking about the here and now.'

'Like what?' He had quick, sharp eyes, Lottie thought, and they were focused on the Super.

'American handguns. Colts. A case of them went missing. And I've had a Colt used in a pair of crimes.'

'I wouldn't know anything about it.'

'Nobody seems to.' McMillan looked reflective. 'We've been asking around. Keep hitting brick walls.'

'Well, I'm sorry. I can't help you, either.'

'You could ask around. Make people believe you might be interested.'

Park cocked his head. 'Why? People know I don't like shooters.'

'I told you, Harry, times are changing. People might imagine you want to change with them.'

The man was silent for a long time, sucking on his pipe. 'What's in it for me?'

'I have two dead women. One ATS, one in the WAAFs. You help me find who killed them.'

Park rubbed his chin. 'You should have said.'

'I'm saying now. But it doesn't go beyond these four walls.'

'I can ask around. No guarantees.'

'I know. Just let me know any names. Even a hint of one.'

'All right.'

'A daughter in the service?' Lottie guessed as she nosed the car back down the track.

'Had. A Queen Alexandra's nurse. Killed at Dunkirk.'

'That explains it,' she said quietly. If he'd lost his own girl, he'd feel the murders of two others. Even the biggest criminals had hearts and weaknesses. 'I was wondering why you told him when we've been keeping it quiet.'

'It won't go any further; I know Harry. And he'll do what he can. He's my last resort.'

'Where now?'

'Let's go and find your friend Ellison,' he said after a moment. 'Maybe he has some news for us.'

'I don't know why you keep calling him my friend.' Her voice was sharp. In the mirror she saw him smiling.

Much of the Ring Road was complete, but there weren't many vehicles around on a Saturday. She made good time over to Otley Road, then through to the Masonic Hall on Castle Grove. Captain Ellison was in his office, a cubby hole tucked away in the attic.

'They tell me this is where the servants used to sleep,' he apologised, ducking his head to go through the doorway. 'I hope they hired small guys. What can I do for you? Have you gotten a break?'

'I was hoping you might have,' McMillan said.

'I'd have called you if I did. I've got a possible, but that's all.' He shrugged. 'Wait and see what happens.'

'Have you had chance to read the file?'

'I spent a couple of hours with it last night.'

'Any ideas?' He smiled. 'As a copper, I mean.'

'Not much beyond the obvious. The killer's been very careful. He dumped the WAAF's body. Do you have any idea where she was killed?'

'Nothing yet.'

'There's something… he must have had access to a vehicle. That's going to limit things. Maybe not a whole lot, but it's something.'

McMillan nodded. 'I talked to a tramp a little while ago. He was out there when the first girl was killed. Thought he heard a car door, and later he thinks he saw someone in an officer's cap running off.'

'The door would fit with the car.' Ellison shook a Lucky Strike from the packet and lit it. 'So we're a little further along.'

'Assuming the witness is right.'

'Do you believe him?'

'I want to.' McMillan was cautious.

'Yeah,' the American agreed. 'I know what you mean. Got to keep an open mind.'

'Except I don't have the luxury of time. I have a pair of murders to solve. That's why you're seeing me again.'

'I'll do what I can, but don't expect anything overnight,' Ellison warned him. 'I've got something, but it's going to take a little while to put it all together. If I storm in I'll just screw it all up.'

'Will you keep me posted? I'll let you know anything we find. Lottie can keep in touch.'

She gave him a look. Teasing was one thing; this was a step too far. But she simply said, 'Yes, sir.'

As they left, Ellison caught her eye and smiled. She gave a quick nod then hurried out to the car.

'"Lottie can keep in touch?"' she said acidly as the Humber accelerated down Otley Road.

'In a professional capacity.'

'It didn't sound that way.'

'You're touchy today.'

'Am I?'

'Yes.'

He sighed. 'Too much on my mind. I'm sorry. But you've had that twinkle in your eye since yesterday.'

Twinkle? That was cheek. Ellison seemed pleasant. Yes, she was looking forward to tonight. But that was all.

CHAPTER SEVEN

ONE thing about the blackout – you could walk past your closest relative and never notice them. As Lottie stood outside Millgarth that evening the coppers came and went but none of them gave her a second glance.

He was already five minutes late. She liked punctuality. If he hadn't arrived by quarter past she'd make her way home. A little hurt but also angry. Lottie had taken time over her appearance, something smart without going overboard. Debbie had given her a shampoo and set with some colour to take out the grey. A Utility dress, the first new piece of clothing she'd bought since the previous spring. Her last good pair of stockings and a hat she hadn't worn in years. She didn't use much make-up, but today she'd spent a good half-hour at the dressing table, trying to make sure she looked just right.

'Lottie?'

She turned at the sound of her name, surprised to feel her heart beating a little faster. She could barely make him out, a darker, solid shape in the blackness.

'I'm here.'

'I'm sorry, I took a couple wrong turns in this blackout. I hope you're not too mad at me.'

'I might forgive you in time.' She tried to make her voice sound light and carefree.

'Where do you want to go?'

'I don't mind. Up to you.'

'This is your city.'

With rationing, where could they find a decent meal? In the end it was Jacomelli's. Nothing fancy but she'd always enjoyed decent food there.

'Do you have somewhere Italian?' Ellison asked as they studied the menu. 'Or a Chinese?'

'No,' she said, surprised at the question. 'Why would we?'

'It's good, that's all. I'm amazed you guys never discovered it.'

He was in uniform. The shirt was freshly laundered and he'd shaved before coming out; there was still a fleck of soap under his ear.

'Maybe they have them in London.' She smiled. 'Things take a while to reach Leeds.'

They talked. She surprised herself, telling him about her life, being a Barnbow Canary in the last war, marriage. Even working as a policewoman, then being dismissed from the force.

'And McMillan is the guy who got you thrown out of the cops?' he asked in disbelief.

'Not really,' she said. 'I disobeyed his direct order.'

'That's quite something.' He pushed the empty plate aside and lit a cigarette. Enough about herself; she'd already said far too much. Seattle, America, seemed far more exotic.

'There's not much to tell,' Ellison said. 'I made it into the army for the end of the last war but not overseas. Joined the cops just in time for the general strike we had in Seattle. Worked my way up. Got married, had a couple of kids. We fell out of love, divorced.' He shrugged.

'Divorced,' she said quietly.

'Plenty of people do it.'

'Not over here. It's…' she searched for the words. 'Not acceptable.'

Ellison gave her an easy grin. 'Different customs. Anyway, we're just going to be friends, right?'

'Yes,' Lottie agreed. She shouldn't have even brought it up. 'Go on, what else about you?

'I'm a big Rainiers fan.'

'Rainiers?'

'Baseball,' he explained. 'Every chance I get during the summer I'm down at Sick's Stadium to watch them play.'

She hadn't understood a word but it didn't matter. The language, the accent, it was all so different. Somewhere over the rainbow, away from here. Where the sun shone.

Finally, the coffee cups empty, ashtray full, he glanced at her and said, 'We can go on somewhere if you like. A nightclub.'

'I don't know any,' she admitted. It was time to set him straight. Whatever impression he had of her, it was probably wrong. 'Look, I don't know how you see me, but I'm not the type to gad about. I do my job and I go home. Sometimes I'll pop off to the pictures with one of my neighbours.' She looked at him. 'I lead a very small life, Cliff, and I like it that way. You're the first chap I've done anything with since Geoff died. And friends, like we agreed, remember?'

'Maybe you need to come out of your shell a little more.'

'Possibly.' Lottie gave a small smile. 'I'd better tell you, though, it's a very comfortable little shell.'

No nightclub. A meal out and conversation was a big enough adventure for one night. He offered to give her a lift home but she refused. Instead, he waited at the bus stop with her until the number seven arrived, the vehicle felt rather than seen as it lumbered through the blackout with just a slit on one side for a headlight.

'Would you like to do it again?' Ellison asked.

'Yes,' she replied after a moment. 'I think I would. Just don't expect anything from me. Friends, that's all.'

'Nothing more than company,' he promised.

McMillan was waiting at the entrance to Millgarth when she arrived on Monday morning. It was still dark, an acrid fog clinging in the air to make people choke and cough. He tossed her the car keys.

'Where, sir?'

'Holbeck.' A single word but he filled it with darkness. It must be bad.

She followed his directions, parking a street away from the fake Egyptian bulk of Temple Mill. Even there she could hear the machines of the day shift already hard at work, churning out uniforms for the troops.

Lottie followed McMillan round one corner, followed immediately by another, until they reached an anonymous brick building. A copper stood outside; he saluted as soon as he recognised the chief superintendent, and opened the door. Muttered voices came from a room at the end of the corridor. In the harsh electric light she saw Inspector Andrews, DC Smith close behind him as always.

The temperature cooled as they approached and Lottie noticed the fur coats hanging on racks along the walls of the room. Cold storage. She felt goose pimples forming on her skin and wished she'd worn gloves.

Closer, she could see a man's legs. He was kneeling on the floor, examining something.

'What—' she began, but McMillan held up his hand.

'Tell me what you know,' he said to Andrews.

THE YEAR OF THE GUN

'About two hours ago, Wilkins, the beat man, was going by and saw the front door open.' The inspector ran a hand over his hair. 'He thought maybe Sid Cohen had come down to pick up a fur coat for one of his customers – he keeps them down here, nice and cold. Wilkins came in, said hello. Then there's a shot, he's lying on the floor with blood coming out of his shoulder and someone's running off.'

'How is he?'

'At the infirmary. He was lucky, just winged, really.'

'Shot.' McMillan's voice was icy.

'Yes, sir.' Andrews nodded. 'That's not the worst of it. Take a look.' He moved aside. The police pathologist was still on his knees, examining the body of a young woman. She lay in the middle of the room, still wearing her smart WRNS uniform. Only the hat was missing.

The doctor turned his head.

'If you're hoping for quick answers, you're out of luck. The only thing I can say for certain is that she was shot. I can probably tell you more after I've had her on the slab.'

'How soon?' McMillan couldn't take his eyes off the girl and Lottie knew he was thinking about his daughter, a Wren stationed on the south coast.

'I can have a report to you by dinnertime.'

'Any identification yet?'

'That's your department, Chief Superintendent.'

McMillan glanced at Andrews.

'I'm leaving it for the evidence men.'

'Fine.' A few more minutes wouldn't make any difference. He cleared his throat. 'Lottie,' he whispered in her ear, voice close to cracking, 'please can you see if she's wearing underwear.'

She didn't want to do it, didn't want to touch a corpse. But they had to be certain. Taking a deep breath, she gently lifted the hem of the skirt. A quick glance.

'No, sir, she's not.' Lottie blushed and kept her eyes on the floor.

He moved away, pulling out the packet of Four Square and lighting one, standing by a small pool of dark liquid in the corridor. When they entered she'd thought it was water. Now she knew. A copper's blood.

'I want Sid Cohen down at the station as soon as you can get him there,' McMillan ordered. 'Where's the evidence crew?'

'On their way,' Andrews said. 'I'm sending Smith to the hospital to get Wilkins's statement.'

'I want people scouring the area. I know it's isolated back here, but was anyone seen running off. The usual.'

'Driving,' Lottie said, and he nodded.

'Or driving. Any cars parked. You know what to do.'

'Yes, sir.'

It was a cold, damp February day, but outside seemed balmy after the hard chill inside.

'Do you understand it?' she asked.

'No.' Angry. Curt. His jaw was set, eyes hard.

It had to be the same murderer. Shot; the MO fitted perfectly. But… the other bodies had been left once they were dead. Patterson had died at the abbey, Goodman had been dumped there soon after. They hadn't been stored anywhere. This was different. It didn't fit.

'One thing,' she said. 'Whoever did this knows Leeds. He didn't just stumble on that cold storage.'

He took a few more paces. 'It rules out Americans, is that what you mean?'

'I don't know,' she said in frustration. Probably. Whatever it was, she felt on the verge of tears. A woman, killed, left there like meat in a freezer, as if she was nothing. Wasn't there already enough death in the world without all this? She blinked and rubbed at her eyes, knowing he was watching her. McMillan put a hand on her arm.

'Why don't you walk back to Millgarth? Take your time. I can drive myself.'

'All right,' she agreed after a moment. 'Thank you.' She turned away, then quickly back. 'Cohen. He's a furrier?'

'Yes.'

'You should get a list of everyone who's worked for him.'

'I'd already thought of it,' he told her. 'But two heads are better than one.' The expression on his face turned bitter. 'Pound to a penny it's the girl from the house on Shire Oak Road. I can feel it.'

'But how? If she'd been with an American up there, how had she ended up here?'

'I don't know,' McMillan said emptily. 'I'm starting to feel like I'm drowning in questions.'

Lottie took her time. With all the paperwork he wouldn't need her for a little while. She needed to let her mind clear, if it ever could. When she agreed to be McMillan's driver she'd never bargained for this. He'd said he wanted her brain as well as her ability behind the wheel. But even long ago, when she was a copper, she'd never seen anything quite as bad as this. That poor girl, left there…

Three murders now. Three women, all from the services, dead in a few days. It seemed impossible, it was… she didn't know the words to describe it. Insanity, it had to be.

'Are you all right, luv?'

'What?' A hand on her sleeve and she turned to see a small woman looking up at her.

'You're stood there crying. I thought you must have had some bad news.'

'I…' She took a deep breath. 'I don't know, maybe I have.' She could feel the wetness of tears on her cheeks and swiped at them with the back of her hand. 'Thank you.'

'You don't look well. Do you need something?'

'I'll be fine,' Lottie assured her and attempted a smile. 'Honestly.'

'If you say so,' the woman said doubtfully, then moved on, arm weighed down by her shopping bag.

Lottie kept a small compact in her uniform pocket. She dabbed at the last of the tears with her handkerchief and repaired the damage. At least she'd look presentable when she reached the station. It was stupid, letting the job affect her that way. She couldn't have stopped those women being killed. All over the world people were dying, every day, every minute. What she could do was help find the killer.

Crying had helped; a little, anyway. The worst of the sorrow was out of her system, but the determination remained.

The door was closed but she could hear voices from McMillan's office. Cohen the furrier must have arrived. She picked up the telephone and asked Helen on the switchboard to connect her to the Area HQ at Castle Grove. Finally she reached Ellison's office.

'Have you heard yet?'

'Heard what?' He hasn't, she thought.

'One of ours has been shot, and we found another body.'

'What?'

Lottie heard the disbelief in his voice. She gave him the bare bones, what little she knew. 'The boss thinks she might be the girl from Shire Oak Road.'

'That's…' For a moment he didn't seem to know what to say. 'It's crazy. Do you know her name? Anything more about her?'

'The evidence bods are going over everything. Wait a minute.' She put her palm over the receiver as a police messenger boy stood holding a piece of paper.

'For the Chief Super,' he said nervously. Too old for school, too young for the service, the Police Auxiliary Messengers did the boring jobs, from filing to running errands.

'Thank you.'

She read it quickly then scribbled a note, tore it off and gave it to the lad. 'Take that to Missing Persons, will you?'

'Yes, ma'am.'

'It looks as if we have a name for her – Pamela Dixon,' she told Ellison. 'Stationed down in Portsmouth. She must have family here. Aged twenty-three. She was a Leading Wren, whatever that means.'

'Nothing on the bullet? Cartridge?'

'Not yet. The pathologist will be doing the post-mortem now, I expect. No idea on the cartridge.'

'I'm coming over,' he decided.

'All right,' Lottie agreed after a minute. 'I have to say, it's looking less and less as if one of your chaps did it.'

'The gun still came from us,' Ellison said. 'That makes it our responsibility. I'll be there pretty soon.'

She'd barely lowered the handset than a fist banged against the door jamb. Detective Constable Smith. He'd been sent to the infirmary to interview the constable.

'How is he?' Lottie asked.

'He's lucky, he took it in his shoulder.' Smith looked stunned. He was young, in the police instead of the army. If he'd thought this was the easy option, he was learning. 'Billy Wilkins, do you know him?'

She did. Past conscription age but not old enough to retire. Conscientious, always a smile on his face. Poor man. At least he'd be fine.

'What did he have to say?'

'All in my report.' He produced the paper with a flourish and placed it on her desk. 'They've already sent him home. A few weeks on the sick and he'll be good as new.'

'I'll pass it on,' she promised.

McMillan's door was still closed. She glanced at the statement Smith had given her. It was fairly complete, finished with Wilkins's shaky signature. She already knew most of it from Andrews. The gunman hadn't spoken, everything had happened too quickly for a proper description. All Wilkins recalled was someone tall and broad in dark clothes who seemed to block out the light. Then the shot and he was on his back as the man ran out past him. He'd seen a few cars in the neighbouring streets but there'd been no reason to remember them. Until this morning he hadn't seen any activity around the building since Cohen had last been there, just before Christmas.

Not that much use.

Another five minutes passed before Cohen emerged, a squat, heavy man in an overcoat with an astrakhan collar. His face was red but there was relief in his eyes. Lottie gave him time to reach the stairs then hurried across the corridor.

'This is where we stand,' Lottie said as she gave him the reports.

McMillan skimmed the sheets.

'Thank God for small mercies, anyway; Wilkins is going to be all right. I need someone looking into Miss Dixon.'

'I've asked Missing Persons to check on her.'

'Good. Get Smith working on it, too. She must have been visiting someone up here.'

'I rang Ellison. He's on his way.'

'Oh, hell. Why?' He frowned. 'I don't need him around.'

'With another body, I thought he should know. Was Mr Cohen able to help?'

'Not really. He only goes down there when one of his customers wants her coat and no-one's asked for one in quite a while. There are keys to the place at his shop and another set at home. He gave me a list of everyone he's employed in the last four years. We'll need to track them down and talk to them.'

'Yes, sir.' She made a note on the pad. 'Anything else for now?'

'I'll want the post-mortem report as soon as we have it.' He checked his watch. 'Why don't you give them a ring and see if they have anything yet. If there's a bullet I want Lawton to examine it as soon as possible.'

'I'll take care of it.' Lottie stood, hands on hips and looked at him.

'What?'

'You. You look like you haven't slept properly in days. I'll get you a cup of tea.' She wasn't going to mention her own little crying fit; no need for that.

'And biscuits if they have them.'

'Don't push your luck,' she warned.

No Wrens reported to Missing Persons. The evidence crew had recovered a cartridge at the cold storage; Lawton was already checking it under his microscope. Nothing yet from the doctor carrying out the post-mortem. One of those times when everything felt in limbo, Lottie thought as she sat with McMillan and Ellison.

The conversation was going nowhere, simply words to fill the silence. They all stopped and turned at the knock on the door.

Lawton, looking as dapper as ever. His suit could have come straight from the tailor, no grime on the white shirt collar, the knot in his tie perfect. Hair Brylcreemed, parting immaculately straight.

'I've done the best comparison I can manage with our equipment,' he said.

'Well?' McMillan asked.

'It's the same as the cartridge we discovered at Kirkstall, sir. I'd go to court and swear on it.'

'That's good enough for me.' He looked at the American. 'Any questions?'

'I guess not.' Ellison looked thoughtful. There couldn't be any doubt that one man had killed all three girls. And now he'd shot a policeman. The only good thing was that the copper had survived.

'How do we keep it out of the papers now?' Lottie asked.

The superintendent gave a deep sigh. 'We can't. Not about Wilkins, anyway. The women, though… it would hurt morale. If it comes to it, the Home Office will issue a D-Notice.'

'What's that?' Ellison asked.

'The government stops all the papers publishing anything about the case.'

'But how can that help?' the American said. 'People might have seen something. They could come forward.'

'And in the meantime we have a population panicking because three women have been murdered here, and service girls singled out.' McMillan shook his head. 'We've weighed it up and made our decision.'

'Your choice. But I think you're wrong.'

'It's the way things are and we have to work with them. The question is, where do we go from here?'

'You've probably already figured this out,' Ellison said, 'But where this happened and with the body stashed there, it has to mean that none of my people are involved.'

'There's still the gun.'

'Yeah, I know,' he admitted sadly. 'I know.'

'If this happened in Seattle, how would you approach it?' McMillan asked.

She knew what that meant. He had no ideas, he was digging for a fresh approach. For anything at all that could provide a spark.

'Right now I'd be hauling in everyone who knew about that cold storage place,' Ellison replied after a moment.

'We're talking to them all.'

'Sweat them properly.'

'Don't worry. We will.'

'Any connection between the dead women?'

'Not that we can tell, but we don't know anything about the third yet.'

'I don't know, then. All I can do is keep pushing from my end. I'm looking at a quartermaster's assistant. With a little luck I should be able to start roasting him tomorrow. If he wants to escape a long time in the stockade, he'll talk. Then we can follow the gun from the other end.'

'If he talks,' Lottie said.

Ellison turned to her with a smile that held no warmth. 'This is the army. If he knows what's good for him, he'll talk.'

'The sooner, the better,' McMillan said. 'Come in,' he shouted to a knock on the door.

The post-mortem report was exactly what they'd expected. Pamela Dixon had been shot, no bullet left in her body, but the wound was identical to the other murdered women. She'd had vaginal intercourse prior to death. Estimating the time of death was impossible; there was no way to tell how long she'd been in cold storage. The pathologist refused to even guess.

DC Smith had contacted the Admiralty about Pamela Dixon. Eventually he'd been put through to her CO in Portsmouth. Leading Wren Dixon had been given a week's compassionate leave for the funeral of her parents in Birmingham.

'Birmingham?' McMillan asked in astonishment.

'That was my reaction, too, sir,' Smith said. 'She's from there. Her story was that an unexploded bomb had gone off. No reason to doubt it. She wasn't due back until tomorrow.'

The chief superintendent lit a cigarette and took a long, deep drag. 'Right. Talk to Birmingham CID. Find out if she really does have family there and if there's any truth in the story. Then you can get on to Portsmouth CID. They need to talk to Dixon's friends, anyone she might have confided in. She didn't end up in Leeds by accident.'

A few more orders then just the three of them remained in the office.

'It's the damnedest thing I ever heard,' Ellison said.

'Maybe she was meeting someone,' Lottie said. 'Having an affair.' It was the only thing she could imagine. The others stared at her. 'Think about it for a minute. It makes sense, meeting where no one knows them. And it would explain why no one's reported her missing – it was all illicit from the start.'

'It's plausible,' McMillan agreed with a nod. 'But how do we go about proving it?'

She thought quickly. 'We need to check all the hotels. They'll want somewhere fairly anonymous, so it won't be a boarding house. Make up an artist's sketch of her face, see if it rings any bells.'

Ellison was gazing at the floor, gnawing at the skin beside his thumbnail.

'OK, that's good,' he said with approval. 'And if she was meeting someone, you should be able to track him down.'

'That doesn't mean he's our man.'

'There's a good chance of it. Even if he's innocent, he still has a hell of a lot of questions to answer.' He looked at his watch. 'I need to go back to HQ, I've got an operation happening in an hour. Can you keep me informed? And I might have something for you tomorrow or the day after.'

McMillan stubbed out his cigarette, adding to the tall pile in the ashtray. 'That's a good idea of yours.'

'I could be completely wrong,' Lottie said.

'It sounds right. And we won't know until we try.'

She hesitated for a moment before speaking again.

'Have you thought..?'

'What?' He looked at her with curiosity.

She didn't want to say it. But the words needed to come out, whether he liked them or not.

'Maybe it's time to call Scotland Yard in on this. They have all the resources, everyone will co-operate with them.'

'And they don't know Leeds from a hole in the ground.' He pursed his lips together. 'Believe me, I've thought about it every night when I've been trying to get to sleep. But these murders all happened here. They're my responsibility.'

'I had to say it.'

'I know. But we'll slog our way through. Let's get people moving and see what they can shake up.'

Through the day there was nothing. Just a sense of growing frustration. Uniforms were checking all the hotels. By evening they'd had no word and Lottie began to doubt her idea. There could be so many other reasons for the woman to be in Leeds.

'We'll see what the morning brings,' McMillan told her as she finished her shift. 'There's nothing we can do.'

That didn't stop her worrying on the bus home, or as she made her tea. She kept all the leaflets from the Ministry of Food in the cupboard over the draining board. Something from Potato Pete tonight, perhaps; use up those spuds. But where did they come up with such stupid names?

The radio was playing in the dining room. The American Forces' Network, crackly as ever, but more lively than anything the BBC broadcast. There was energy in the swing music that the staid British dance bands could never capture. That American eagerness for life. A bit like Cliff Ellison.

Stop it, she thought. He was a very pleasant man, but that was all. Soon enough it would be spring. Already the evenings were longer. This weekend she'd probably be able to start turning over the soil in the garden. Digging for victory.

She and Geoff had always grown what they could, long before it became a necessity, setting aside an area for fruit and vegetables. The front might show a sharp, pristine face to the world, neatly mown green lawn and rose borders, but the back was more haphazard and utilitarian.

Working in the garden was where she missed him most. They'd always done it together. Sunday mornings, rain or shine, only taking a break during the winter months. Geoff had taught her about plants, although God only knew where he'd learned.

Now the whole street had muddy patches in their gardens for growing food. He'd have been pleased by that.

CHAPTER EIGHT

'RIGHT,' McMillan said into the phone. 'We'll be there in a few minutes.'

He marched out of his office, pushing his arms into his overcoat.

'We might have something,' he said. 'Get your skates on.'

In the Humber she played with the choke until the engine was purring evenly, then set off through town. The Queens Hotel stood next to the railway station. It had a sleek, modern design, white stone that stood out against the dark Victorian fustiness of Leeds.

She'd never been inside before; the closest she'd come was the little newsreel cinema down the street which showed the Pathé news. But the hotel's style carried beyond the façade to the Art Deco desk. DC Smith stood by it, talking to a fat, sweating clerk.

'Tell the Chief Superintendent what you told me,' Smith prompted.

The clerk cleared his throat. 'Room 315 was supposed to leave yesterday.' He glanced at the faces to make sure they all understood. 'But we had no record of departure, so this morning I went up with my pass key. There was a Do Not Disturb notice on the handle; the chambermaid said it's been in place since the guests arrived.' He paused, expecting questions, but none came. 'Inside there was a suitcase. The bed had been slept in. No sign of anyone there, though.'

'Who took the room?' McMillan asked. 'When did they arrive? How did they pay?'

'It's right here.' He pushed the hotel register across the counter and pointed with a stubby finger. 'A week ago. Captain and Mrs Jackson. Our guests pay when they leave.'

A home address in Birmingham. She jotted it in her notebook. It didn't look as if Pamela Dixon had been going to her parents' funeral after all.

'Does anyone remember them, what they looked like?'

'I was working then,' the clerk said. 'We get so many people coming through, especially these days. They were both in uniform, I remember that. But…' he shrugged. 'I'm sorry.'

'I need to take a look at the room. No one's cleaned in there?'

'No, but we have another booking—'

'It'll have to wait. Smith, I want the evidence people down here. Fingerprints.'

'Yes, sir.'

'Let's take a look, shall we?'

The room was smaller than Lottie expected. It smelt empty, neglected. Stale tobacco in the air, a dozen cigarette ends in the ashtray. Only one had lipstick, she saw. A double bed, but the covers were only turned down on one side; a dent in the pillow. A door led through to the en-suite bathroom. Very posh, she thought. Make-up by the sink, a toothbrush on its own in the glass.

A hairbrush sat on the dressing table, and next to it, on the floor, a small suitcase, the lid tossed back to show a woman's underwear and a nightgown.

'Like the *Mary Celeste*, isn't it?' she commented.

'There's definitely something wrong here,' McMillan agreed.

Lottie checked the wardrobe; nothing hanging inside. The windowsills were empty too.

'She was here, wasn't she?'

He nodded. 'What I'd like to know is who was with her and where the hell he is now.'

Plenty of different fingerprints, but it only took a few minutes to find a match for Pamela Dixon. On the suitcase, the hairbrush, in the bathroom.

'Take prints from all the people who work at the hotel,' McMillan ordered. 'Eliminate everyone you can. Send all the prints to Records, see if there are any matches.'

'There's one big question,' Lottie said eventually. She'd been sitting quietly, sipping a cup of tea and thinking. 'Miss Dixon obviously arrived with someone. But as far as I can see she never slept at the hotel and she ends up dead in a cold storage in Holbeck. Clothes in her suitcase, but she's still in uniform.' She looked at McMillan. 'How?'

'If I had the answer to that one, the killer would already be in custody.'

'And the two other deaths?'

He shook his head. 'I don't know. I just don't know. Whoever she was with is the obvious suspect.'

'But he'd need to know Leeds,' Lottie pointed out, 'and have a key to Cohen's place.'

The telephone rang and he picked it up. 'Yes. That's fine.' He frowned. 'Are you certain? Positive? OK, thank you.' He put down the receiver slowly. 'That was the pathologist,' he said, lighting a cigarette. 'The underwear we found at Shire Oak Road belonged to Pamela Dixon. He checked hairs under the microscope; they match.'

'But that means he killed three girls in three nights.'

'More than that, it means he has to be someone who's local, who knows Shire Oak Road, Kirkstall Abbey, and Cohen's cold storage.' He counted out the points on his fingers. 'And he has American friends.'

'Doesn't that narrow it down?'

'Not enough. Not by a long shot.' He let out a weary sigh. 'We don't have any names.'

'So what do we do now?' Lottie asked.

'Start trying to unpick this mess and see where it leads us. Let's just hope Ellison can find something at his end.'

'Maybe one of her friends in Portsmouth will know who she was meeting here.'

'Maybe.' He said it like a man without much hope in his soul.

McMillan told her to give out the tasks, and she saw the disappointment on the faces of the men. More work, not less. Another job piled on the growing heap, each more urgent that the last. But there was no point in apologies. They meant little and they were soon forgotten. This was what they did.

'I'd like to take a look at the luggage Dixon brought with her,' Lottie said. 'And what she had in her pockets, too.'

'Go down to evidence,' McMillan told her. 'It's all there. What are you thinking?'

'Nothing.' She shrugged. 'Maybe it'll give me an idea.'

Down in the cellar, the evidence room had the kind of aching, permanent cold that penetrated to the bone. Her fingers felt frozen as she opened the catch on the suitcase and pushed back the lid, taking out each item and laying it on the bench. The underwear was nothing unusual. None of the banned lace or frills. Cotton, not silk; no one had been giving her extravagant gifts. Most of it had the St Michael tag from Marks & Spencer. A pair of darned stockings. A folded Utility dress with the CC41 label and another, cotton, older; she hadn't even hung them up to take out the wrinkles.

The cosmetics were ordinary enough. Probably black market, but there was nothing unusual in that. Lottie's face powder was from under the counter and she didn't like to think what might be in it.

Old hairbrush, a lipstick that looked as if had been made by heating several old ones together. There was absolutely nothing unusual about Pamela Dixon at all. Nothing to give a hint of who she'd been, how she'd seen herself.

She tipped out the contents of a paper bag pushed into the pocket in the lid of the case. National Identity Card in Dixon's name. A travel warrant from Portsmouth to Birmingham and back. That was interesting: no mention of Leeds, but it fitted in with the funeral story. No letters, nothing that could incriminate anyone. Pamela Dixon was almost anonymous.

'Anything from Birmingham yet?' Lottie asked McMillan when she returned to the office, brushing dust and dirt off her uniform.

'The police there are supposed to be checking.' He sorted through the sheets of paper crowding his desk. 'Haven't heard back yet.'

'Her warrant is Portsmouth to Birmingham and back, and she didn't have a train ticket for Leeds.'

'She could have hitchhiked,' McMillan said.

'Bit iffy if you have an assignation.' She chewed her lip. 'Why Leeds? It's the other end of the country to where she's stationed.'

'It could be to make sure no one would recognise them.'

Yet that didn't feel quite right, Lottie thought.

'Unless one of them is very well-known, they could have picked a hundred other places that were closer.' She paused. 'Maybe she came to him. It makes sense. If he's the killer, he knows Leeds, after all.'

McMillan was nodding. 'It would fit.' His face brightened a little. 'It might even answer one or two questions.'

'Not enough to give us anything solid, though.'

'It's a start,' he assured her and tapped his fountain pen against the desk. 'He signed himself as Captain Jackson.'

'What about it?' Lottie asked.

'There are thousands of captains around. It's not a rank that stands out. Just high enough to gain some respect, but not be noticed. And a young man can be a captain these days.'

'So maybe he's not in the service and got a uniform from somewhere?'

'I don't know,' McMillan admitted. 'I'm throwing ideas in the air. But if he wasn't really in the army, I think Dixon would have worked that out quickly enough.'

'Maybe she did,' Lottie suggested. 'Perhaps that's why she's dead.'

'Possibly. But that doesn't explain the rest.' He tapped with the pen again. 'They have a perfectly comfortable hotel room but they go out and find a cold, dirty house on Shire Oak Road. Why?'

She couldn't picture a reason.

'Another thing,' Lottie said, seeing the room in her mind. 'They're lovers, but the bed in the room has only been disturbed by one person sleeping there. Surely the first thing they'd do once they were alone…'

'And she'd had sexual intercourse before she died.' He stared at her. 'What's the line from that book? "Curiouser and curiouser"?'

'Who's questioning the staff at the Queens?'

'A couple of Specials. It's all we can spare.'

'I could talk to the chambermaids,' she offered.

He weighed her words for a long time.

'I can't. I'm sorry, but not when there are other coppers around. It's not allowed,' he reminded her kindly. 'You know that as well as I do. I know you're good, but…' He let the sentence trail away. And he was right. She was an auxiliary. Her duties were limited, and they didn't include any real police work. When no one else was around it was a different matter. If others could see, they might complain.

'I'll go to the canteen and fetch us more tea, then.' She tried to sound bright, but inside she felt disappointment. They had women police constables on the force, more than just the two that existed twenty years earlier, but they were stretched with work, too. Everyone was these days.

It stung, but she should have known. McMillan would stretch the rules when he could, but even he daren't break them completely. The same way he'd always been. She was the one who flouted orders.

He was still staring into space when she returned carrying two cups. Lottie put his on the desk and left quietly.

'Come on,' McMillan said from the door of her office. 'We're going back to Holbeck.'

'Something new?' She put her cap on her head and slipped into her raincoat.

'I want another gander at that cold storage. Too many people there before.'

People were streaming out of the factories on their dinner breaks, standing on the steps, lighting cigarettes and drawing down the smoke. Women outnumbered men. Hundreds of them, hair tied up in turbans and scarves, many wearing boiler suits, trousers, or overalls. She parked as close as she could to Cohen's building.

'There wouldn't be people around to see him shifting a body first thing in the morning, especially with the blackout,' McMillan said as he gazed around. 'Nowhere that overlooks this place, either.'

He strode by the special constable guarding the building with a quick salute. Lottie gave the man a smile. On duty there hour after hour was a thankless task.

The storage room had that animal smell of pelt. No matter how they treated the skins, that never seemed to fade. She had a cheap fur coat in the wardrobe at home with the exact same scent.

'Why would people keep their coats in storage in the middle of winter?' she wondered out loud. Sables, minks, others she couldn't identify, but all expensive and soft to the touch.

'Maybe the owners have gone away or died.' He was crouching, looking at the rough chalk outline on the floor that showed where Pamela Dixon had been. 'No attempt to hide her. No blood anywhere on the floor in here. Anyone walking in would have seen her right off. Unless…' He paced around the small room. 'You see those long coats in the corner?'

About ten of them, all ankle length, almost touching the floor.

'Yes,' Lottie replied, not sure what he meant.

'What if he'd hidden the body behind those and he was disturbed pulling it out?'

'I don't know.' She wasn't so certain. 'Wilkins—'

'What about him?'

'He said he hadn't seen a vehicle outside here.'

He could have parked close by. Kept it away from the door to avoid suspicion.' He shook his head. 'I don't know, it's all guesswork. One thing's certain, though; he was pretty sure he wouldn't be disturbed. He knew the fur business.'

'And Cohen's business in particular.'

'Yes.'

McMillan stood in the doorway, surveying the scene, then turned and started down the corridor. More chalk marked where Wilkins had been, another cross showed where they'd found the cartridge.

'He must have been around here when he shot Wilkins,' he said. 'Then he ran.' Out in the light again, he began to walk around the block. 'Three dead women, one wounded copper, and we still hardly know a damned thing more than when we began.'

'Maybe some of the interviews will tell us more.'

Someone had to remember something, Lottie thought. One little thing, just one, would seem like a leap forward.

She could feel McMillan's frustration; it came off him in waves. By the time they reached the Humber he was ominously silent. She'd seen this before. Better not to say a word until he was ready to speak. She turned the ignition, put the car in gear and began to drive back to Millgarth.

That was where he needed to be. He might not know it, might not want to be stuck in his office, but he needed to assess every statement that was taken, to find the little strands and connections worth following. Someone had to be in charge of the big picture, and rank meant it was him.

'Go out along Chapeltown Road,' he ordered as she moved along Briggate, past the bricked-up front of Marks & Spencer. With the war, their new shop hadn't opened; the Ministry of Works was using it.

'Yes, sir.'

'Park here,' McMillan told her eventually. She glanced at him in the mirror. Years before, back when she was a WPC and he seemed to give her a lift home so often, he'd drop her off at this parade of shops. Did he remember? Without a word he disappeared into the grocer's. Wilson's; still the same name. The business looked run down, but they all did now, with so little stock. Just a few faded packets and boxes on display in the window.

She was lost in the past when he returned with a paper bag. 'Potternewton Park,' he announced.

At the entrance he showed his warrant card to a council worker. After that Lottie could drive where she liked along the path. Eventually she halted under some old, bare oaks.

'My God, is that real ham?' she asked as he passed her a sandwich. 'And white bread?' She hadn't seen that in a long time.

'Wilson owed me a couple of favours.'

Only one slice of meat, and margarine, not butter, but it was still heaven. Like eating the memory of how things had been before '39. They sat in silence, never minding the cold, listening to the birds calling as they ate.

McMillan swallowed the last of the bread, crumpled the paper and wiped his hands clean. He lit a cigarette and said, 'I suppose we'd better get to work.'

Lottie raised her eyebrows. 'Do I get a chance to finish my food first?'

He grinned. 'If you hurry up. Can't spend all day dawdling.'

On the way back into town he was more genial. The mood had passed and he was back to his usual self. A sheaf of reports waited on his desk. Lottie opened her notebook and sat with a pencil as he went through them.

'Here we are,' he said, drawing one from the pile. 'Birmingham. Pamela Dixon's parents are both alive and well. Hadn't heard from their daughter since Christmas… not close… didn't know anything about her personal life since she joined the Wrens.'

It didn't matter if they were close or not. She couldn't begin to imagine what they must be feeling now. The numbness, the loss. Nothing but memories to sift through and years of emptiness ahead. Worse still that Pamela had been murdered. You could make some jumbled sense of natural causes; she knew that from her own experience. You could even find a kind of redemption from a death in battle. But a killing like this left nothing at all. Nothing but bleakness.

'None of her friends on base seemed to know she was meeting anyone.' He was reading from another piece of paper. 'That's what they claim, anyway. The DS who did the interviews isn't certain he believes them. As far as Dixon told them, her parents had died and she was going to the funeral and to sort through the house. She was cagey.'

'Had she been up this way before? Did anyone ask?'

He skimmed the rest of the document. 'Not mentioned.'

'She met the man somewhere. If it wasn't down there, we need to look at where she's been. Had she been in Leeds before?'

'Good point.' He jotted something on his blotter. 'I'll have CID down there dig a bit deeper. But none of her friends mentioned a regular boyfriend.'

'Married man,' Lottie said suddenly. 'She'd keep that quiet, wouldn't she?'

'True,' he agreed with a slow nod. 'Married man, someone who knows Leeds and is familiar with Cohen's business. Possibly in the service, an officer with access to Americans or the black market. Has money, too,' he added. 'The Queens isn't a cheap place to stay.'

'That definitely narrows it down.'

'If we're right,' McMillan warned. 'I can't afford to stake everything on one idea.'

'It's still worth pursuing.'

'We will, don't worry about that.' He glanced at his watch. 'I have a meeting with the chief constable at two; you hold the fort. Anything really urgent, ring through to the Civic Hall and disturb me.'

She read through the reports as she added them to the file. There was nothing he hadn't already noted, just reams of the background that made up every murder case.

Lottie settled down with Graham Greene, but she'd only managed five pages when the telephone began to ring. Helen on the switchboard.

'Is he in? He's not answering.'

'He's out talking to the chief.'

'I've got a woman on the line who says her daughter went out last night and still hasn't come home.' She paused for a fraction of a second. 'The girl's in the Land Army, home on leave. I thought…' The other deaths. Everyone knew, just not officially.

'Put her through.'

Mrs Kemp lived out towards West Park, not far from the POW camp. Her daughter Lily was twenty-three, had joined the Land Army four years before. Stationed in Wales. She was home on a three-day pass. The evening before she'd gone into town, meeting some friends at the pictures, then probably on dancing.

'She didn't come back last night,' the woman said, trying to push the fear out of her voice. 'I thought, well, she's young. I remember what I was like. And there's a war on. But when she didn't show up this morning, I started to worry.' Her voice faltered. 'And she's due back in Wales tonight. Her dad's at work.' Her voice cracked. 'There's only me here and I don't know what to do.'

'Give me your address again, Mrs Kemp. We'll be there in a little while.' She tried to sound soothing. 'Look, there's probably a rational explanation. There usually is, you know.'

She had to persuade an officious switchboard operator to put her through to the chief constable's office. McMillan listened, then said, 'Pick me up. Soon as you can.'

Just a few telephone calls before she left: the infirmary, St James's Hospital, the mortuary, even central records to be certain the girl hadn't been arrested. But she wasn't in any of those places.

She followed Queenwood Drive out from Headingley, turning along Spen Lane until she found the house. In the distance the tall barbed wire fence and towers of the POW camp stood against the horizon on Butcher Hill. This one held Germans; that was what she'd heard.

The front door of the house opened even before they'd reached the drive. Mrs Kemp, drab, ordinary, hands moving around each other, the skin on her face taut with worry.

She didn't have much to add to the story. The names and workplaces of the two girls Lily was supposed to meet in town and a photograph in uniform taken the summer before. Nothing memorable about her face. A pleasant smile, slightly timorous.

'We'll look after this,' Lottie said. 'I promise. Do you know where Lily was planning to go with her friends?'

'She never said. Just the pictures and dancing, that's all.' Mrs Kemp bit her lip. 'She's always been a good girl, always come home before. Something's happened to her, hasn't it?'

'You don't know that,' Lottie said. She took hold of the woman's hand and looked her in the eye. A calm voice and a uniform could reassure people. 'We're going to look for her. What was she wearing when she went out?'

A floral dress, stockings, black shoes with a court heel. All things she kept at home for her visits. A heavy wool coat in dark blue. No hat.

'Not in uniform,' McMillan said as he settled on the back seat of the Humber.

'I know. But maybe he's spreading his net wider.'

'Maybe,' he said doubtfully. 'I don't see why he'd suddenly change. There's no shortage of women in uniform in town.' He sighed. 'Let's go and talk to the friends she was meeting.'

But they both told the same story. They'd been waiting together outside the Odeon on Briggate by quarter past seven, in ample time for the next showing of the film at half past. Lily never arrived. Finally, with a minute to spare, they'd bought their tickets and gone in. Afterwards to a club on Vicar Lane and the last bus home. They hadn't seen her at all.

Late in the day, dusk growing, but he still ordered officers out to search the grounds at Kirkstall Abbey until it was dark.

'There's nothing more we can do,' Lottie said. She gazed at the photograph on her desk. 'How many hundreds of young women were out in Leeds last night?'

'Get copies of that picture made. I want every man on the beat to have it. Details – height, weight, everything. Missing.'

'The papers will get hold of it.'

He nodded. 'I'm going to give it to them. Lily Kemp was in civvies. We don't *know* what's happened to her. I'm not going to mention the other three, and nor will any reporter if they know which side their bread's buttered. The fact she wasn't in uniform gives us something we can use.'

'She's dead, isn't she?' Lottie said.

McMillan let out a sigh. 'Probably. Number four. Too many. Far too many.' He lit a cigarette. 'Get that picture out and give our American friend a ring. See if he's come up with anything yet.'

An American voice said Ellison wasn't in his office but he'd ring back later. She typed Lily Kemp's details on a piece of paper, glanced at the photograph again and took them to Olivia, one of the young WAPC clerks. At the change of shift all the men on the beat would have the information.

Nothing to do now but wait. They had nowhere to turn, no one they could question. No one would remember her in the pubs or clubs. Just another face to be served and forgotten.

Something had happened between the time she left home and when she was due to meet her friends. Not something – someone. A man.

Had they met on the bus? Possibly, she decided, but that felt unlikely. This was a killer who drove. It had to be in town.

Could she have been early and stopped somewhere for a drink before meeting her friends?

Plenty of places between the bus station and the cinema, and there was nothing too strange about a woman going into a pub alone these days. If he'd found her, if it was the same man, it had all been by chance. Doubtless he'd been prowling, keeping his eye open for a victim, but finding the right woman depended completely on luck.

'It's worth checking,' McMillan said when she suggested talking to pub barmen in the area. 'Right now I'm willing to try anything.' He gave a snort. 'I don't suppose you know any mediums?'

An hour passed. McMillan's door was closed but she could hear his voice on the telephone, a long, involved conversation. Lottie sat in her office, trying to read *The Power and the Glory*. But her mind kept drifting. By half past six Ellison hadn't rung and she felt weary. No more word on Lily Kemp. Each hour that passed made it more certain that her name could be added to the roll call of the dead.

Finally the superintendent told her to go home.

'We're not likely to learn anything more tonight. And if we do it probably won't be good.'

Outside the bus window the world was black. She'd learned to judge where they were by the length and steepness of the hills then the flat stretches of road. As the bus pulled away from the stop and started up a small gradient, she stood.

She felt weary. All the killings, seeing the poor, sad corpses left her drained, all her emotions at rock bottom. Upstairs at home she changed into an old dress, taking off the scratchy black uniform stockings and rubbing her calves. The house was chilly, the fire just lit, but the air felt good on her legs.

Lottie had just started down the stairs when the knock came on the door. With the blackout curtain in place there it was impossible to see who was there. And at the front door, too. That was formal; neighbours would come to the back.

'Who is it?'

'Cliff Ellison.'

Lottie froze for a moment. She'd never told him where she lived. She hadn't invited him round. How..?

'Wait a minute.'

The elaborate routine of switching off the lights before drawing back the curtain and unlocking the door. Then he was inside, a faint, masculine scent that seemed to fill the hall.

'Come through,' she told him when they could see each other. 'In there.'

She settled him in one of the armchairs by the fire, where Geoff used to sit. It was strange to see another man there. Not wrong, just… different.

'Would you like some tea? I haven't eaten, I could make some supper.' Hush, she told herself. You're wittering.

'Tea would be good,' he said with a soft smile. 'I guess you don't have coffee.'

'No.'

In the kitchen she busied herself with the kettle and teapot. Yesterday's leaves, but they'd have to do. She felt nervous with him in the house. Whether that was in a good or a bad way, she wasn't certain yet. When she reappeared, resting the tray on a battered old pouffe, he had stood up and was glancing through the titles on the bookcase.

'You don't look the type to be interested in engines and radio.'

'My husband was. Usually he was rebuilding something on the table.' She glanced across to it, on the other side of the room. 'How did you get my address?' She stared at him. 'And why?'

He sat down, stretching out long legs towards the fire.

'I got a message that you'd called. But when I tried your number they said you and your boss had both left for the day. I persuaded the girl on the switchboard to give me your address by saying it was important.'

Helen, she thought. They might have a few words about that.

'I see.' Lottie raised an eyebrow. 'And is it?'

'No,' he admitted, a sheepish smile on his face. 'Unless you count the fact that I'd like to take you out for a drink as important.'

'We are drinking,' she reminded him sharply. 'Tea.'

'I know. But… never mind.' He shook his head and raised the cup. 'Cheers.'

'Have you found out anything more about the guns?'

'Not yet. I'm getting closer.' He brought out a packet of Lucky Strikes. 'Do you mind if I smoke?'

'Go ahead.' She brought an ashtray from the sideboard and placed it on the arm of the chair.

'I've got to keep things very quiet right now so I can arrest my guy and make the charge stick.' His voice became intent. 'Nothing a lawyer can wriggle them out of. Years in the stockade.'

'I rang to tell you there's another missing girl.'

CHAPTER NINE

'ANOTHER?' He sounded as if he couldn't believe it. He listened carefully as she gave him the facts about Lily Kemp, nodding his head at times, his features soft in the firelight.

'I don't see what else you can do,' he said when she'd finished. 'It's a waiting game now. Hope she turns up alive.'

'I don't think she will,' Lottie's voice was bleak. She picked up the poker and pushed it into the coals. The flames jumped.

'I'm sure John's doing all he can,' Ellison told her quietly. He reached out and put his hand on top of hers. She drew back quickly. He meant it kindly, but it wasn't what she needed now. Not what she wanted, either.

'He is, but… I feel helpless.'

'I had a few times like that when I was a cop. A missing kid is the worst. Your heart feels like it's going to stop. I was lucky, I always found the ones I was looking for. But there are always going to be some who never come home again. You can't go beating up on yourself and thinking "what if?". An old patrolman told me that when I was a rookie. He was right.'

'I don't want to talk about this any more tonight,' Lottie said. If he was going to sit in her living room, he was going to cheer her up. 'Tell me about Seattle.'

'That might take another cup of tea.' He gave her a wry smile.

'There's probably one more in the pot.'

He made America more real than it was in films. Not as perfect, perhaps, but Seattle still sounded like paradise.

'There's this long bridge, the Aurora bridge. On a clear day, when you drive over it you can look off to your right and see the Cascade mountains. Turn your head to the left and there's Puget Sound, all blue water. Past that, over on the peninsula, it's all the Olympic mountains.'

'It sounds beautiful.'

'It is,' he agreed with a wistful smile. 'I've never gotten tired of it yet and I see it pretty much every day. Saw,' he corrected himself.

'You'll be back there again soon. It'll all be over.'

'Yeah.' He sighed. 'It does kind of seem like we're starting the last chapter, doesn't it? But there's Hirohito and the Japs after that. We had a lot of them round Seattle. All in internment camps now.'

'All?' That seemed impossible. A whole population?

'Every single one,' he told her. 'Happened a couple of years ago, moved everyone from the West Coast to inland states. Built these camps for them. I was in the service by then, but it was all over the news. The feeling was pretty strong after Pearl Harbour.'

'I can imagine.'

He stayed another half hour, sliding out into the darkness with just a quiet goodnight.

'Let me know what happens tomorrow, will you?' he asked as he started the Jeep.

She arrived at Millgarth early, before it was light. Bad dreams about Lily Kemp and the other women kept waking her. Finally, a little after five, she was up, pottering around and killing time until she could reasonably leave for work.

McMillan was already at his desk. Shaved, wearing a clean shirt, but he hardly looked rested.

'Anything?' she asked.

He shook his head. 'We'll have more people out looking today. I kept a patrol out by Kirkstall Abbey all night, just in case, but nothing. You don't fancy getting a couple of teas from the canteen, do you? I'm parched.'

Helen was down there, with a Cheshire cat grin on her face.

'Did lover boy come round, then? I didn't think you'd mind me giving him your address. I'd have given him mine if I thought he'd turn up.'

'It was fine.' Lottie gave her own smile, sweetly enigmatic.

'Well, go on then. Details.'

'I had some information he needed. That's all.'

Helen raised an eyebrow. 'Really?'

'Really,' Lottie said. She gathered up the teas and left. That would leave her wondering, if nothing else.

McMillan was on the telephone, listening, adding a word of his own here and there before finally putting the receiver down.

'The Assistant Chief Constable,' he explained. 'The Watch Committee want us to go public with all the murders. The Chief is arguing against it, says they'll crucify us for not revealing it earlier.'

'What have they decided?' Lottie sat across from him, seeing the strain on his face.

'Still up in the air. He just wanted me to know.' He ran his palms down his cheeks. 'He said I can have all the men I need, but I can't magic them out of thin air. We don't have the people.'

'Then maybe you need to use me more,' she suggested.

'It might come to that.' The phone rang again. He listened, then said, 'Can you keep him out there for a few minutes. Take him to a café and buy him something hot. I'll pay.' Another paused. 'I know it. We'll see you there.'

'Where?' Lottie asked.

'Smith's café by Kirkstall Bridge. George Chadwick's found that other tramp.'

The windows were covered in condensation. A few faded posters, almost transparent with grease spots, hung on the walls. Chadwick sat at a table, arms crossed, watching a small man in a tattered overcoat devouring a plate of powdered egg, fried bread and baked beans.

'This is Leslie Armistead, sir.'

The man looked up. A pale, bland face, a timid expression, blue eyes. The type who wouldn't say boo to a goose.

'I'm Chief Superintendent McMillan.' He sat, leaving Lottie to find a chair at the next table. 'Did Constable Chadwick tell you what I'm looking for?'

'Yes, sir.' He bobbed his head, staring down at his plate.

'Did you see anything that night at the abbey? Hear something, maybe?'

'The shot. But when they arrived, too. Voices, you know.'

'Voices?' McMillan asked quickly. 'Could you hear what they said? Accents?'

'Not really.' The man shook his head. 'Just…'

'What?'

'She sounded English, but him… I couldn't hear well but he was…' He paused, trying to think. 'Different, I think.'

'Different how?' McMillan leaned forward, elbows resting on his knees, his voice urgent.

'Not from here, you know?'

Lottie realised she was holding her breath.

'Here? Leeds, you mean? Or England?'

'I don't know.' Armistead glanced up apologetically for a second then quickly lowered his head. 'Maybe American, like in the pictures?' He sounded uncertain.

'American? Could you make out anything they said?' McMillan asked slowly. 'Any words?'

'He said "Come on, baby."' The man seemed to colour with embarrassment.

'Where were you?' Lottie asked quietly.

'In one of the rooms off the cloister.' He seemed to grab on to the question. 'I know somewhere dry there.'

'Did you have a fire?'

He shook his head. 'Blackout. Can't have fires. Enemy aircraft might spot them.' For some reason, Lottie found that sweetly patriotic. He had nothing, he lived rough, but he still cared about the war effort.

'You were close enough to hear them,' McMillan said. Lottie could feel the pulse beating in her neck. 'Did you stay there, Mr Armistead?'

'No. They were walking round the cloister, I thought they might find me. I know my way round the abbey. I went out, by the old lodge.'

'How long after the voices did you hear the shot?'

'Five minutes.' He paused. 'Maybe it was ten. I was settling down again.'

'What did you do then?' McMillan asked.

'Stayed there. I remember guns.' Fear crept into his face. 'They scare me.'

'Did you see or hear anything else, Mr Armistead?' Lottie asked quietly, but the man began to shake his head quickly. If he had, he wasn't going to say.

The Chief Superintendent stood, took a shilling from his pocket and placed it on the table.

'Thank you. You've been very helpful. I appreciate it.' He tilted his head for Chadwick to join them outside.

'Good stuff, sir?'

'Very, if it's true. Do you believe him?'

'Never known Leslie Armistead to lie, sir,' Chadwick answered.

'Fine,' McMillan answered after a moment. 'I want you to keep an eye on him. Don't let him vanish again. I think there might be a thing or two he hasn't said yet.'

'I'll do my best. Do you want me to have a go, see if I can find out more?'

'If you think he'll tell you. It would save me some time.'

'Yes, sir.' Chadwick grinned under his heavy moustache. 'He's a good lad, really, is Leslie. Just too meek for this world.'

'We'd better go out to Castle Grove Area HQ. I need to see Ellison as soon as possible.'

'On our way.' She sped up to overtake a bus on Kirkstall Road before turning up the hill to Headingley. 'An American voice.'

'I know.' She checked the mirror. He was staring emptily out of the window. 'What do you make of it? Was he telling the truth?'

Lottie took her time replying.

'In his mind I think he was,' she said.

'What does that mean?'

'He believes he heard an American.' She tried to explain it. 'Inside, he's sure of it.'

'You're not sure? He seemed quite convinced.'

'The more I think about it, the less likely it seems. Especially with everything else we know now.' Her eyes flicked to the mirror, watching him. 'Don't you agree?'

'Yes,' he told her. 'But I'm trying to keep an open mind.' He gave a dark smile. 'And it might prove useful.'

The sentry recognised the car and their faces, waving them through without checking identification. Inside the old building Lottie hurried to keep pace as McMillan climbed the stairs to the attic. Ellison was in his office, head bowed as he wrote. He looked up at the footsteps, his expression changing from surprise to concern.

'I hadn't expected to see you so soon, John. Have you found him?'

McMillan ignored the question and sat down. 'I've just had a very interesting conversation.'

She watched Cliff's face as he listened to the story. He pushed his lips together and narrowed his eyes, then reached for a cigarette, squinting through the smoke.

'So where does that leave us on the other killings, and that body at the furrier's?'

'I don't know. But what about Shire Oak Road – the neighbour saw a woman carried out to an American Jeep. And we have someone else missing…'

'I know. Lottie told me last night.' He immediately realised he'd said too much. But McMillan ignored it.

'There's something going on and I'm damned if I can make head or tail of it. But it really looks as if we're going to need to work together.'

'I've got men ready to arrest the people selling guns in—' Ellison looked at his watch '—thirty minutes. Want to stick around and see?'

'I don't have time. But I do still need any information you can give me on an American officer with a mole on his cheek. He's the one who was looking at the house.'

'I've been checking, no joy yet. But I haven't forgotten.' His expression softened. 'I'll let you know as soon as I have anything at all. Meantime, we'd better start liaising daily and keep each other up on things.'

'Agreed.' McMillan paused. 'I need this solved quickly and cleanly. I'm under a great deal of pressure from above.'

'Yeah, I guessed,' Ellison said gravely. 'I'll do everything I can.'

A handshake and they left. She looked over her shoulder but he was already concentrating on the papers once more.

CHAPTER TEN

THEY'D just crossed Shaw Lane, on the way back into town, when he spoke.

'Last night?'

'I wondered how long that would take you.'

'I hadn't realised you two were so close.'

'We're not. I'd rung him earlier. On your orders, remember,' she added. 'He wangled my address from the switchboard and stopped by.'

'Very cosy.'

'Stop it,' she said. Her voice was firm and he held up his hands, palms out.

'Sorry. None of my business.'

'No, it's not. And there's no business, as you call it.' She could feel the heat rising up her neck. Not embarrassment – anger. 'Shall we just leave it at that?'

'I need you to work with him. I hope that won't be any sort of problem.'

'It'll be fine. Don't worry.'

'Good. I'm relying on him to take care of the American end.'

'How do you think it all ties together?' Her flash of temper had passed. She was breathing calmly again. Back to more important matters.

'Honestly, I'm damned if I know. I start pulling at one thread and something completely different pops up.'

'What about this American connection?'

THE YEAR OF THE GUN

'If it even exists. Remember that. All we have is the word of one tramp.'

'And the American at Shire Oak Road. That old chap who saw the Jeep there,' she said. 'We know Pamela Dixon was there from the knickers we found.'

'If you can untangle it you can have my job,' he said. 'None of it makes the slightest bit of sense to me.'

McMillan closed the door to his office and a few seconds later she heard his voice on the telephone. Sitting at her desk, she tried to draw a chart, to put any connections on paper. But they didn't know enough to join the dots. The only names they had were the dead women. And one still missing.

One where there was still hope.

For an hour there was nothing to do beyond doodle and read more of the Graham Greene novel. Then he came out and beckoned her.

'Can you get us a cuppa?' he asked. 'I've been on the phone to the chief. My throat's like a desert.'

Lottie shook her head at him, but returned after a few minutes with two mugs and a pair of digestive biscuits. Down in the canteen Helen and Margaret had been at a table, flirting with a pair of uniformed coppers, too busy to notice her.

'Had my ear scorched,' McMillan said. 'Orders are to get it solved, as if it was something simple.'

'Did he offer any brilliant suggestions?'

'Merely that my intelligence and experience would take care of it.' He raised an eyebrow.

'Lily Kemp?' she asked.

'No word yet. People have been searching out at Kirkstall.'

'Maybe she's alive somewhere,' Lottie said.

116

'I wish to God I could believe that.'

Silence filled the room slowly.

'There's got to be something in the fact he chose Cohen's cold storage,' Lottie said. 'That he had the key for it.'

'I've got Smith and others going over that. I've drafted in a couple of men from Wortley and Chapel Allerton to help. Probably half the names on the list are in the forces now. And there might well be some Cohen's forgotten.'

'None of them are American, I take it?'

McMillan shook his head. 'That would be too easy. We're in for the long slog on this, no doubt about it.' He dunked the biscuit for a moment then ate it, thinking. 'What have we missed?'

She was about to answer when someone rapped hard on the door. Pegg, the sergeant brought out of retirement to man the front desk. His face was red after climbing the stairs.

'Beg your pardon, sir, but we've had a message. Body in the river at Kirkstall.' He paused. 'A young lady. I thought you'd want to know, what with…'

'Thank you.' He was already standing, reaching for his coat and hat.

'I'll bet you anything it's Lily Kemp,' he said. Lottie darted the Humber in and out of traffic, not caring who sounded their horns.

'We'll find out once we get there.' But she knew he was probably right.

A procession of vehicles was already parked at the kerb. The pathologist's car, the coroner's van – five in total.

'Looks like we're last to the party,' McMillan said wryly.

The earth was hard under her shoes as she marched across the grass towards the crowd gathered on the bank. One uniform was interviewing an older lady. She was sitting on a bench, distressed, kneading a handkerchief in her fist. A pudgy terrier lay placidly at her feet. Had to be the woman who discovered the body.

The corpse had been pulled up on to the bank. As they arrived, the pathologist was putting his instruments away in a large leather bag.

'Well?' McMillan said. It came out almost as an accusation.

'She didn't drown.' The duty doctor was a lanky man, half a head taller than anyone around him, with sandy hair, glasses, and washed-out features. 'Can't really tell how long she was in the water. Eight hours is my guess, maybe a little longer.'

'Then what killed her?' McMillan asked.

Lottie knew the answer as well as he did. But he needed to hear it.

'She was shot. Now if you'll excuse me, I have house calls to make. On the living.'

She had the photograph of Lily Kemp in her uniform jacket, but she didn't need to look at it again. The face was imprinted on her mind. Now she was seeing it, all the life gone. Hair matted by the water, blood gone from her cheeks and lips, eyes closed. Just the innocence of death. As she looked, McMillan whispered in her ear. She looked at him, pleading silently, but he simply stared at her.

'Move everyone away,' she told him. Only when they'd gone ten yards back towards the ancient buildings did she lift the hem of the dress. The soaked material clung to the skin. Finally, though, she could see, and gave the woman some faint decency again.

He watched her and she shook her head. As if there was ever any doubt about it, Lottie thought. The killer's hallmarks, a bullet hole and no underwear.

McMillan interrupted her thoughts. 'How fast do you think the river's flowing?'

She glanced at the water. It hardly seemed to be moving at all.

'Why?' she asked. Then it clicked.

'I've had men watching the abbey all night. He must have slipped her in the water further upstream. It can't be too far. Come on.'

Back in the car he ordered her to drive slowly.

'There,' he said after about half a mile.

She parked and saw why he'd chosen the spot. No houses anywhere near, just a short walk down the bank to the River Aire. She started to follow the path but he held her back.

'We'll get the evidence people out here. They might be able to find something.'

'If there's anything to find,' Lottie pointed out. 'He didn't kill her here. You can see that; this is strictly for dumping.'

He turned. In the distance the old, ruined tower of Kirkstall Abbey stood above the treetops.

'What is it about that place, do you think? Why does he want to have the bodies there?'

'I don't know. But we need to find out.'

'I'll give him this, he's sly.' McMillan said. 'He must have seen the men watching the abbey and come up with the idea of floating the body down.' He slammed his palm down against the stone wall. 'Dammit.'

Back in the car, returning to Millgarth, he said, 'He must have been planning to haul Pamela Dixon from cold storage out to Kirkstall.'

'I've been thinking about that,' Lottie said. 'I wonder why he didn't bring her out immediately.'

In the mirror she could see him watching her.

'Any ideas?'

'Well,' she began, 'it looks as if she was his first. Maybe he hadn't decided on a place to leave the bodies yet.'

'Possible,' McMillan agreed. 'He came to a decision soon enough, though. He killed Kate Patterson out there. And dumped Anne Goodman's body there the night after that.'

'So why did he leave Dixon there for so long?'

'Maybe he was waiting until it was safe.'

She shook her head. 'I don't buy it. That was taking a chance,' Lottie said. 'He couldn't know when Cohen would come down to the cold storage for something.'

'Don't ask me. I can't find a scrap of logic in it.'

'What if he put the body there because he didn't know what to do with it and he had to go on duty? If he was in the service.'

'It's a thought.' He nodded. 'But then why didn't he get rid of her the next night instead of finding another victim?'

'I don't know,' she admitted. He was right, not a scrap of sense in the whole thing.

When she'd been a full police constable Lottie had worked on a murder case. Her one and only. It had seemed thrilling, every day a challenge. She'd worked with McMillan then, too, when he was no more than a brash, cocky detective sergeant. Now she just wished the killing would end, that they could catch the murderer, then life might return to whatever passed for normal these days.

The old sergeant nodded welcome as she followed McMillan past the front desk and up the stairs to his office. A head poked out from the CID room. Detective Constable Smith.

'Got something for you, sir.'

'Go on,' McMillan said once they were all seated.

'You wanted me checking those men who'd had access to Cohen's keys.' He looked around eagerly.

'What have you found?'

'His name's Terry Cruickshank. Worked as a salesman at the company until he was called up. He was in the Signals, stationed up at Catterick. Went AWOL in November. His name's on the deserters' list.'

They all knew what that meant. If he was arrested for some other offence he'd be handed over to the military police. There just weren't enough coppers to go searching for deserters. Once in a while they'd conduct a sweep and take a few into custody. But it was a losing battle.

'Possible,' McMillan agreed.

'There's something else, sir. We had him in for questioning in '38. Assault and rape. We had to let him go because there wasn't enough evidence. Reading between the lines, he was probably guilty.'

'Good work. I want the last known address for him. Lottie, find a couple of uniforms. We're going to see if we can track down Mr Cruickshank.'

The Humber felt cramped with four people inside, gas masks tucked in the boot. The bobby next to her smelt as if he hadn't washed for a day or two; she tried to breathe through her mouth as she drove out to Gildersome.

Industry had crept out from the city, edging along Gelderd Road, almost reaching the old Jewish cemetery. Gildersome itself was little more than a village perched at the top of a hill south of Leeds. Houses along a couple of main streets, it was sleepy, hardly a soul around. Still plenty of farmland off to the south and west.

'Turn here,' McMillan ordered at Street Lane.

The house was part of a dark Victorian terrace. Number seventeen, the ninth one out of ten.

'Park farther along.'

It was basic. One man at the back of the property, another with McMillan at the front door. Lottie knew she wouldn't be allowed to take part in this. Fine; there was nothing she could add, anyway. She didn't have the size or the strength. Instead, she took the Graham Greene novel from her pocket, settled back and began to read.

The men returned in a quarter of an hour. No luck; she could see it in the boss's face.

'His mother says she hasn't seen him since his last leave. She's had the local coppers out there twice looking for him. Claims she wouldn't have him in the house now, anyway. Cowards not welcome.'

'Do you believe her?'

'I do. We searched; no sign of him in there. I think he knows she wouldn't be waiting with open arms. We'll get the word out to the snouts. He's around somewhere.' She could see the look on his face: frustration at not finding Cruickshank mixed with the satisfaction of one solid lead.

'How do you think he ties in with the Americans?' she asked McMillan after they'd returned to the station.

'He's on the run. He'll be in contact with criminals. One thing leads to another.'

'I'll ring Ellison. If he's arrested anyone he can try the name on them.'

'Good thinking. Maybe we can get a little something from that end.'

'Cruickshank.' She said the name into the receiver. 'Terry Cruickshank. He was in the Signals. Went AWOL from Catterick in December, wanted as a deserter.'

'Got it,' Ellison said breezily. 'What rank?'

'I don't know.' She told him what else they had on the man.

'Yeah, he'd go top of my list, too. I'll ask.'

'Your people selling guns, did you arrest them?'

'All but one. He must have been off base or hiding. I'll catch up with him soon.'

'Are they talking?'

'Making sweet, sweet music.' She could almost see his smile. 'I'm going to have a bunch of names for you guys later today.'

'We'll be glad to get them. Especially if Cruickshank's is one.'

'I need to get back and sweat them some more. Remind them that they're looking at a long time in the stockade.' He hesitated. 'I'm sorry I let the cat out of the bag yesterday.'

'It doesn't matter.'

'OK, good,' he said. 'I'll send those names over later. And…' he began, but stopped himself. 'Never mind. I'll see what I can find for you.'

Officers trooped in and out of the superintendent's office, both uniform and plain clothes. All trying to track down Terry Cruickshank. With a name, the machinery could begin to creak into action.

There was nothing for Lottie to do except sit and read. She was twenty pages from the end of the book when someone tapped on the door. He had to be American, she thought. A broad, shy face, big body with cropped dark hair, dressed in a leather jacket with a worn canvas bag slung over his shoulder.

'Are you WAPC Armstrong?' He read the name off the front of an envelope.

'I am,' Lottie told him. Definitely a Yank, with an accent straight out of *Gone with the Wind*.

'For you, ma'am. From Captain Ellison.' He handed it over, gave one of those flat salutes and left.

She ripped it open. There was the list he'd promised, eight names, and another sheet with a scrawled note:

These are the local guys the thieves here have been dealing with. The man from stores swore he'd never taken and sold any guns. I told him one had been used in a murder and that meant he could face trial in England. A lie, but he didn't know that. He says he sold them to someone called Harry. That's the only name he has, but he told me the man has a scar on his cheek. I pressed him pretty hard on Cruickshank, but he said he'd never heard of him. I believe him.

Cliff

Someone called Harry with a scar on his cheek? Lottie didn't have to reach far into her memory. She'd met him a few days before at his house in Whitkirk. The man who said he'd help McMillan. The man whose daughter had died serving with the QA Nurses in France. The man who said he hated guns.

She took both sheets over to McMillan's office and placed them on his desk, the list on top.

'From Ellison,' was all she said, standing as he read through, nodding at the names, then turned to the letter.

'So much for anything Harry Park tells me.' He let go of the paper and it fluttered down to the desk. 'I'm going to crucify the bastard for this. Cruickshank must have got the gun from him.' In one angry movement he was on his feet. 'Let's go.'

He stopped at the CID room, passing over the list: everyone on it to be arrested. Get warrants for each property Park owned and search them top to bottom. Then he clattered down the stairs to the Humber. She didn't need to ask the destination, simply headed out along York Road.

Park's wife met them at the door, growing alarmed as she saw the expression on McMillan's face.

'Is he in?'

'Yes, but—'

He barged by her, through to the living room. Lottie followed, standing by the door in case Park tried to run.

'What?' Park stood, dumping the newspaper from his lap on to the floor. 'What the hell are you doing—?'

'Harold Park, I'm arresting you for receiving stolen property.'

'You're joking.' He looked genuinely outraged.

'The American's been arrested,' McMillan told him. 'He told them everything. You know, I believed you when you said you hated guns.'

'I do.'

'You hated them enough to buy some.' He took out the handcuffs but Park moved away. 'Don't, or it'll be resisting arrest.'

'Call the solicitor,' Park told his wife as the Chief Superintendent pushed him out to the car. 'Tell him to go to Millgarth.'

No talking as they drove back to town. Once, pulling away from a light, she had to fight the clutch to put it into gear. Not a good sign, Lottie thought.

At the station Park was booked in, fingerprints taken, personal items removed and sealed away, before being placed in an interview room.

An hour later he was still there with the Chief Inspector. Lottie waited in the corridor, feet aching from standing so long. As men reported in with names from the list brought into custody, she wrote in her notebook. But no sign of the weapons. The searches of the places Park owned had brought nothing – yet. It was far from over.

The hard slap of a hand on wood grabbed her attention, then McMillan's voice through the wall, yelling at full volume. The whole station must have heard him.

'I don't give a monkey's. One of those guns has been used to kill four people. We know you bought them, we have a description from the Yank quartermaster who sold them to you.' A muttered response. 'You're not bloody innocent, don't even try to deny it. I want to know who has those guns and you're going to tell me.'

He stormed out of the room. The door slammed behind him, rattling in the jamb.

'Sir—' she began, but he walked right past her, out into the cold February air. By the time she caught up he was already drawing deeply on a cigarette.

'He's guilty. I know it, he knows it. By now his bloody lawyer knows it.' McMillan flexed his fist. 'He's just lucky I haven't beaten it out of him.' For a moment she wasn't sure if he was joking. But his eyes were deadly serious.

'They've arrested six from that list. Got them in cells spread all around Leeds so they can't talk to each other.'

'Good. Anything from the search?'

'No,' Lottie told him. 'But he might well have places we don't know about. And he's hardly going to keep pistols anywhere obvious, is he?'

'He's going to tell me where the hell they are.'

'We could get the statement from the man Ellison's arrested. It might give you more to work with.'

He nodded. 'See what you can arrange. Harry Park won't be going anywhere for a day or two.'

CHAPTER ELEVEN

'THERE'S a copy of the American's statement—' she placed it on the desk '—and full reports from all of Park's properties.' Lottie glanced at McMillan. 'No guns.'

She'd arrived early at Millgarth to go through all the papers and collate everything ready for him.

'These are the statements from the names on the American's list. We still can't find two of them, they seem to have vanished. Four confessions to receiving and black market trading so far. Not a bad haul. Maybe it'll cut down on the amount offered for sale.'

'You sound cheerful this morning,' McMillan said.

'A good night's sleep. You don't look too happy.'

He shrugged and said nothing. His face was more lined and careworn than ever. Raw at the edges, caught between the devil and the deep blue sea. But hardly surprising.

'I'll be fine as soon as I get an admission from Harry Park,' he said. 'Did you do much last night?'

'Went to a film at the Odeon with Margaret from Records and Helen off the switchboard.'

'The coven.' He smirked.

She raised an eyebrow. 'You'd better not let them hear you say that.'

'I know.' He sighed. 'Good film?'

'Very. *Double Indemnity*. They almost get away with a crime except for the hunch of the investigator.'

'Has to be rubbish, then.' McMillan smiled. He read the statement Ellison had sent. 'Harry can't worm his way out of this one. It's almost as good as a photograph.' His eyes moved to the clock. 'How about a cup of tea, then I'll have another crack at him?'

By midday there was nothing more. No confession. Some shouting, but few results. Lottie sat in the canteen, finishing *The Power and the Glory*, closing the book as she swallowed the last mouthful of something that pretended to be Swiss roll and drank the dregs of her tea.

Helen came in to the room, looked around, then strode over purposefully.

'I've been looking all over for you. Your American's been on the phone twice, wanting you or the Chief Super, and there are orders not to disturb him.'

'He's not my American,' Lottie insisted. 'I'll ring him back. Did he say what he wanted?'

'Just that it was important.' She cocked her head. 'Who do you think he resembles more, Cary Grant or James Stewart?'

'Who?' Lottie asked. Good God, had the woman gone daft?

'The one who keeps ringing you, of course.'

Lottie just shook her head and walked off.

'Could your boss come out here?' Ellison asked. 'I'd like him to talk to my prisoner, get his questions in before I send him off to the stockade.'

'He's spent the morning interrogating the man who received the guns.'

'Any luck?'

Without thinking, she lowered her voice. 'I don't think so.'

'If he can get out here in the next couple of hours, fine. If not… I'll have to send this guy on his way.'

'I'll tell him. And thank you.'

She knocked on the door of the interview room and entered. Three sets of eyes turned to her. Park, unshaven, bruises on his cheek, one eye swollen shut. Next to him, a sleek lawyer with a worried look on his face, briefcase open at his feet, a notepad and pen in front of him. McMillan sat across the table. A mountain of cigarette ends filled the ashtray. The air was thick enough to cut.

'What?'

'A word, please, sir.'

He pinched the bridge of his nose with a thumb and fore-finger as she explained.

'We'd better go,' he said. 'Can you find me some Aspro? My head's pounding.'

'Of course.'

'His name's Kroger,' Ellison told them outside the door. 'Corporal in the stores. Was, anyway. He's going to spend the next few years doing some very hard time at Fort Leavenworth.'

'Have you wrung him dry?' McMillan asked.

'Got all I need. I figured you might have a few specific questions.'

'I appreciate that.' The cloud of the headache had passed from his face. Aspirin, and the window in the car rolled down to bring fresh air; they'd helped.

'I'd better warn you, he's not a pretty sight.' He turned to Lottie. 'He's a soldier and a traitor. I'm not going to be gentle with him.'

'It happens. Our suspect hurt himself when he fell down the stairs on the way to his cell,' McMillan said flatly.

Lottie said nothing. She didn't like it, but she understood the necessity. Better to bite her tongue.

A soldier with a rifle stood behind the door; he snapped to attention and saluted when he saw the captain.

'Outside,' Ellison ordered. 'No one comes in.'

The prison sat hunched over on a chair, wrists and ankles shackled. A trail of dried blood ran from the corner of his mouth to his chin.

He looked so young, she thought. Twenty-two? Twenty-three? Dark eyes, short curly black hair. There was a curious innocence to his face, pleading in his eyes.

'Listen up, Kroger,' Ellison said. 'This is an English cop. He's going to ask you some questions about selling the guns. And you're going to answer him, understand?'

'Yes, sir,' the man answered with a cracked, faded voice.

'Tell him everything and it'll look better at the court martial.'

It didn't take long. Kroger was terrified, embarrassingly eager to co-operate. The words flooded out of him. How often he'd met Park, what he'd sold, where it had taken place, even the dates. The man even gave a more detailed description of his buyer; Park wouldn't have any room to squirm.

Back outside, smoking a cigarette, McMillan gave his thanks.

'Any chance of getting him to testify on my case?'

'Nope. I'm keeping this guy under wraps. Quiet trial and back to the States to start serving his sentence. We're already going to look like fools. No need to make it worse.' He gave a rueful smile. 'Politics trumps law. Sorry.'

'Now all I need is for Park to confess,' McMillan said as they walked into Millgarth.

'With all you have now?' How could there be any doubt about it? 'He has to.'

'We'll see.' His voice was doubtful. 'I'm more concerned about those guns.'

'Charge him with receiving stolen property,' McMillan told the sergeant. Park stood beside him, handcuffed, shoulders slumped in defeat. The solicitor stood clutching his briefcase, smiling. His client would still go to prison, but this was a victory all the same.

Five minutes later, McMillan had all the detectives assembled in the office. Lottie stood behind him, taking notes.

'Park admitted buying the guns. Said he'd give me the names of everyone he sold them to, in return for reduced charges.' He shook his head. 'I must be getting soft in my old age.' The men chuckled. He held up a list. 'Here they are. I want every last one of them and I want those shooters. We know one of them's been used to kill. It's been sold on, and I want to know who has it. All clear, gentlemen?' McMillan looked at the faces, all of them serious now. 'Good. Go and get them.'

'Cruickshank?' she asked when they were in his office. 'Did you find a link to Park?'

'Harry said he'd never heard of the man. I think he was telling the truth.' He ran his fingers through his hair. 'This time there was no reason to lie.' He glanced at his watch. 'You might as well go home. There's nothing more to do until they come back.'

'What about you?'

'I'll catch forty winks here. It's going to be a long night.'

She didn't know why, but at home Lottie primped herself a little. A touch of precious lipstick; it was so hard to find these days that she kept it as a luxury. A little powder. One of her good dresses from before the war. She'd taken it in a little and raised the hem an inch.

There was no indication he'd come. He hadn't given a hint. She just felt he'd show up, and for once she wanted to look her best. The boss had his copper's hunch; she had her woman's intuition. But by the time she'd cooked her meal, washed up and hung her apron behind the kitchen door, he still hadn't arrived.

Maybe she was wrong, Lottie thought, tuning the radio to the BBC. An orchestral concert from somewhere or other. Classical music. She wanted something jollier, more rousing. Her fingers searched out the American Forces Network, one of the big bands playing that song again. *Imagination.* Then she heard the knock on the door.

Good to know that her skills had not vanished with age.

'I'm sorry,' Ellison said when she led him into the light of the dining room. 'I'm intruding. You're dressed up to go out.'

'Not really.' She smiled. 'I fancied a change, that's all. Would you like a drink?'

'Tea again?' he asked warily.

'That's what I have.'

'Or we could go to a pub? There's got to be one nearby. They seem to be pretty much every block here.'

'It's about ten minutes' walk,' she told him. 'Probably longer in the blackout.'

It was closer to twenty minutes in the end, but they took their time, her arm tucked through his, guiding him past St Matthew's Church, down Allerton Hill, taking their lives in their hands as they crossed the blackness of Harrogate Road.

The Regent seemed like an island of warmth and light. People turned to stare as they entered, then returned to their drinks.

Old, threadbare red velvet on the seats. Dark, polished wood-work. Beer for him, gin and tonic for her. Lottie glanced around, looking for any neighbours, but there were no faces she knew.

They spent an easy hour chatting. Neither of them mentioned work, as if they'd chosen to put a fence around it. He sipped at his pint as if it was an obligation.

'You don't like English beer?'

'I still haven't made up my mind. It's different. Stronger. I'm more a Rainier kind of guy.'

She didn't understand. 'I thought that was the name of the team you mentioned.'

'Baseball, yeah.' He laughed. 'At Sick's Stadium. That's named for the Sick family that brews Rainier beer. We have a mountain called Rainier, too. It all comes from there.' He paused and thought. 'I guess we have a bunch of mountains, really.'

The conversation moved through geography, history, family, and finally to the future.

'What are you going to do when it's all over?' she asked.

He didn't hesitate before answering. 'Go home, spend some time with my kids, catch a ball game or two and go back to my old job. What about you?'

'I'm not sure yet,' Lottie admitted. 'Sell the house. I'm just rattling round in it. Find something to do with my time. Not easy at my age.'

'You're not old,' he assured her.

She shook her head. 'There's a whole new generation out there. They're going to need work when they come home. And places to live. They have to find their lives, never mind go back to them.'

'That's very philosophical.'

'It's true, though.' She shrugged. 'I have money. Geoff left me comfortable. Once the war's finished I'll just need to find a purpose.'

'You might meet someone.'

Lottie eyed him sharply. 'I don't know that I want to.'

But Ellison smiled. 'Stranger things have happened.' He drained his glass. 'Come on, I'll see you home. It's been a long day.'

'For me, too.'

At the front door she was ready, half-expecting something. But when he put his arms around her Lottie surprised herself. She didn't pull back. Instead she let herself settle against him, just for a quick moment, smelling the mix of soap and tobacco on his skin.

She moved away and he let his arms rest on her shoulders.

'What do you think? Should we do this again?'

'I think that could be a good idea,' Lottie agreed. 'Maybe I can cook us something. How about lunch on Sunday? It'll be short commons with all the rationing, but maybe some snoek if you're lucky,' she said.

He didn't understand.

'Fish,' she explained. 'Well, that's what the government claims.'

'How about this? You cook, I'll bring the food,' he offered. When she didn't answer, he continued, 'I'm serious.'

'All right, then,' Lottie said, surprised. Who was she to turn down food?

'Maybe some of that roast beef and Yorkshire pudding.' She could sense him grinning. 'And I can see what it's like round here in the daylight.'

CHAPTER TWELVE

'YOU look like you haven't been home.'

His clothes were creased and rumpled, face pale with heavy, dark circles under his eyes.

'I haven't,' McMillan said. He stretched then ran a hand over his cheek. 'Borrowed a razor so I didn't look as if I'd been sleeping rough. There was too much to do here.'

'Did they find the guns?'

'All but one.' He lips curled into a hard smile. 'None of them had been fired, thank God. We have a few gentlemen looking at a long time behind bars. Two of them are deserters, too; icing on the cake.'

'The one still missing?' Lottie asked. 'Can you trace it to Cruickshank?'

'The person who was supposed to have it has dropped out of sight.' He raised an eyebrow. 'Bit of a coincidence, don't you think?'

'What now?'

'Now… do you think you could pop to the canteen and find us some tea? That would be a good start.'

'What did your last one die of?' But she was smiling, one hand on the door knob.

'Overwork,' he told her, voice gruff. 'I'm very demanding.'

'There's a biscuit, too.' She placed it next to the mug. 'Don't say I never spoil you.'

'Could you get on the blower to Ellison and tell him we have most of his guns? Thank him for the information, too.'

'The chief constable will be happy, all those weapons out of bad hands.'

'Do you know what he said when I told him? "What were the bloody Yanks thinking, letting them walk out of there?"' He shrugged. 'Can't win.'

'I checked on the way in,' she said. 'No women reported missing.'

McMillan shook his head. 'Don't get your hopes up. He hasn't had enough yet.' He searched through a pile of papers, drew out a flimsy carbon copy of a report, the ink smudged, and pushed it across the desk to her. 'The post-mortem on Lily Kemp. Exactly the same as the others. No bullet or cartridge, but it has to be him. He's still hungry.' McMillan lit a Four Square and blew out smoke. 'It's not *if* he strikes again. It's *when*.'

'Unless we catch him.'

'Every copper in Leeds and all the surrounding areas has Cruickshank's description. So do the newspapers and the BBC.'

'You're certain it's him?'

McMillan sat back in his chair. 'He's what I've got; everything points to him. For now, I'll take that.'

'There's something we're forgetting.'

'What?'

'Shire Oak Road. The American seen there.'

'I haven't forgotten,' he told her. 'I just haven't worked out how it all fits yet. Maybe Ellison can come up with something now he's solved his case.'

'I'll remind him.'

McMillan yawned broadly and covered his mouth. 'I need to go home. I'm too old for two days and a night without sleep. You'll have to manage without me. I can't think any more.'

'What if the brass wants you?'

'Tell them. What are they going to do, sack me?' He smiled and for the first time that morning, it reached his eyes. 'Anything really urgent, come and get me. Just ring first and tell Sarah.'

'Do you want a lift?'

They both laughed. Memories: twenty years before he'd been the one who asked that, pulling up in his little Peugeot.

'Just look after things here.'

Apart from the filing there wasn't much to do except ring Ellison. She put it off, making excuses to herself – he'll be busy with the paperwork from yesterday, he'll be preparing for court – until the clock ticked past eleven.

After the evening before she wasn't sure what to say. It had all felt pleasant and natural out there in the darkness. She'd enjoyed his company, maybe a little too much. But now, in the grey February daylight, it all seemed different. She was Lottie Armstrong. Middle-aged, a little bit frumpy and stuck in her ways. She wasn't looking for excitement. She didn't need romance; she'd had that with Geoff and nothing was ever going to be better. And she certainly didn't need a divorced man who lived half a world away and who'd be off somewhere else in a month or two. Someone who might not even survive the war, she reminded herself.

Twice she put her hand on the receiver; twice she lifted it off again. Finally she dialled the number. This was work. It was more important than her silly emotions.

'That's good news,' Ellison said when she told him.

'There's still one out there,' Lottie reminded him. 'That's the one doing the killing.'

'I know. If I get any tips—'

'And there's still that house on Shire Oak Road,' she continued. 'Maybe you can help us from your end with that.'

'I didn't have any luck before but I can try again,' he said after a moment. 'You're very businesslike today.'

'It is business,' she said.

'Yeah,' he agreed. 'But…'

'We have four young women dead. All of them shot with a gun that came from your camp.'

'Lottie…'

'What?'

'We're on the same side, remember? Trying to help each other. I'm not fighting you. I'll dig deeper into anything about that house, OK? See if I can find the guy who was seen there.'

'Yes. Thank you.'

She ended the call, stared into space for a while, then went down to the canteen for some dinner. Woolton pie, runny and tasteless. There were shortages of everything, they had to make do, but why did the food have to look so unappetising?

Lottie sat in the corner with a cup of tea and tried to read. *Random Harvest*. She'd enjoyed the film but never looked at the book. But she could only concentrate for a line or two before her mind started to wander.

On the phone she'd considered telling Ellison not to come on Sunday. In the end she said nothing. He sounded so eager at the prospect of a home-cooked meal. That couldn't hurt. No more hugging, though. That was for the best. Friends, exactly the way they'd agreed.

A little after three and the afternoon was dragging. For once the heating in the building was working, and it was warm enough to leave her drowsy. She'd filed, cleaned the desk in McMillan's office and her own, taken more tea breaks that she'd ever normally be allowed. And it still wasn't time to go home. She kept trying to read, but the words swam in front of her.

The telephone had only rung twice during the day; now the bell startled her. Helen from the switchboard.

'I've got a chap desperate to speak to the Chief Super. Can you take it?'

'All right,' Lottie agreed. 'What's his name?'

'He won't say. He's in a phone box, I can hear the coins dropping.'

'Put him through.'

'This is Detective Chief Superintendent McMillan's office. Can I help you?'

'I want to talk to him.' A local voice, a slight wheeze when he spoke. It could be one of his narks.

'I'm afraid he's not here. I can take a message for him.'

'Tell him Terry Cruickshank wanted to talk.'

'I know who you are.' She sat upright, suddenly attentive and awake. 'I work with Mr McMillan.'

'Where is he?'

'He's out for the day.' She tried to keep her voice level and calm, as if he was just another stranger.

'Tell him it's not me.'

'What's not you, sir?'

'I've heard. People have told me. He's looking for me. He says I've shot girls.'

'I know.'

'It's not me.' His voice rose. He sounded at the end of his tether, almost ready to start weeping. 'I didn't do that, all right?'

'Do you have the gun?' she asked.

'Gun?' The idea seemed to astonish him. 'No. Why would I need a gun? I told you, I didn't do it.'

'Sir, why don't you go to a police station. Tell them who you are and the Chief Super will come and talk to you. I promise you. I'll go and get him myself.' She could feel the sweat on her palms. She needed to keep him talking, to find out where he was.

'You'll have me for it.' She heard him drop more coins into the slot. 'I know you lot. You'll see me hang for it.' There was a frantic, desperate edge to him.

'Sir, if you're not guilty, you'll be fine.' She tried to sound soothing, just to keep him on the line, to try and gain his trust. The man was still guilty of desertion, but that was nothing in comparison to murder. 'Where are you? We'll come and meet you. Talk it over.'

'Just tell him. Tell him it's not me.' Lottie heard him slam down the receiver then the buzz of a dead line.

He'd said his piece. Cruickshank wouldn't ring back.

But was he telling the truth?

'Hello, Sarah, it's Lottie. Is he up and about yet?'

'I heard him stirring a few minutes ago. Is it really urgent? He was dead on his feet when he got home.'

'I'm sorry. Could you give him a shout, please?'

'He'll be along right away, he says. How are you? He's not working you too hard, is he?'

'I'm fine. But I'm worried about the way he's pushing himself.'

'Once all this is over he's taking retirement. I'm putting my foot down.'

Nothing seemed to worry Sarah McMillan. Lottie had known the woman for the better part of twenty years and never seen anything upset her. She took life in her stride and got on with things.

'Here he is,' Sarah said.

'Has something happened?' His voice was still slurred at the edges with exhaustion.

'You could say that. Terry Cruickshank telephoned. He wanted to talk to you.'

'What? When?'

'Just now.' She gave him the gist, then went through it once more, in detail.

'That's what he said?' McMillan asked. 'Word for word?'

'Yes.' Every syllable was imprinted on her mind.

'How did he sound?'

'Hunted. Scared. As if he couldn't take much more.'

'Do you believe him?'

Lottie paused before answering. 'I don't know. I think so. It would be a good way to divert attention, though, wouldn't it?'

'But…' They both knew the implication. If Cruickshank was guilty and they started looking elsewhere, he could get away. If he was innocent and they only focused on him, someone else was free to murder. 'I'm coming in,' McMillan said. 'I want to go over everything we have.'

She wanted to tell him that everything would still be there in the morning. But why waste her breath? He'd never listen.

'Do you want me to pick you up?'

'I'll take the bus. I want you there if he rings back.'

'He won't,' she said with certainty.

'Just in case,' he told her.

She typed it all out and placed it on his desk. Every inflection was sharp in her mind, along with the fear underneath it. But was it the truth, or was Cruickshank a very good actor? She wouldn't put money either way.

McMillan spent half an hour going over the conversation with her, every word, every sentence. He wanted to know exactly how the man had sounded, whether he'd stumbled over his words as he spoke.

'He was in a telephone box?'

'Yes. Definitely.'

'Could you hear anything in the background? Traffic, anything at all?'

Lottie thought, trying to recall. She'd been paying attention to the voice, nothing else. Finally she shook her head. 'Sorry.'

'It was a long shot, anyway.' He glanced at the clock. 'You might as well get off home. I'm going to be here for a while.' He reached across for the files on the murders. Papers at least six inches deep.

Before she left for the evening, Lottie took him a cup of tea.

'You're an angel,' he said.

'Remember that the next time you're upset with me.'

The next morning she found him in his office, head down on a file, snoring as if he'd just invented it. Gently, Lottie shook him awake, smiling as he blinked and raised his head.

'I must have dropped off for a minute,' McMillan said.

'You're safe, the door was closed. No one saw.'

He stretched and winced. 'I don't even know what time I fell asleep.'

'You must have needed it.' Good Lord, she thought, she sounded like a mother. 'Did you find anything?'

'Nothing worth a damn. As far as I can see, Cruickshank is still our only real suspect.'

'No girls reported missing last night,' Lottie said. It had become the first thing she checked each day at the station. Maybe the madness had passed, she thought hopefully.

'That's no consolation for the ones who are dead, is it?' McMillan's voice was empty. 'We need to complete the chain.'

'What do you mean?'

'Bring in the man who sold him the gun. We still haven't found him. He seems to have vanished. But that way there'd be no doubt Cruickshank's our man.'

'Until then?'

'We keep an open mind,' he told her with a sad smile. 'And keep doing everything we can to track down Cruickshank.' He stood and stretched again, groaning. 'First order is to clean my teeth, have a shave, and put some food in my belly. Can you take a look at the new reports and see if there's anything important?'

Among all the official bumf was a handwritten envelope, simply addressed to Chief Superintendent, Millgarth Police Station, Leeds. She slit it open and took out a sheet of thin, cheap notepaper.

I told the girl who works for you. I didn't kill anyone. I would never kill a girl.

Terry Cruickshank

She breathed out slowly, removing her fingers so the letter fluttered to the desk. Very carefully, she took a cellophane bag from her desk drawer and eased the paper in with a pencil, then did the same with the envelope. The postmark was too smudged to read, and thick, wavy lines obscured the king's head on the stamp. Maybe the lab boys would be able to find more.

Lottie stirred at footsteps in the corridor. McMillan appeared in the doorway.

'I think you'd better take a look at this.'

It only took him a few seconds.

'Get this to the evidence people. I want to know everything they can find as soon as possible.'

She rang for one of the messenger boys to carry it over.

'Tell them it's the highest priority they have right now,' Lottie said. 'And make sure you're careful with it. It's evidence in a murder case.'

That made the lad stand taller and he gave a salute before he dashed off.

'Close the door,' McMillan ordered when she entered his office.

'What is it?' She sat, notebook and pencil ready.

'The sergeant in charge out at Otley rang me at about eleven last night about a girl who was due home at ten o'clock. Her mother reported it and he got straight on the blower to me.'

'But—' She'd checked; no missing girls.

'Arrived home an hour later. She'd missed the last bus, had to hitchhike in the blackout. Got a talking-to from her mother.'

'Was she in the service?'

He shook his head. 'Just seventeen. Works in a shop. A bit of a flibbertigibbet, evidently. I don't want this going any further. But people are getting worried. They've read about Lily Kemp in the papers.' He lit a cigarette. 'Do you know something?'

'What?'

'When the sergeant phoned me, I thought at least people are scared now. They're going to be wary.' He looked at her. 'Ghoulish, isn't it?'

'If it stops someone else dying…'

'I know.' He exhaled. 'Now we still have to catch Cruickshank, or whoever the hell's behind all this.'

'What do you make of the letter?'

'I'm sure he wrote it,' McMillan said. 'But it doesn't change anything. I still want to arrest him. Nothing more from the Americans, I take it?'

'Not yet.'

'That whole angle is nagging at me. I can't make it fit with everything else. Come on,' he decided, 'let's take another run out to Shire Oak Road. Maybe things will make more sense if I see it again.'

But they didn't. He paced around all of the rooms then out into the garden, rain darkening the shoulders of his mackintosh. Lottie stayed just inside the front door, trying to imagine what kind of cheerless party Pamela Dixon had taken part in here. It couldn't have been loud or the neighbours would have rung to complain. But the place was hidden from the street and most of the other houses by a wild, overgrown hedge. Safe, away from things.

She flicked a switch on the wall but nothing happened. No electricity. There must have been some kind of light; torches, lanterns. They couldn't have been blundering around in complete darkness. She searched around quickly. No sign of wax anywhere; they hadn't used candles. And no curtains, nothing covering the windows. Any glimmer inside would have been visible for miles across Meanwood Valley. The air-raid wardens would have come knocking…

'I've had an idea,' she told McMillan as he came back in, shaking his head in frustration.

The man at the ARP station had small, round glasses and a carefully clipped white moustache. What remained of his hair was pomaded and shining, carefully combed across his scalp. He was dressed in a clean boiler suit, insignia neatly sewn on the shoulders.

'Here we are.' His finger traced down the page of the ledger and peered closer at the notes. 'We received a telephone call from one of our chaps down in Meanwood. Someone must have worked out it was on Shire Oak Road and we sent a warden down there. The building looked deserted and there were no lights showing when he walked around the property.'

'What time was this?' Lottie asked. She felt deflated. He'd arrived at the house too late.

'Hold your horses, young lady. I'm not done yet.' She felt herself bristle at the reprimand. 'The door to the house was open. He walked in, saw some rubbish. But he noted that people must have been there recently, he could still smell cigarette smoke. This was at a quarter to one in the morning.' He lifted his head and smiled. 'Is that what you wanted?'

'Thank you,' McMillan said. 'I'd like to speak to the warden.'

'Yes, sir.' The man smiled. 'Of course.'

'You wrote that you could smell cigarette smoke in the house,' the chief superintendent said. 'Is that right?'

'Yes.' Daniel Johnson blinked. He'd limped along the hall, leading them to the kitchen, the metal scrape of a calliper every time he moved his right leg. Polio, she thought; poor man, no wonder he wasn't off in the services. He looked to be in his late twenties, hair already receding, his body thin and awkward. 'It was still strong. They can't have been gone too long.'

'Did you see a vehicle nearby?'

'Not that I noticed.' He frowned as he tried to recall. 'No, I'm sure of it.'

'Did you hear a Jeep at all while you were in the area?' Lottie asked him.

Suddenly Johnson became animated, nodding eagerly. 'Yes. The engine has a special sound.' From the corner of her eye, Lottie could see McMillan watching. 'I was coming up the street towards St Michael's church and I heard one going towards town.' He glanced around, embarrassed. 'There's not much traffic around at that time so it stuck in my mind.'

'How long was this before you reached the house?' the superintendent asked.

'Five minutes. Ten at most.'

'Thank you, Mr Johnson. That's very helpful.'

'It doesn't prove anything,' McMillan said as she drove back to town. Moving away from Hyde Park Corner, the clutch slipped again. Second time, Lottie thought. She needed to take the Humber to the garage. 'We can't even be certain he really did hear a Jeep.'

'Come on. You saw him; he was telling the truth. We have a better idea of the time it all happened now.'

'True. That was good work.'

Roadworks took her all the way down to City Square, circling the roundabout with the statue of the Black Prince. Air-raid shelters stood on the surface. They hadn't been used for a long time; with luck they'd never need them again. She hoped so. Stone staircases led down, below the square. A pantechnicon was parked by the kerb, clear of the tram lines, two soldiers with rifles guarding the back doors.

'They must be dismantling Regional Command Defence HQ,' he said, staring out of the window.

'What's that?' She'd never heard of it.

In the mirror she saw him smile. 'Under the square. If London fell they were going to run the country from here.'

'I never knew.'

'Of course not. It was all very hush–hush. Now there's no threat of invasion they're removing it.' He sighed. 'The tide's turned. You know they're even talking about standing down the Home Guard.'

'Really?' If that happened it would seem as if the end was definitely in sight, Lottie thought.

'That's what I've heard. Now we just need a second front.'

'Do you think that's why all these Americans are here?' She waited on Vicar Lane to turn down George Street.

'It has to be. Probably won't be too long, either.'

For a moment the image of Cliff Ellison moving on filled her mind. Saying goodbye, never seeing him again.

'You're miles away,' McMillan said.

'Sorry.' She could feel herself redden. She pushed down on the accelerator and the Humber jumped down the road.

'Just get us back in one piece,' he muttered.

They sat in the yard behind Millgarth, watching drizzle on the windscreen and listening to the tick of the car's engine as it cooled.

'We've got two separate strands here,' McMillan said. He raised his left hand. 'The killings at Kirkstall Abbey. Until I get evidence to the contrary, Terry Cruickshank's responsible for those. Agreed?' Lottie nodded. His right hand went up. 'And we've got Pamela Dixon. We know from the underwear we found that she was out at Shire Oak Road, and we discovered her body in a cold storage unit. We have every reason to believe an American was out at the house, too. But she was killed with a bullet from the same gun.' He stared at her; she nodded once more. 'Which is where these two strands come together.' He clasped his hands. 'How did that happen? And who's the American?'

'So far we haven't done too well finding answers.'

'Luck. Unless someone gives us a tip, half the time that's what solves a case. That and not giving up.' McMillan lit a Four Square. 'We could do with a lot of it right now.'

No reports at the desk of any missing women. Could the killer have satisfied his hunger for the moment? Or was he running scared now?

Lottie rang the police garage. They could book the Humber in next week, not before. Didn't matter if it was the chief constable himself. No, they couldn't promise how long it might take. Depended on parts. Yes, they could provide another car, but no promises as to what it might be.

Frustrated, she went to the canteen and brought a couple of mugs of tea to McMillan's office. He was on the telephone.

'That's something,' he said into the receiver. 'But I need this man. How many officers can there be around here with a mole on their cheek?'

She waited, curious. He pushed a paper across the desk for her. The report from the lab on Cruickshank's letter. It was definitely him; the fingerprints matched those on file from when he was questioned in '38. But that still didn't answer the big question: was he telling the truth or creating an elaborate lie?

'And I need to solve four murders,' McMillan said. 'This man could be key.' He paused. 'I've been told a Jeep was definitely heard leaving the house that night.' She looked at him; he raised his eyebrows and shrugged. He listened, sipping from the cup. 'That would be very helpful. Thank you, Cliff. We'll be up there later.' He put the receiver down gently and turned to her. 'He hopes to have an answer for us this afternoon. It's taken enough pushing.'

'Maybe…' she began then stopped. She couldn't defend Cliff; he'd delayed an investigation. It seemed as if he'd been deliberately dragging his feet. It couldn't be, though; that was stupid. 'Never mind.'

'How do we make Lady Luck smile on us?' he wondered. 'It used to be that I could go anywhere in Leeds and find out what I needed.'

'Not now?'

He pursed his lips and shook his head.

'The higher the rank, the more removed from everything you become. You lose the touch, the feel for it. Half the narks I had are probably dead now. The rest are off fighting.'

'You have plenty of people working for you here.'

'I know. But… all that means is a lot more sitting around here and waiting for information rather than being out there getting it for myself. That's what makes the job exciting, watching people when they tell me things, so I can look at their eyes and know if they're lying.'

'We have a list of his associates.'

'And they've all been questioned.'

'Not by you,' Lottie said. 'What else do we have to do for a few hours?'

He weighed the idea then laughed. 'Come on, then. It won't make me popular, but I'll never win a beauty contest, anyway.'

'Maybe if you lost a few pounds.'

CHAPTER THIRTEEN

THEY sat in canteen of a big welding shop in Hunslet, where a *Careless Talk Costs Lives* poster was peeling away from the wall. Then in the porters' room at the infirmary, where a man with thick glasses blinked every time he answered. And finally out to Crossgates, the Royal Ordinance Factory. Close enough to the sprawling old Barnbow munitions factory where she'd worked during the last war. Where she'd met Geoff.

She knew the streets round here. She knew the smell of them, the taste of the air. It was funny how it all came back as soon as she stepped out of the Humber. So many houses now where there had once been fields and farms. But this factory stood apart, buildings full of noise and heat. Casting metal for artillery guns.

The heavy-set woman had thick smudges of dirt on both cheeks, a pair of dark goggles hanging by their strap around her neck. Her hair was tied up in a scarf, and tiny welding scars covered the back of her hands. She eyed them suspiciously.

'I've not seen him.' Her voice was a rasp. Standing outside the building in the damp grey air she took a Woodbine from the pocket of her overalls, lit it and gulped down the smoke. 'Don't want to, neither.'

Vera Dodds had been Terry Cruickshank's girlfriend, according to his mother. She'd already been questioned once by DC Smith and had given the same answer then.

'When did you see him last?' McMillan asked.

'Came round after he deserted. I told him to get lost.' She put her hands on her hips. 'I'm doing my bit for the country. If he can't do his, he can sling his hook. No time for yellow bellies.'

'How did he react?'

'Stormed off like a little lad in a tantrum.' She shook her head in disgust. 'Sod him.'

Someone shouted. Dodds turned her head towards the open door of the building. Inside, showers of sparks came from the welding machines every few seconds. 'I said I'd be back in a minute,' she shouted, then turned back to them. 'Bloody slavedrivers.'

'Do you know where Terry might be?'

'In a ditch somewhere for all I care.' She nipped the burning tip off the cigarette and put the dog end in a tin. 'Is that it? Only we've got an order to get out.'

'Yes,' he said, then added, 'If you hear from him, please ring us.'

'Course.' She smiled and for a moment the hardness vanished from her face. 'Strange to think I liked him once. Funny old life, isn't it?' She shrugged, turned and vanished.

'Terry doesn't seem to have many friends, does he?' Lottie said as the car bumped out of the yard. Back to Selby Road, a quick glance at the place that had been the making of her before 1918.

'I wish one of them would turn him in.'

'Where now?'

'We'll start at the office,' he said with a sigh. 'Maybe there'll be something new. And happen pigs can fly, too. After that we'll go and see the Yanks.'

The drive to Castle Grove Masonic Lodge seemed all too familiar now. It seemed impossible to believe that a fortnight before, she hadn't even known the place existed.

Today there was a bustle of troops, men in battledress with steel helmets, weapons and packs, all clambering into the backs of lorries. Half of them were covered in mud, shouting and laughing. They seemed filled with a sense of drive and direction.

'Looks like they've been on exercise,' Lottie said.

'Yes,' McMillan answered slowly. For a moment she wondered if he saw a reflection of his young self in the dirty faces. He'd fought, marched with a rifle and been in the trenches.

Ellison was spick and span, the creases sharp in his trousers, not a shred of lint on his jacket.

'Coffee?' he asked as they seated themselves in his cramped attic office. 'There's got to be a fresh pot round this place somewhere.'

'It's fine,' McMillan told him with a smile. 'It's not a social call. You said you might have an answer for me this afternoon. The officer with the mole on his face.'

'I know.' The muscles on his face tightened. 'I've tried, believe me. But we've had half the men out on manoeuvres today – I guess you saw some of them outside. I haven't been able to go round. By tomorrow, I promise.'

'I hope you can deliver this time.' There was very little warmth in McMillan's voice.

'I'm a man of my word, John. Always have been.' He extended his right hand and the Chief Superintendent shook it. 'If he's around here at all, you'll have him.'

As they left, Lottie could feel Ellison's eyes staring at the back of her head. She looked back for a moment and saw pleading and guilt on his face. She gave a hint of a smile then closed the door.

'What the hell's he up to?' McMillan slammed a hand down on the car seat. 'What's going on in there?'

She didn't answer; she had no idea. But Ellison was hiding something, trying to put them off. That was certain.

'He knows who it is,' McMillan continued. 'I could see it on his face. He's probably known since I first gave him the description.'

'Why would he shield someone?' Lottie asked.

'A friend. Senior officer, maybe. I don't know.' He was frustrated, angry. 'He holds the cards. Dammit. If he comes back and says he can't find anyone, what am I going to do? Call him a liar?' He hesitated. 'He's your friend. Couldn't you have a word with him?'

'What?'

'At least find out why the hell he's holding back.'

Lottie kept on driving and didn't say a word. She could feel her outrage building. He might be her boss, but he could go and whistle for that. Finally, once she'd calmed a little she said, 'Give him a chance. He's come through for us once.'

'Sorry,' McMillan said. 'I shouldn't have asked.'

'No,' she agreed. 'You shouldn't.'

She wanted to believe in Ellison. It boiled down to that. She hoped that under it all – beneath the soldier, hidden behind the copper – he was a good man. An upright man. She'd just have to wait and see what tomorrow brought.

The morning gave them good news and bad. Still no women reported missing, no more bodies discovered. That was hopeful.

But by eleven Ellison hadn't rung, and McMillan was pacing around his office like an animal in a cage.

Eventually he appeared in his overcoat, hat in his hand. 'Come on, we've given him a chance. We're going out there.'

He didn't speak on the way. Lottie frowned as she drove, paying attention to the car. The clutch was definitely on its way out. Putting it into third was like a wrestling match and it didn't feel secure when she nudged it into second. All she could do was hope it would last until the appointment next week.

She was still worrying about it as she parked at Castle Grove, rushing to follow McMillan into the building and up the two flights of stairs to the attic. Ellison's door was closed. He turned the knob: locked.

'He didn't know we were coming,' she reminded him.

'Then let's find out where he is.'

It took them five minutes to track down a corporal who seemed to know where everyone should be.

'The Captain?' he asked in surprise. 'He's going to be gone all day. His meeting's been set up for a while. Was he expecting you?'

'No. I'll come back tomorrow.' McMillan was almost at the door when he stopped and turned. 'Tell me – do you know an officer with a mole on his cheek?'

The corporal smiled. 'Sure, sir. Everybody knows him. That's Colonel del Vecchio.'

'Del Vecchio?' He looked at the American with curiosity. 'What does he do?'

'He takes care of transportation and welfare. You know, billeting when it's needed, entertainment, dances, things like that.' The man leaned forward and lowered his voice. 'His first name's Charles so we call him Good Time Charlie.'

Lottie grinned and the corporal winked at her.

'How long has he been stationed here?'

'No idea, sir. He was here when I arrived back in September. He already seemed to know his way around pretty well.'

'And where can I find him now?'

'Out and about.' He picked up a coffee cup and drank. 'The colonel doesn't spend too much time here. Pretty much comes in to collect his messages and that's it.' Another grin. 'He's kind of a maverick, but he sees the guys are looked after, so no one cares.'

The Chief Superintendent took a card from his wallet. It gave his rank, where he was stationed, and the telephone number at Millgarth.

'Would you ask the colonel to give me a ring? I'd like to talk to him.'

'Sure thing, sir.' He gave a salute as they left.

'Well?' He waited until they were back on the road before speaking.

'Don't ask me.'

'Ellison knew all along.' His voice was bitter. 'He's been covering for this del Vecchio. So much for co-operation.'

Lottie didn't know what to say; he was right. She'd hoped Cliff would do what he said. He'd *promised*. And it turned out he'd been lying all the time. Lottie felt an emptiness inside for trusting him, for liking him. Maybe it was a sign. A lesson that she ought to know better at her age.

'Do you think this colonel will ring?'

'No. But leaving the card might keep him on his toes.'

'How does that help us, though?'

'It probably doesn't.' In the mirror she saw the smile in his eyes. 'But I couldn't resist.'

They were on Woodhouse Lane, close to the Headrow. She started to change down into second but it wouldn't engage. Coolly, she pulled to the side of the road.

'What's wrong?' McMillan asked.

'Clutch. It's been having problems. Now it's given up the ghost. It was already booked in for a new one. Sorry – foot traffic only back to Millgarth.'

With the gas mask container bumping against her hip she felt laden and awkward. Next to her, McMillan seemed to waddle as he walked.

'I'll have the garage come and tow it,' she promised. 'And I'll whistle up some transport for us.'

A Morris 8 was all the motor pool had to offer.

'It's nine years old, but it's in good nick,' the mechanic said as he handed her the keys. 'Not as fast as that Humber, but it'll get you there.' He smiled, showing the black gaps in his teeth.

'How long before our car's mended?'

He shrugged. 'I'll take a look and order the parts. Depends.'

'Any chance of new tyres, too? The old ones are worn to nothing.'

The mechanic didn't even bother to look up. 'I'll see what I can do. Don't you know there's a war on?'

'Is that what it is? I thought perhaps we were having a big fancy dress party.'

She and Geoff had owned a Morris 8 before the war. She knew them, liked them. But they'd kept theirs with more pride than this vehicle: the coachwork was dull brick red, the roof black, all the shine gone. Four doors, the running board bent. Inside, the leather on the seats was cracked and worn. Still, what could she expect? At least they had a vehicle. The engine turned over well, it went into gear easily, and the brakes were sharp as she stopped before turning on to the road.

By the time she reached Millgarth the Morris felt familiar. Not much power, he'd been right about that. But it would be fine for a few days, as long as they didn't have to chase any criminals.

McMillan was on the phone when she peered into his office. He beckoned her in.

'Yes,' he said. 'I know you told me you'd ring today.'

She raised an eyebrow and he nodded. Ellison.

'Is that right? You haven't been able to identify anyone like that at all?' He waited. 'I see. No, I appreciate you trying, it's very helpful. Just one question, if you don't mind.' He paused. 'You've really never seen Colonel del Vecchio? You're based in the same building, after all.' A moment later he held the receiver away from his ear. 'He seems to have disconnected.'

'What now?'

'We can hope this mysterious colonel rings me. But I wouldn't hold your breath. And I suspect we're personae non grata up at Castle Grove now.' McMillan hesitated a moment. 'I'm sorry.'

'What for?'

'Well, you're friends with Ellison.'

'I think that's probably over now, too. It doesn't matter, anyway. It wasn't anything special.'

That was what she told herself again as she settled behind her desk. She barely knew him and that was just as well. She didn't need a liar in her life.

Damn the man, anyway.

CHAPTER FOURTEEN

L OTTIE had been in the office for three hours when she heard him slam down the phone. Even through the closed doors the noise seemed to echo. She stiffened. There'd been a sense of anticipation in the air all morning. Now she waited, ready.

McMillan was already shrugging into his coat when he appeared.

'We've got a tip. Cruickshank.'

She dashed down the stairs, out into the cold air. The day was bright, a weak sun in a clear sky. But it was bitter, her breath steaming. Lottie pulled out the choke in the Morris. Start, she thought as she turned the ignition key. The engine caught at the first attempt

'Where?' Lottie asked as she put the car into gear. Smooth, easy. Thank God.

'Chapel Allerton. We're meeting some uniforms at the station there.'

She knew the area; it was little more than ten minutes' walk from home. She did most of her shopping there; she was registered with the butcher on Harrogate Road and bought her bread from Perkins, when they had any for sale.

The police station stood on a corner, the sandstone pitted and darkened over the years. Next door was the library she seemed to visit every week now.

Lottie pulled in to the old cobbled yard. Two men were waiting, a sergeant and a Special.

'Got a report that he's in a house on Town Street, sir.'

'How reliable?'

The sergeant extended his hand, holding it flat and moved it from side to side. So-so.

'Still worth investigating, sir.'

McMillan nodded his agreement. 'This is your patch, what's the best way to approach it?'

'Nothing fancy, sir. You and me at the front door and Richards here on the back.' He nodded towards the special constable; the man was older, running to fat, but still built like a prop forward.

'Is he there now?'

'That's what I've been told, sir.' It was a cautious answer, she thought, as if he wasn't completely certain. But she kept her mouth shut. No one would appreciate her saying anything, and she certainly wouldn't be involved in any arrest.

'Then let's bring him in.'

Lottie had walked along Town Street often enough. It was a grimy terrace across from the graveyard, run-down houses, a sweet shop standing in the middle. Not that there was much to sell with everything on the ration. She leaned against the car, hands deep in the pockets of her coat as the men marched off. One way or another they'd be back soon enough.

As she waited, her mind strayed to Ellison. Just the way it had when she was sitting at home the night before. She didn't understand him, didn't see how he could have deceived them like that. Why? But when she said it didn't matter now, she was lying to herself; if it didn't, the whole thing wouldn't still be preying on her mind. Thank God it had never developed from the start of a friendship. At least there was that saving grace.

They returned empty-handed and silent. McMillan thanked the officers and waited until they'd disappeared into the station.

'Waste of time,' he said. 'Cruickshank was never there.'

'Who gave the tip?'

'I didn't ask. The sergeant looked too embarrassed at dragging me out here. Wild goose chase.'

'Not even that,' she said. 'At least you can eat a goose.'

It made him smile: food, clothing, petrol, anything in short supply, had become material for jokes.

Saturday. After she dropped him at Millgarth, Lottie was done for the week. Leeds was packed with shoppers searching for something, anything, to buy. She wandered around the market, coupon books in her purse, then on to Matthias Robinson, Marks & Spencer, and Schofield's. The only thing she needed was stockings, and they were like gold dust. The best way to get a pair was to know an American; they had nylons to spare. But she didn't fancy her chances of being given any now.

The tram home felt achingly slow. A cup of tea, change into old clothes, hair up in a turban, and out in the garden with a spade and fork for a while before dark. This cold snap was just right for turning over the earth. Soon she had a rhythm, humming as she worked, odd snippets of songs that came into her mind: *Blueberry Hill, Paper Doll, Underneath the Arches, The White Cliffs of Dover, Imagination*. One to another, no reason behind them.

An hour and she stood, stretching out her back.

'You've been hard at it.'

She turned at the voice. Dr Smith next door, standing on the other side of the privet hedge and holding out a mug of tea. 'I thought you might be ready for this.'

Smith was a sweet, plump woman, a GP who lived with her mother, as well as a pair of cats that caused havoc around the neighbourhood. She kept a small vegetable patch by the far fence, next to the Anderson shelter, but never had much luck.

'Might as well while I have the time.'

They chatted for a couple of minutes, then Smith's gaze shifted.

'Looks like you have company,' she said quietly. Her eyes twinkled. 'A fella.'

Lottie turned quickly. She wasn't expecting anyone, especially not a man. And certainly not Cliff Ellison. But there he was in his uniform, standing in the drive, an uncertain expression on his face. He took a short step towards her and Lottie lifted the fork.

'I think you'd better go.'

Ellison raised his hands a little. 'I came round to try to explain.'

'I'm not the one you need to talk to.' Her voice climbed over his. She was surprised at just how cold she sounded. Betrayed.

He looked down at the ground. 'I know, but… I guess I *need* to tell you.'

Lottie shook her head. 'I don't think I *need* to hear it. I'm sorry, you've had a wasted trip. If you want to talk to him, Chief Superintendent McMillan will be in his office on Monday morning.'

'I could have gone down there this afternoon and found him.' Ellison stood his ground. 'But I wanted to talk to *you*.'

'No. I don't want to hear it.' She turned away to start digging again.

'I didn't have any choice, you know.' Ellison spoke a little louder to make sure she could hear. He wasn't about to let it drop, Lottie thought, and she wasn't big enough to throw him out. With a sigh, she pushed the tines of the fork into the ground and walked across to him, arms folded.

'Didn't have a choice about what?' She stared into his eyes, daring him to lie to her again.

He glanced around the garden, looking hesitant. 'Look, can we do this inside? I don't want everyone knowing.'

'Fine,' Lottie agreed after moment, then led the way. She took off her muddy shoes and left them on the mat, untied the turban and shook out her hair. In the dining room, she turned to face him, stopping him a few paces away.

'Right,' she said. 'Tell me. And this time I hope it's the truth, Captain.'

He took a deep breath. 'I was under orders not to say anything about del Vecchio.'

'Why?' She wasn't going to give him an inch.

'Do you know what he does?'

'Finds billets and organises entertainment. That's what we were told.'

'Yeah.' Ellison nodded slowly. 'He does some of that.'

'Go on. What else?'

'I'm not supposed to say.' He took a breath. 'But he's OSS.'

'What on earth is that?'

'Spying.' He paused, waiting for a reaction, but Lottie was listening and thinking. 'I don't know the details. I don't want to know. But we protect him at all costs. That's the order.'

'Your Colonel del Vecchio might be able to help us solve a murder.'

Ellison stared at her. 'You don't get it. You won't ever get to speak to him. A lot of our guys behind enemy lines depend on him. He's their lifeline.'

'You need to tell the boss this.'

'Nope.' He was adamant. 'No one's supposed to know what he really does.'

'Then why are you telling me?' she asked. But she already knew the answer. Because he liked her and he didn't want to see that fall apart.

'Because… because I need you to know why I did it. Not saying anything wasn't my choice.'

'I see.'

'I'm trusting you, Lottie, that you won't run to John on Monday morning and tell him.'

'Don't you think he deserves the truth?' She felt the colour rise in her cheeks. How dare he put this responsibility on her? 'We're trying to catch someone who's killed four girls, for God's sake. And remember, I've known John McMillan an awful lot longer than I've known you.'

'True,' Ellison agreed quickly. 'But please.'

'No,' she told him. 'I'm not making any promises. For all I know, this is another cock and bull story to try and get back in my good graces.'

'It's not.' His was on the verge of shouting, stopping himself then running a hand through his hair. 'It's the truth.' Calmer, he added. 'You understand exactly why I'm telling you. I can see it in your face.'

She did, but God, was she that obvious? She'd never been good at disguising her feelings.

'That doesn't matter,' she told him.

'Look, I like you. I've never tried to hide it. Do you think I wanted to lie to you and John? I'm a cop, too. But I have a duty to the army.' He pushed his lips together. 'And right now the army's my boss.' He paused, stayed quiet for a few seconds. 'I wanted to come and tell you. It's up to you now. If you want to tell John, I can't stop you. You don't want to see me again, that's your choice, too.'

'I haven't said what I'll do yet.' The words came out as a dry croak; she had to clear her throat. Give him another chance? Seeing him standing there, looking humble, a hangdog expression, it was impossible not to like him. Whether she could trust him again, though, was a different matter.

'I didn't want to have to lie,' he said. 'If it didn't bother me, I wouldn't be here now.'

She wanted to believe that guilt had prodded him. That the army hadn't taken every scrap of integrity from him.

'All right,' she said finally. 'You can still come for your dinner tomorrow.'

'Thank you.' He took a step forward but she raised an eyebrow to stop him. 'I'll bring the food, like I said.'

'Fine,' Lottie told him. 'But please don't make more of it than it is. I'm simply giving a soldier a home-cooked meal.'

'That's fine.' He gave that open, American smile. 'Home-cooked will be a real treat. It's been a long time.'

'You'd better come around eleven. The meat will take time to cook.'

'Yes, ma'am.' Ellison grinned.

'Now I want to do some more in the garden before it's dark.'

He knew where he stood now, she thought as she pushed the tines deep into the soil. Tomorrow would tell its own story.

Talk was stilted, coming in fits and starts. He turned up with the biggest piece of beef she'd seen since rationing began, the meat red and bloody as if it had come straight from the butcher's shop. He stood, leaning against the larder door, watching her peel potatoes and carrots, trying to make small talk.

Another clear, crisp winter's day. She'd woken to a rime of frost inside the bedroom window. Even now it was cold enough outside to make breath bloom. But in the living room the fire was warm and inviting, and in the kitchen she sweated as she worked. The smell of roasting meat filled the air.

He ate enough for three, only using his knife when he had to cut the food, then putting it down again. Finally, the plate empty, he pushed it away.

'That was great. Thank you.'

'You supplied the food.'

'But the skill's in the preparation. I'm not much of a cook. And I've never had Yorkshire pudding before.' He grinned. 'Not made properly, I mean.'

'What do you eat back home?'

He thought for a moment. 'Mostly I grab something when I'm out. There are plenty of diners around. Hamburger, spaghetti, brisket if I want something to fill me. Hot dog if I'm not too hungry. By the time I get home I'm usually too tired to fix anything. Just grab a beer from the icebox and sit out on the back porch.'

Lottie felt as if she'd only understood half of that. It was probably easier not to ask for an explanation.

'How long do you think you'll be stationed in Leeds?' She gathered the crockery and cutlery, took them into the kitchen, then lit the gas under the kettle.

'What made you ask that?' he asked when she returned.

'Just wondering.'

'I don't know.' He stared at her. 'Honestly. We don't have any orders, nothing like that. We talk about it on base. But I guess we'll be on our way sometime soon. It wouldn't make much sense just to come to England then stop, would it?'

'No.'

As they drank tea she switched on the radio, letting the dance bands play softly in the background.

'About del Vecchio,' he said eventually.

'Maybe it's better if we let that lie. You said your piece.'

'Just one thing more: if it had been up to me, he'd have talked to you.'

'It wasn't only that. It was the *way* you lied about it.'

'I'd been told I couldn't even admit he worked at the base.' Ellison took out his packet of Lucky Strikes and lit one. He seemed on the verge of speaking. Finally he said: 'If John really wants a word with del Vecchio he's usually in the bar of the Metropole around six every Monday evening.' Ellison stared at her. 'I didn't tell you that, OK? Just some little bird somewhere.'

Lottie smiled. 'I'm sure he'll be grateful.'

'I hope it helps.' He stood. 'I ought to get going. No days off for me. But thank you. I really mean it.' He rubbed his stomach. 'The meal was great.' His face cracked into a smile. 'And you've got a cute place, now I've finally been able to see it in the light.'

She hadn't expected him to leave so soon. It was probably for the best. If he stayed, the conversation would only become more personal.

'I'm glad you enjoyed it.' She held out a hand; he shook it. 'And thank you for the food.' The joint had been delicious. There was enough left to scrape out two more meals, too.

'There's a little bit more.' He reached into the breast pocket of his jacket and brought out a bar of chocolate. Hershey. 'I don't know if you like candy. If you don't, maybe someone else will.'

In spite of herself, Lottie had to smile. Chocolate, too?

'It'll find a home here, believe me. That's very generous.'

'You're welcome.'

With a nod, he went by her. By the time she reached the front door he was halfway down the drive, turning to give her a flat American salute.

'I'll call you.'

She stood and watched until he pulled away in the Jeep.

CHAPTER FIFTEEN

'WHO told you that?' McMillan looked up in disbelief, cigarette poised halfway to his mouth.

'A little bird,' she said.

'I can guess what kind. Is it true, do you think?'

'As far as I know. Cliff's trying to make up for what he did before.'

He took a deep breath. 'Do you fancy a drink at the Metropole after work?'

She laughed. 'I bet you make that offer to all the girls.'

'Sounds as if you have offers of your own.'

Lottie glared at him in warning; that topic was off-limits.

As soon as she arrived at Millgarth, Lottie had checked the missing persons register. Only when she saw there were no reports did she realise she'd been holding her breath.

That was still good news – as far as it went. There could still be others out there, ones they might never discover. And it didn't help them catch Cruickshank. Or whoever the killer really was.

Two tips during the day sent them haring off. McMillan complained about the slow speed of the Morris. She let him rant; it was simply his frustration at the way things were progressing.

But neither hint panned out. The first was nothing, the second a man with a faint resemblance to Cruickshank. By five o'clock they were parked on Commercial Street with nothing to do for an hour.

'Come on, I'll buy you tea,' he offered. Men bringing food yesterday, offering her a meal today: who was she to complain? Betty's was busy, the waitresses bustling around in their black and white uniforms.

The cooks did their best, but nothing could disguise the shortage of food. A small selection on the menu. As tasty as they could make it, but not filling, and a poor choice of sweets.

'How do you want to tackle del Vecchio?' Lottie asked when they were finished. She dabbed at her mouth with the serviette. At least the place made sure its linen was white and starched. Keeping up appearances, even as the war rolled on.

'We need to catch him on his own.'

'Are you going to arrest him?'

'For what?' McMillan asked. 'All we've got to connect him to Shire Oak Road is the testimony of that chap you talked to. The commissioner for oaths.'

'Ask him to help with inquiries, then?'

'I'll be satisfied if I can get him somewhere for a quiet word.' He checked his watch. 'Come on, we'll walk down.'

The Metropole Hotel was a place that had seen better days. The colours on the carpet were faded and worn, the staff old and slow. But it was like everywhere else these days, just hanging on and hoping things would be better soon. That the war would end. Servicemen and women in uniform sat and talked, and a murmur of noise came from the bar.

'I'll be back in a minute,' McMillan told her. She saw him talking to a man in a well-cut lounge suit. No more than a minute, and they parted with a quick shake of hands.

'What was that all about?'

'Wait and see,' he answered with a sly smile. 'Let's have a look for our friend. Shouldn't be too hard to spot with that mole on his cheek.'

It was easy. He was at a table in a corner, wearing his uniform. The small lump stood out on his face. DelVecchio sat in earnest conversation with a man wearing a heavy overcoat, bald head glistening under the lights.

'We'll wait until they're done,' McMillan said. 'I'll order drinks. Stand where we can see them.'

With so many different uniforms around, Lottie knew she blended in. Who knew what was what? From its colour, the WAPC skirt and jacket could easily belong to the navy. She sat back, enjoying the people-watching and trying to guess who were couples and who was passing time. She sipped her gin and tonic. Even now, tatty at the edges, there was still an echo of grandeur about the Metropole. Geoff had brought her here for their tenth anniversary, and she'd felt overwhelmed by the Art Deco splendour of it all. But that seemed like a lifetime ago.

And now she was back again for work: a different kind of treat. This was like being a real copper again. She glanced at her reflection in the mirror and saw she was grinning like a loon. People would start to wonder.

Half an hour later the man with delVecchio put down his empty glass, stood and left. He didn't glance at them as he went by. McMillan waited until he'd left the bar, then he was on his feet, strolling over to the American, Lottie close behind.

'Colonel?'

DelVecchio looked up, cocking his head, curious. The mole on his cheek stood out against the skin.

'Hi, do I know you?'

'No, sir. But I've been trying to catch up with you.' He brought out his warrant card. 'Detective Chief Superintendent McMillan, Leeds City Police. I'd like a chat with you, if I may.'

Del Vecchio didn't look concerned. 'And if I don't want to?'

'Then we'll have a talk anyway, sir.' His voice hardened. 'We can do it here or somewhere more private.'

The colonel seemed to weigh the choice for a second, then stood in a single, fluid motion. He was easily six feet tall, with thick dark hair. Not handsome; his features were too puffy for that, and the mole was a beacon on his cheek. But he carried himself confidently, an air of cockiness about him.

McMillan led the way down a corridor, away from the reception desk. He stopped at a door, turned the handle then stood aside for the American. So that was what his little word earlier had been about, Lottie thought. A favour from the manager. Somewhere out of the way for an interrogation.

'What do you want to know?' Del Vecchio pulled out cigarettes and a Zippo lighter.

'About you and a house on Shire Oak Road in Headingley.'

'Yeah? What about it?' His eyes narrowed a little.

'You were there, giving the place the once-over.'

The smile returned. 'That's right. Someone told me it was empty. I thought it might make a good billet for my guys.'

'But?'

'I took a look at the place. It was a wreck, it was going to need too much work.' He shrugged. 'That's all.'

'Unfortunately, it's not.' He waited for the colonel's reaction.

'Is that right? What else?' He didn't seem especially curious, Lottie thought. As if he already knew.

'A few days later a man was seen leaving the house after midnight, carrying a young woman. They drove off in a Jeep with the American insignia.'

'So?' He shrugged. 'She's drunk, he takes her home. Happens every night somewhere.'

'She left her underwear behind in the house,' Lottie added.

Del Vecchio glanced at her before replying. 'She's probably not the first to do that, either.'

'A few days later her body showed up in a cold storage unit.' McMillan paused for a heartbeat. 'She'd been shot with a Colt.'

Del Vecchio leaned forward, elbows on the table, suddenly very earnest.

'Are you trying to say—?'

The Chief Superintendent cut him off. 'I'm trying to find a killer. I want to know what you know. And I want it now.'

'Do you know who I am?'

'You could be big-arsed Duncan from Dundee for all I care. It doesn't put you above the law of the land.' McMillan slammed a palm down on the desk. 'Someone's killed four women, all the same way. I want him. Now...' His voice calmed again. 'Shall we start over?'

'Start what? I already told you what I know.'

'No, Colonel, you've told me nothing. That American who left the house with a girl; that could have been you.'

Del Vecchio gave a smile with no warmth. 'I guess it could,' he agreed. 'But it wasn't.'

'Prove it. Tell me where you were a week ago on Wednesday.'

Del Vecchio stubbed out his cigarette and lit another. 'I don't remember. I'll have to check with my social secretary.' He shook his head, blew out a trail of smoke and stood. 'I'll tell you what I'm doing right now, though. I'm walking out of here and it really won't be a good idea if you try to stop me.'

He had size and age on his side. Very likely some deadly experience, too, Lottie thought.

Del Vecchio's face showed his mood, patience exhausted. 'I'll spell it out for you, OK? It wasn't me there that night, and I don't know who it was. This is the first I've heard of it. Goodnight.'

He brushed past McMillan, shouldering him out of the way, then walked around Lottie with a short nod. The door closed softly and they were alone, the silence enveloping them.

'Come on,' the Chief Superintendent said finally. 'Let's call it a day.'

There wasn't much to discuss, and only one question to ask as they walked back to the car.

'Do you believe him?' Lottie asked.

'Some of it,' he said wearily. 'I don't like him, but my gut says part of that was the truth.'

'Which part?'

'We go home and hope we know that in the morning.'

The day arrived with a bitter wind from the west to make the February cold even worse. Standing at the bus stop Lottie was glad for her heavy greatcoat and scarf. There'd be little crime today; weather like this would keep even the crooks off the streets.

By the time she reached Millgarth a few flakes of snow were whipping around. She was grateful for the warmth of the building as it wrapped around her. The first stop was the missing persons' book. No young women reported in the last twenty-four hours. It had been several days now. Lottie started to feel she could breathe more easily. Maybe the madness had abated. Maybe.

Upstairs, she hung up her coat and rested her gloves on the steam radiator to keep them warm, then made her way to McMillan's office with two mugs of tea from the canteen.

'Better drink it fast,' he told her. 'I've been waiting for you. We need to go to Harehills.'

'What?' She felt her heartbeat quicken. 'Have they caught Cruickshank?'

A shadow passed across his face as he shook his head. 'Not yet. The chief authorised a reward – the usual, information leading to arrest and conviction.'

'How much?'

'Fifty pounds.'

She let out a low whistle. It wasn't feminine but she couldn't help herself. Fifty pounds? It was a fortune. 'That should bring something.'

'I hope so.' He drained the mug. 'Right, let's go.'

'I want you to ask most of the questions when we get there,' he said as they drove through Sheepscar, caught behind a tram.

'Me?' Lottie asked in surprise. 'Why?'

'It's a young woman home on leave. She says someone tried to attack her last night. Andrews questioned her but he didn't get too much, she was still upset. He left a WPC with her.'

'All right.' She felt a shiver run through her body. Doing real copper's work. This could get to be a habit. 'Let me talk to her on her own, then, without you there. She might find it easier to speak without a man around.'

'If it helps,' he agreed. 'We want Luxor Drive. It's around here somewhere.'

Cobbles on the road. Back-to-back houses, paint peeling in long strips from the window frames. The Morris was the only car parked on the street.

'What's her name?'

'Caitlin Johnson.'

'Caitlin?' She'd never heard that before. 'What type of name is that?'

'Irish. Probably from a grandmother.'

The woman police constable answered the door. Seeing her, so smart and eager, was like gazing into a mirror and catching a reflection of herself twenty years younger.

'Through here, sir,' the WPC said. She didn't even seem to notice Lottie.

The young woman at the table wore a dress of printed cotton, torn at the shoulder. She'd tried to mend her hair and her make-up, but she was still dishevelled, eyes frightened as a rabbit, dark tracks of mascara tears still visible on her cheeks. Her features seemed too small for her face, crowded together, giving her an awkward look.

'Is there another cup in there?' Lottie picked up the teapot. Empty. 'I'll make some more, shall I?'

A dark blue uniform jacket hung on the back of the chair, a pair of eagles on the lapels. Nothing she recognised, but there were so many branches of the services these days. It was like a maze.

'I'm Lottie.' She sat on the empty chair. 'You must have been terrified.'

'Yes.' The woman held out her hand, still shaking slightly.

They were alone in the scullery, the door closed, heavy heat coming from the range.

'Do you feel up to talking about it, Caitlin?' She didn't take out her notebook. Nothing official, nothing to put her on her guard. Just two women talking.

Johnson was home on a three-day pass from the Air Transport Auxiliary.

'The job's nothing glamorous,' she said with a timid laugh. The smile suited her; it made her face come alive. 'I don't deliver the planes or anything. Ground crew. Control tower.'

She'd gone out with some of the girls she'd known from school. They'd stayed at home to work in the factories, she'd joined up; it was a chance to get away and meet people she'd never know otherwise.

'By nine we'd had a couple and went off to dance a bit.' She tried to laugh again but it came out forced, cracked. 'Maybe meet a bloke. Well, I did that all right.'

'Is that the dress you were wearing?'

Johnson glanced down at it as if she'd never seen it before. 'Yes. And a coat. But…'

'It doesn't matter. What was he like?'

'He was wearing civvies. Nothing special, suit from the fifty-shilling tailor. Nice enough in a pinch.'

Lottie brought out the photograph of Terry Cruickshank they'd taken from his mother and laid it on the table.

'Was this him?'

Johnson shook her head as soon as she saw it. 'No. Not even close. I've never seen this one before.'

The man who'd been with her claimed to be an army officer on leave. Pale hair Brylcreemed down, thin moustache, a hint of a Leeds accent. About five feet nine.

'He seemed nervous,' Johnson said suddenly. 'Eager. I thought he just…' She looked down for a moment.

'What happened? Take your time, I know it's not easy.'

Johnson lit another Player's, adding the match to the pile in the ashtray.

'He said he knew somewhere we could go. I wasn't sure – my mum had told me about what happened to that girl.'

'But you went with him?'

She gave a curt nod. 'I'd had a few and I was in the mood. Anyway, he said it wasn't far. We went down this ginnel and suddenly he was all over me. Pulling at my clothes. Got my wrists pinned over my head. He scared me. Then I felt something against my stomach.'

'Go on,' Lottie said quietly.

'It was cold. Hard.' She looked up for a moment. 'Metal. I thought I was dead. I just brought my knee up. As soon as he let go I started screaming and ran. Kept going until I found a policeman.'

'Where did it happen?'

'One of those little lanes off Lower Briggate.'

'Which side? Do you remember?'

'The copper I found asked me that. I don't know. I just ran.'

McMillan would have men out searching all the courts down there. There might be some small piece of evidence to find.

'When are you due back on base?'

'Day after tomorrow.' She stubbed out the cigarette in a flurry of ash. 'How am I going to sleep? Every time I close my eyes it's like it's happening all over again.'

'Talk to your doctor,' Lottie suggested. 'He can give you something.' She paused. 'You don't have to tell him what happened.'

Johnson nodded. 'Was it… him? You know.'

'It sounds like it,' she answered cautiously. If it was, Cruickshank had been telling them the truth. They were back to square one. 'Was there anything else about him?'

'No. That is… no.'

Lottie waited a moment, then said, 'What? Tell me, please. It might help us catch him.'

'He had a ring. Not a wedding ring, it had a square piece with some initials on it.'

'A signet ring?'

'Yes, that's it. On the little finger of his right hand.'

'What were the initials, could you see?' Lottie held her breath.

'It was old, all worn, and the light in the dancehall wasn't good.'

'It doesn't matter.' She put a hand over Caitlin's and squeezed it very gently. 'You've done well, thank you.' And they had something. A good description.

CHAPTER SIXTEEN

'I OUGHT to get rid of half of the men in CID and just use you instead,' McMillan said when she gave him all the details. 'So it's not Cruickshank.'

'That's how it looks. She was definite when I showed her the photograph.' Lottie started the engine. 'Where now?'

'Millgarth. I want that description circulated as soon as possible. Maybe someone will know him. Hell's bells.' He slammed a hand down on the armrest. 'We're right back where we began.'

At the station she typed everything on to Banda sheets and passed it over to be duplicated for the beat bobbies. She could hear McMillan on the telephone. He came out of his office shaking his head.

'I've been on the blower to Sid Cohen, the furrier. Thought he might know the man. No such luck.'

Before he could say more, DC Smith came dashing from the detectives' office, a piece of paper in his hand.

'This bloke, sir,' he began, 'I think I know who he is.'

'Who?'

'If it's the same one, his name's George Hilliard. I had him for nicking lead back when I was in uniform. Sounds about the same, and he had a ring like that.'

'There's plenty of distance between stealing and murder.' McMillan glanced at Lottie. 'Can you get his sheet? Let's take a look.'

A couple of minutes in Records and she was walking back with the file, scanning the page. Aged thirty-two, there was a resemblance to the man Caitlin Johnson had described. He'd been arrested a few times for theft, possession of stolen property, once for assault. Jail each time. But nothing since 1940. On the way back to McMillan's office she checked the deserters' register. Yes, the name was there: Hilliard, George J. Came home on leave in the middle of 1943 and never reported back to camp.

'He's been AWOL for eight months,' Lottie announced as she handed over the file.

McMillan took a glance. 'Look up every address we have on him,' he told Smith. 'I want each one of them searched top to bottom.'

'Yes, sir.'

Lottie could sense the electricity crackling through the air. He took the photograph from under the paperclip and handed it to her. 'Go back and see Miss Johnson. I want her to take a look at that.'

She nodded and left. It was strange to be driving without his bulk in the back seat. Emptier, somehow. The skies had cleared; now it was just another frigid day. Roundhay Road was blocked by a broken-down lorry. She ended up taking the back streets, guided by memory and good luck until she found Luxor Drive.

Caitlin Johnson's mother let her in. 'The doctor's been. He gave her something, she's settled down in her bed.'

'It's quite important,' Lottie said. 'I'll only be a moment.'

'Go on, then.' She inclined her head to the stairs. 'Just be quick. Rest would be a blessing for her.'

The girl wasn't quite asleep, but on the edge of it. Her eyes opened at the sound of footsteps.

'Me again, I'm afraid.' Lottie sat on the edge of the bed. A threadbare cotton sheet, a pair of rough blankets, eiderdown, candlewick; there'd be ample warmth in there. 'I need you to look at something for me.' She held out the picture.

Johnson began to scramble under the covers.

'It's all right.' Lottie kept her voice low and soothing. 'It's fine. Is this him?'

'Yes.'

'We have policemen out looking for him. Don't you worry, we'll find him. He won't bother you again, I promise. You're safe now.' She stayed, talking until Caitlin was calm again, settled and dozing.

'Did you get what you needed?' Mrs Johnson asked as she was leaving.

'Yes,' she said. 'I did.'

'No doubts at all?'

'None. Poor lamb was scared out of her wits.' The line crackled a little. Lottie stood in the telephone box, watching traffic pass on Roundhay Road.

'At least we know who we want now.'

'Cruickshank was telling the truth.'

'I know.' She heard him cough. 'There's still so much about this that I can't work out.'

'Maybe it'll all make sense after we arrest Hilliard.'

'Maybe,' he said bleakly.

She found a small café, almost every chair filled. The air was warm and the meat and potato pie suspiciously full of meat. No wonder it was busy, she thought; she'd come back if they were always this generous.

The owner, grey-haired and smiling, gave her a wink as she paid. 'Your lot are always welcome here.'

Millgarth seemed to be bustling. Men walked around with determined expressions. She could hear McMillan talking on the phone, an anxious edge to his voice. As she passed his open door he waved her in.

'I'll be out there in a few minutes,' he said, and slammed the receiver down.

'What is it?'

'A pair of Specials were out checking places where Hilliard had lived.' From the furious look in his eyes she could see what had happened.

'They let him get away?'

'Through the back bloody door and ran off. They couldn't catch him. So now he knows we're after him and he could be anywhere. Dammit. Come on, we're going to take a look at the place. Smith's already there, talking to the owner. Randall's with him,' he added ominously.

Long ago, Wilf Randall had been a promising light heavy-weight boxer. These days he was years past his prime, beyond conscription age, but still intimidating, even if he'd run to fat. And not shy with his fists, from all Lottie had heard.

'Whereabouts?' She took the car keys from her pocket.

'Out along York Road. Gipton.'

The estate had been built ten years before, a green, airy new beginning for people uprooted from the slums in the city centre. Semi-detached houses, gardens. He directed her around the streets.

'There.' He pointed to a house close to the end of the cul de sac. 'Do you mind talking to the Specials and getting their story? If I have to hear how incompetent they were I might go through the roof.'

She smiled. 'Of course.'

'I can't believe it.' He held his thumb and finger half an inch apart. 'We were *this* close.'

The unpainted wooden front gate hung open. A privet hedge hid the front garden. A special constable stood by the front door, moving from foot to foot to try and keep warm. He saluted as McMillan strode past.

'Were you one of the pair who came out here?' Lottie asked. She tried to sound sympathetic. And she did feel sorry for the poor man.

'Me and my oppo.' He had the good grace to look embarrassed.

'Where is he?'

'Off beating the bushes.' He shrugged. 'You never know.' He turned his head to glance at the house. 'I suppose we're not in the super's good books.'

'That's putting it mildly,' she told him. 'I'm WAPC Armstrong. I work with Mr McMillan.'

'Wilson.' He gave a small, sad smile. 'Joined up after the army wouldn't have me.' He raised one leg to show a surgical boot. 'Right leg's shorter than the left.' He was a young man, probably barely twenty-one, with an expression that looked eager to please.

'Why don't you tell me what happened.' He started to reach for his notebook, but she stopped him. 'Off the record.'

'Well,' Wilson began, 'we'd been to a couple of other places searching for this Hilliard bloke. No luck; you know how it is.

Either they'd never heard of him or they didn't want to know. Knocked on the door here, fella answered it. The next thing I know, we heard the back door slam. Bert took off running. He's my partner. But he's asthmatic. Managed about a hundred yards. Got a glimpse and that was it. I sent him off to phone the station.'

'You didn't think one of you should've been watching the back door?' Lottie asked.

Smith hesitated for a moment, then admitted, 'We didn't reckon he'd be here. Not after them other two houses.'

'If I were you I'd keep out of the chief superintendent's way until the war's over,' she advised. What else could she say? Wilson already knew how stupid he'd been. She had no power to punish, and she wouldn't have done it, anyway. Everyone made mistakes. There was no point in saying anything. When she'd been a WPC, all those years ago, her record hadn't been spotless.

With a nod to Wilson, Lottie entered the house, and followed the voices to the dining room. A fire burned low in the grate, most of its heat gone. One man sat on a straight-backed chair, wrists handcuffed behind him. Blood spattered his face and white shirt. Big old Wilf Randall stood close by, face flushed, rubbing his knuckles, a satisfied smile across his face.

DC Smith had his jacket off, shirt sleeves neatly rolled up. He grabbed the man in the chair by his hair, pulling the head back sharply.

'Where would he go? Do you need my mate to jog your memory again?'

'I don't know.' He sounded desperate, on the verge of tears. 'I don't bloody know.'

She looked across at McMillan. He was watching everything, eyes narrowed, hands bunched in the pockets of his overcoat.

A few more minutes with no answers and he left the room. Lottie followed.

'They'll manage to get something from him,' he said. 'Probably nothing very useful.' He lit a Four Square and stared out at the back garden. 'Must have gone over the fence.'

'The man who tried to chase him has asthma.'

'This close,' he said quietly.

'Has anyone searched here?' Lottie asked.

'Top to bottom,' he answered. 'Nothing of his. No gun.' He nodded towards the other room 'The fellow in there insists our friend was only visiting. I'm inclined to believe him.'

She saw the bare trees and thought about the bitter winter cold. 'Does Hilliard have an overcoat?'

'Still hanging up in the hall.'

'Then he'll be perishing soon enough.'

'Easy enough to steal a coat,' McMillan told her. 'Come on, we're not going to get anything else here.'

As they passed Wilson, she gave him a wink. He deserved that, at least.

'Where are we going?' she asked McMillan.

'Good question,' he said as he settled on the back seat. 'Back to Millgarth, I suppose. Since we don't have Hilliard.'

A message waited on her desk: the Humber was ready. A quick trip to the garage and the relief of being behind a familiar steering wheel.

'Gave it a service while I had it here.' The mechanic winked. 'You won't have any trouble with her for a while.'

And it did feel sharper, more powerful. Much, much better than that Morris. There was real power under the bonnet.

McMillan was waiting in the yard as she arrived, and climbed in as soon as she came to a stop.

'Kirkstall Abbey,' he ordered.

'Not another body? Please say it's not.' She couldn't bear the thought of that. Not now.

'Someone thinks they saw Hilliard.'

Thank God for the Humber, she thought. It had the speed and the acceleration she needed. She dodged in and out of traffic, ignoring the blare of horns as she passed between a lorry and a Corporation bus. She knew it was safe. Tight, maybe, but safe.

She made record time, pulling in by the abbey behind two more cars. Immediately, McMillan was slamming the door and hurrying down the path. A uniformed inspector she didn't recognise seemed to be in charge. Coppers and Specials were fanning out, going through the ruins and the undergrowth by the river.

Lottie kept her distance. This was a time to fade into the background, simply to be there when she was needed. The earth was hard under her feet, and the wind whistled along the Aire valley as it came down off the Pennines.

It was hard to believe people had chosen to live out here when this was a truly wild place. The monks who'd founded the abbey must have been hardy men. But they had faith, that was what drove them. Who had anything so powerful these days? All she believed was that they'd beat the Germans and the Japs one day. Soon, she hoped.

But that would need another front, troops marching through France and Belgium to take Germany. Many of them would be Americans. Cliff Ellison would be among them. He'd leave and become nothing more than a memory, and perhaps a name on some letters. Much safer to keep her defences up. He was only here for a little while.

She was suddenly aware that McMillan was calling her name, dragging her away from her thoughts.

'Yes, sir?'

'I want you to liaise with the inspector here. He's in charge of the search. I think Hilliard's gone, if he was ever here, but we'll keep looking. It's the best we have for now. Worth a try.'

'Yes, sir.' She gave the uniformed officer a nod and the phone number at Millgarth. 'Something made me wonder,' she said as they walked back to the car. 'He must have got here sharpish from Gipton It's a fair distance and the buses aren't that regular.'

'I know,' McMillan agreed. 'I don't really expect to find anything. But we'd have looked a right bunch of Charlies if he'd been here and we hadn't checked. Just take the report when it comes in.'

It was already dusk. The men would only be able to search for a few more minutes. They wouldn't find anything. Hilliard was somewhere in Leeds, but not here. All they had to do was find him before he killed again.

CHAPTER SEVENTEEN

S HE saw the Jeep as soon as she turned the corner. He was sitting behind the steering wheel, huddled in his greatcoat and reading a book, looking up and smiling as she approached.

'Hi,' he said. 'I thought I'd take you by surprise. I hope you don't mind.'

Too late for that, she thought. He was already here. All the neighbours would have peered through the blackout curtains and seen him. Not the first time, either. Tongues would be wagging again in the morning.

'You might as well come in.'

She lit the fire, glad when the heat started to fill the room. It was already bitter out and the temperature would fall further tonight. In the kitchen she put the kettle on the gas then looked through the larder with a frown.

'I can make a sandwich if you're hungry, but the only bread is the National Loaf.' Lottie made a face. 'Good for you but it tastes disgusting.'

'I think I'll be fine with tea. I hadn't heard from you. I hoped you'd forgiven me.'

'It's been busy. Let me make the tea and I'll tell you.' When she returned he was smoking, a packet of cigarettes balanced on the chair arm behind the glass ashtray. 'We found del Vecchio.'

'I heard.' He grinned. 'Came in ranting and raving about the Limeys going after him. Thundered round for thirty minutes yelling at anyone who came close, then took off again.'

'Yes, he seemed a charming man,' she said drily. 'We had another woman attacked.' She saw his eyes widen. 'She got away unhurt, and we have an identification. Almost caught him, too.'

'He escaped?'

'Let's just say the boss isn't happy. What have you been up to?'

'Nothing too important. How did you identify this guy?'

'Luck. And someone's memory.'

The conversation seemed to founder. The flow had vanished. Lottie felt as if she was sitting with a perfect stranger. Why, she wondered? Ellison was a pleasant enough chap. Maybe that was the problem. Lottie finished her tea.

'Would you mind if we called it a night?' she asked. 'I came home with a pounding headache.'

'Of course.' Before she knew it, he was only his feet, looking solicitous. 'Is there anything I can do?'

'It's fine. A good sleep and it'll pass.'

'I'm sorry for just turning up.'

'Don't worry about it,' she said. 'I'll lie down for a while.'

She felt relief go through her as she closed the front door behind him. She did have a headache, it wasn't a lie; but it was only minor. Mostly she wanted to be on her own, not have to talk to anyone. It all felt like too much effort.

McMillan was in a foul mood. He glared at her as she entered, then snapped his questions, demanding this and that. After an hour of it she marched back into his office and stood, hands on hips.

'What?'

'You,' she told him. 'It's like being round a grumpy bear.'

'We could have ended this yesterday if those Specials—'

She cut him off. 'Well, they didn't, and that's the end of it.' Lottie moved over to the door, closing it quietly. 'I wish they had, too. I dread going through the missing persons list every morning and hoping there's no one on it.'

He grunted.

'I've known you a long time, John McMillan.' She leaned forward and lowered her voice to a hiss. No reason for the whole building to hear. 'You're acting like a child having a tantrum. We don't have Hilliard. Taking it out on me and everyone else isn't going to make him give up. We're all trying to do the same thing.' She stared at him until he finally turned his face away. She'd said her piece; with luck it had struck home. She opened the door again. 'Anything else for now, sir?' He shook his head slowly and she returned to her desk.

Of course he was angry. They all were. But there was no excuse for having a short fuse around people who were trying to do their jobs. He was in charge, he needed to set an example. Lottie could sense the frustration inside him, building up like a head of steam. Letting it out on everyone around wasn't fair, though. He needed to be reminded, and she was probably the only one in the station who could do it without setting off an explosion.

Five minutes passed, then the door to his office opened. He emerged holding a clutch of papers and held them out to her.

'Would you mind filing these, please?' Polite and calm. He gave a tiny nod, then vanished down the stairs. The storm had blown over. When he returned he was carrying two mugs of tea and put one on her desk. His peace offering.

'Do we have anything new on Hilliard?' she asked.

'No. And I still can't make head or tail of how the cold storage and Shire Oak Road fit into it all. There's nothing to tie him to them. It's like trying to do the *Times* cryptic crossword.'

She understood, but for a fraction of a second it dredged up memories. Geoff had enjoyed the cryptic. The acrostic, too. He rarely completed them, but he could never resist the challenge.

'And it doesn't explain an American leaving the house carrying a girl,' she said.

'I know.' He scratched the back of his scalp. 'The old buffer next door to the place swore he saw that star insignia, but maybe he just imagined it.'

'But that would mean Hilliard had a Jeep, though. He didn't make that up. That ARP fellow heard it.'

'Stealing a car's nothing. I could do it myself.'

Lottie raised an eyebrow in disbelief.

'I could,' he insisted with a grin. 'A professional car thief showed me.'

'At least you'll be useful if I lose the car keys.'

'We'll only discover the truth when we arrest Hilliard,' he said. 'Still, Cruickshank's off the hook.'

'Hilliard's going to be running scared now.'

'Good,' McMillan said firmly. 'That's what I want. People make mistakes when they're scared.'

'He must have a place somewhere.'

He nodded. 'We're looking. That man he was with yesterday didn't know where it was. We made sure we got the truth out of him.'

In her mind's eye she could see him, the blood and the bruises.

'Did he give you any other names?'

'A couple of friends. Smith and Randall have been out looking.' He checked his watch. 'We should have something soon.'

As if on cue, the telephone in his office began to ring. In less than a minute he was back.

'Come on.' He gave a dark grin.

Bitterly cold and grey. She had to scrape frost off the windscreen. At least the heater worked since the service; she turned it all the way up, and rubbed a hand across the glass to try and clear the condensation.

'Where?' Lottie asked.

'East End Park.'

It wasn't far, a twist and tangle of streets through some of the poorest parts of Leeds. Past the grey, looping bulk of Quarry Hill flats, then Marsh Lane, the railway goods yard still a ruin where German bombs had landed back in 1940. Faded, flapping posters on walls urged people to support the Spitfire Fun and Ark Royal Week. Up through the Bank, where half the houses had been demolished before the war, the rest still packed to overflowing with people who could afford nothing better. Then Cross Green and pulling to the kerb, the only car by the scrubby green of the park.

'Over there.' He pointed to a house with a green door and a tiny front yard; a through terrace, by the look of it. 'Where Hilliard lives. We got a tip.'

'You're sure he's not there now?'

'Positive. The man on the beat checked a little while ago. I told him to carry on. I want to search this place myself.'

The man who answered the door had a liquid, bronchitic cough, pulling out a grey handkerchief to spit in it. Cloudy eyes, thin as a garden rake, a wheezy voice. He'd been expecting them.

'Upstairs,' he said. 'Not seen him in a few days. He's paid up to the end of the month, mind.'

'You have a key for his room?'

'Course.' A short, sullen reply.

'Unlock it for me.'

It wasn't much, twelve feet by twelve. A single bed with a cast-iron frame. Tattered rag rug on bare boards. A small desk, a wardrobe in the corner by the window, a suitcase on top. McMillan looked round.

'I can smell him.' He took in the dirty clothes piled in the corner, the drawers that were closed, the tangle of sheets and pillows. 'I'll take the desk, you look in the wardrobe.'

The door pulled back with a squeak. One side had shelves for shirts and underwear, the other a rod for hanging clothes.

'I think you'll want to take a look at this,' Lottie said.

Two army uniforms on hangers. One for a private, probably Hilliard's own, smelling oddly musty. The other was for an officer. A captain. The peaked cap sat on top of a shirt.

'Well, well,' McMillan stood behind her. 'He certainly likes to play dress-up, doesn't he?' He tossed the captain's uniform on the bed and started digging through the pockets. Just an empty matchbox, nothing more.

She went through the other clothes, Hilliard's own uniform, forage cap pushed through an epaulette, and an old suit with a Burton's label inside. Dust and lint in the pockets, nothing to help them. Shirts, underwear, socks, shoes; she didn't find anything hidden in the folds. The suitcase was empty. He remained anonymous.

There was very little in the desk, either. A spare collar stud, a couple of scraps of paper, names and addresses scribbled in pencil; something to be checked later. But the man was a deserter, he'd probably keep anything important with him. Lottie stripped the sheets from the bed, lifted the mattress and looked under the frame. The only thing there, in the dust, was a copy of *Health and Efficiency*. In a strange way it made Hilliard more human, more fragile.

'We'll take the uniforms and the suit with us,' McMillan said. 'I'll have the evidence boys over here later to see if we missed anything.'

'Doesn't look like there's much to miss.'

'You never know. They'll tear it apart properly. In the meantime we'll get them to examine these clothes. Might be some blood they can identify, or some hairs. Anything to nail him down.'

The evidence laboratory was over in Hunslet, a rickety affair in the basement that had once been the home of the police surgeon. The officer in charge, huddled in his white lab coat, tutted as they walked in.

'Those could have picked up all sorts on the way here.'

'Maybe they did,' McMillan replied. 'But I'm interested in any blood, whatever you can find to tie the wearer to those murdered girls we have.'

She could hear it in his voice; he wasn't in a mood to argue the toss. The lab man nodded after a moment.

'Where now?' she asked as they walked back to the Humber.

He produced the scraps of paper with the names and addresses he'd taken from Hilliard's room. 'Let's find out what these are about.'

The first man on the list admitted that the writing was his, but nothing more until he heard the description.

'Him.' He shook his head. 'Met him in a pub. He said he could maybe lay his hands on a case of this or that. I told him I might be interested, wrote down my address. He never turned up.'

'Was he in uniform?'

'No, civvies.' He glanced from McMillan to Lottie. 'Why, who is he?'

'Just following up on something, sir. But I'd steer clear of the black market if I were you. The judges don't look kindly on it.'

The second address brought more of the same. A taxi driver.

'I remember him. Said he knew where I could get petrol off the ration. Told me he worked with the Ministry.'

Hilliard must have been in civvies again, she thought.

'What happened?'

'I wrote my address down, told him to come round. That's the last I saw of him. Honest.'

She believed him. It fitted. On the run from the army, Hilliard was getting by, making deals. Some must have worked or he'd be broke. And he was still going around with a gun.

As they pulled into the yard behind Millgarth, a police van was screeching out, bell ringing. Lottie raised an eyebrow as she glanced in the mirror but McMillan ignored her, already on his way into the station.

'Shooting, sir!' the desk sergeant shouted. 'Noble the jeweller on Commercial Street.'

McMillan didn't say a word; he simply turned. She was ahead of him, running to the car, starting the engine and pushing down on the accelerator as he closed the door.

'It's him,' he said. 'I can taste it. He's getting desperate.'

DC Smith was already talking to the owner of the shop, a man in his sixties who kept wiping his forehead with a handkerchief, even in the cold wind. Uniforms were all around, interviewing witnesses. Lottie spied a woman trying to stay small and out of sight in the corner.

'Hello,' she said as she approached. 'I'm Lottie Armstrong. Do you work here?'

She nodded, staring with wide, scared eyes.

'Yes.' The word barely came out.

'What's your name?' Lottie smiled at her. She looked to be about twenty, hair neatly set, a face and figure that looked younger. Shy, petrified. She needed a little calm and comfort.

'Angela Dobson.'

'Were you here when it happened?'

Another nod. 'Me and Mr Noble, we were in the shop.' She pointed to a counter with a glass top. Half the display cases beneath were empty. He must have got away with a good haul of rings and watches.

All around them there was noise. Men, loud, angry, commanding. Too much masculinity, she thought. If she took the girl away from the commotion she might be able to say what happened.

'Why don't we go and get a cup of tea, eh?' Lottie suggested. 'We'll let them blunder around in peace.'

She guided Angela gently by the elbow. McMillan gave her a curious look as she left; she tilted her head to indicate the destination. Fields' café. Genteel, soothing. Above all, quiet. As soon as they were seated she ordered a pot of tea then said nothing, taking off her cap and primping her hair a little.

'WAPC?' the girl asked as she saw the cap badge.

'Auxiliary.' Lottie smiled. 'Not a proper copper.'

She was mother, pouring, asking about milk and sugar. Finally, once Angela had lit a cigarette, it was time.

'Why don't you tell me about it.'

Angela took a few moments, remembering, composing herself.

'We'd just been moving the stock around a bit. Mr Noble likes to do that so customers have something a little different to see when they come in, it might catch their eye. Then the door opened and a man was standing there.'

'What did he look like?' Lottie asked quietly. She listened to the description. It had to be Hilliard, and still without an overcoat.

'He pulled a gun from his jacket.' Without thinking, Angela mimed the motion. 'I've never seen a real gun before. Just at the pictures.' Her voice halted as she relived it all.

'He won't come back. You're safe.'

'I know.' She swallowed and looked away. 'I'm sorry. You must think I'm a baby.'

'No, I don't. I think I'd faint if someone held a gun on me.'

'Really?' Angela stared at her, uncertain.

'Honestly,' Lottie told her. 'They terrify me.' It was perfectly true. She loathed the things. Soldiers might need them, but she was glad the British police were unarmed. 'He had the gun out. What did you do?'

Angela settled her small hands on the crisp white tablecloth.

'He started to shout that he wanted everything, and pointed the gun at Mr Noble. It felt like it must have lasted about ten minutes, but I suppose it all went very quickly. I just kept my back against the wall, hoping he wouldn't see me.' She fell silent, and was quiet for a long time. 'I couldn't move, but he kept pushing Mr Noble to go faster. I think he must have been scared, he kept looking around. He wanted rings and watches, he was stuffing them in his pockets as fast as Mr Noble could reach them out. Then the money from the till. As soon as he had everything, he fired into the wall twice and ran off. I started screaming.'

'He wasn't firing at anyone?'

'No. I'm certain of that.'

Why fire the weapon at all, Lottie wondered? He already had them frightened. Did he need to prove something?

For a few minutes she made small talk, steering Angela's mind away from it all, hearing about living with her mum in Bramley and the boyfriend she had in the navy who was somewhere in the Pacific now.

Finally they returned to the shop. She could sense Angela's reticence as they approached.

'Go on,' she said. 'I think you were very brave. Everyone else will, too.'

'Are you sure?'

'Positive. On you go.'

'Do you think she'd be able to identify Hilliard?' McMillan asked. They were sitting in the Humber, out of the cold.

'Her description was very good. What about Noble?'

'He's all over the place, completely numb. Evidence managed to get the bullets out of the wall and there were two cartridges on the floor.'

'There's no doubt, really, is there?'

'No. But the more evidence the better, for when we get him in court.' He gazed out of the car window at the shoppers milling past. The first most of them would know about the robbery would be in the newspaper or an item on the radio news. 'There was very little cash on the premises, just a few quid. He's going to need someone to buy his loot.'

'Fences?'

'The beat bobbies will be talking to every fence who handles jewellery. I want to know if Hilliard approaches them. They'll behave; they'd better if they want to stay in business.'

'What will he do, then?' She couldn't imagine where else he'd be able to sell everything.

'Pubs,' McMillan answered without hesitation. 'You know what it's like: there's always something dodgy for sale there these days. And we know he's tried that before from that pair we talked to earlier. He'll be out tonight, trying to make a little money. It's his only option.' He sat, smoking. In the mirror she could see him watching her as he thought. 'What are you doing for the next couple of evenings?'

'Why?' There was a heavy note of suspicion in her voice.

'I just wondered if you'd like to invite your American friend out to sample a couple of the hostelries in town, that's all.'

'And perhaps we'll just happen to run into Hilliard?' Sarcasm curled around her words.

'You never know.'

'He has a gun. He's just used it. And you know full well how many girls he's killed.' She shook her head and exhaled slowly. 'I'm sorry, but it's a stupid suggestion.'

'I need people out there who don't look like they're on the force.' He paused for a fraction of a second. 'It would be like being a real copper.'

Lottie knew her eyes must be blazing. 'He's armed! For God's sake, John, do you really want to send your people up against that?'

'It's what we do,' he replied. 'Have you forgotten that? Part of the job. And Ellison's a soldier. He can wear a gun.'

'Oh, wonderful.' She glared at him. 'The two of them can play Dodge City and the rest of us hope we get out alive. Don't be ridiculous.'

'Then what suggestions do you have?'

'I don't know.' The only thing she knew was that his plan put innocent people in danger.

'If you can come up with something better I'll gladly listen.'

'That's your job,' she reminded him.

'It is, and I'm asking for your help with it.' A long sigh. 'He's got nowhere to turn, that's obvious. Not if he's robbing a jeweller's in broad daylight. Believe me, if I had any great ideas, I'd use them.'

'You don't even know where he'll go to try and sell them,' Lottie said.

'City centre. People with a little cash, out for a good time. He knows Leeds, he knows the pubs in town. It's where he found the girls he killed, after all.' He waited, letting it sink in.

'That's still an awful lot of places. How many? Thirty? Forty? Then there's the nightclubs on top of that. How are you going to cover all of those? It's a needle in a haystack.'

'I'll find people who'll do it and move them around. They just can't seem like coppers, that's all. He'd smell them a mile away.'

'I don't see how it can work. It's wishful thinking.'

CHAPTER EIGHTEEN

S HE knew better. At her age she knew much better. For God's sake, what she really wanted was to be at home, sitting in front of the fire, knitting as the radio droned. Instead she was in a draughty pub looking out of the window towards Kirkgate Market. Not that she could see anything with the blackout curtains in place.

There was no joy in the General Elliot. People eking out their drinks, dour expressions, money counted out in pennies, not silver.

'What do you think?' Ellison asked. He'd sounded so eager when she rang from the station to suggest an evening together. Even telling him to come armed hadn't made him question anything.

It was a stupid idea. She still thought so, but she was here. She'd agreed because she couldn't come up with anything better, because the boss seemed at the end of his tether, and because Hilliard needed to be off the streets. There were three other couples circulating, she knew that. WPCs – real ones – enjoying a night out with their brothers or fathers or boyfriends.

But she knew there was another reason for doing this. McMillan had hit the nail squarely on the head; it was like being a real copper. That was why she'd loved her brief experience of detective work twenty years earlier and the bits and bobs on this investigation. The feeling wouldn't go away; she still craved those moments. They sent the blood rushing through her system and made her come alive. Her skin had prickled as she walked into the pub and glanced around.

'He won't come in here,' Lottie said. 'No one's going to spend more time than they have to in a place like this.'

'OK.' He finished his half of bitter and they left. In her head, Lottie was mapping out all the pubs around here. She fixed on the Star and Garter on Call Lane. It wasn't far, and it had a reputation for liveliness. They'd try there next.

It was loud and bustling as soon as they were through the door. Lights blazing, plenty of life. Men and women in civvies and uniform. People smiling. This had possibilities. But there was a desperate edge to all the joy. It felt forced, every moment a last chance at pleasure. Things had never been like that before. This was what the war had done, she thought. It had made life urgent.

Lottie was wearing the Utility dress she'd bought after work; her second piece of new clothing in as many weeks. Splurging, she thought. Seven coupons. Like the other, it fitted surprisingly well, flattering her, and she'd been pleased by the quality of the material and stitching when she inspected it. No problem with the coupons; she still had plenty. With her good stockings, careful touches of the little make-up she still had, she'd felt stylish when she'd met Ellison in town.

She was flattered that he'd agreed to come. But did he want to help, or simply to spend time with her? Perhaps the motive didn't matter so much. And so far he'd been a gentleman. Holding doors, buying her glasses of lemonade, making easy, genial conversation.

As he queued at the bar she had a chance to examine the faces around her. No sign of Hilliard. None of the women seemed to be admiring new rings. They'd give it half an hour and see if he showed himself. If not, try somewhere else then call it a night.

All the chairs were taken, and she leaned against a pillar. The air was heavy with smoke. Ellison joined her, lighting up a Lucky Strike.

'Do you see him?' he asked.

'No. There's plenty of time yet.' It was only half past eight, the pubs would be open for quite a while.

'How many people does John have doing this?'

'Us and three other couples.'

'To cover all the pubs in downtown Leeds?' He gave a disbelieving whistle.

'I know. I told him, believe me. It's ridiculous, really. I should never have agreed.'

'Well, I'm glad you did.' He raised his glass in a toast to her.

'You're a policeman,' Lottie said. 'What do you think of the idea?'

'Honestly?' He thought before answering, 'I reckon it's nuts. This guy's armed, we know he's killed…'

'You're armed too, remember.' Her glance moved to the holster on his hip.

'And you asked me not to draw my gun unless there was no other choice,' he reminded her.

'I know.' She glanced around at the press of people, all enjoying themselves and forgetting the war for a few hours. 'Start shooting in a place like this and people will die.'

'Don't worry. I've only ever shot someone once.' He grinned. 'I've told you, it's not the Wild West. Or gangster movies.'

'So Seattle's very law-abiding?'

Ellison shrugged. 'It has its moments, the same as anywhere. Back before the war there was always something happening down at the port. It's still pretty raw. You know how long Seattle's been around?'

She didn't have a clue. But it was America. That was a young country, wasn't it?

'Two hundred years?' she guessed.

He smiled. 'Try less than a hundred. The first white people sailed into the bay in 1851.'

It seemed an impossibly short stretch of time. Just over ninety years. Half the buildings she knew in Leeds were older than that. She couldn't imagine fashioning a big modern city in nine decades. It showed how different America really was. That energy. That desire.

'The climate's pretty similar to here, actually.' Ellison continued. 'I told you that, didn't I? You know what they say about Seattleites? We don't die, we just rust away.' He grinned at the joke but she wasn't paying attention. Someone had come into the pub.

No coat, a suit that looked as if he'd slept in it, a bulge in the jacket pocket. It was Hilliard. He must have popped in to see a barber; he was neatly shaved, his hair cut and combed. Without even ordering a drink he began moving from couple to couple. Showing something glittering, pulling up a sleeve to display three watches.

'Let's move to the door,' Lottie said quietly.

'He's here?' Ellison looked around. 'Yeah. Got him. It doesn't look like anyone's interested.'

Lottie's heart was hammering in her chest. Her palms felt clammy.

'He'll probably stop and try to sell us something before he leaves.'

They picked their way through the crowd until were standing by the entrance.

'How do you want to play this?' he asked quietly. The pair of them glanced at Hilliard as he worked the room. No success yet and his face was looking pinched and haunted.

'Let me talk to him,' Lottie said. 'You pin his arms from behind, make sure he can't move. I've got a pair of handcuffs here.' She patted her old patent leather handbag.

'You have cuffs in that thing?'

'The boss lent me a pair for this.' The auxiliaries had no power to make arrests. But if she brought in Hilliard, no one would make a fuss. 'Look out, he's heading back this way.'

'What if he doesn't stop?'

She didn't know. They'd have to make something up.

'Just grab him on the way out,' she said.

Hilliard was close enough for her to smell his hair tonic. He spotted her and turned on his false smile. Did she really look like an easy mark, Lottie wondered?

'Sir,' he began, 'Madam.' It was strange to see his face, to hear his voice, to stand so close to a murderer. 'You look like someone who likes one or two of the nicer things in life.' A quick wink in her direction.

Inside, she was shaking, but Lottie tried to sound casual.

'Can't really find them these days, can you?'

He winked again. 'Depends if you know where to look.'

'And you do?' she asked.

Ellison was edging behind the man, both hands ready.

'Course.' Hilliard grinned and opened his fist to display six or seven rings. 'See?'

'Those look expensive.'

'Bargain of the year, love. All real stones, too. Genuine article. None of that costume junk.'

'Really?' She tried to sound surprised and disbelieving. 'Let me get my specs.'

Lottie gave a short nod as she opened her bag. It was the signal. Ellison clamped his hands on Hilliard's arms as she reached for the handcuffs. The American was bigger and stronger.

'Got you, asshole.' He seemed to smile as he spoke.

But Hilliard had fear on his side. Desperation. He lashed out with his foot, catching her on the left knee with the hard tip of his shoes. Lottie let out a cry as her legs crumpled. The rings dropped from his fingers with a quiet tinkle. He twisted and slid and lashed out until Ellison couldn't keep hold of him any longer. It had all taken no more than three or four seconds. As soon as he was free, Hilliard banged the door open with his shoulder and dashed out into the night.

The American went straight after him, drawing his gun as he disappeared. And Lottie was left in the pub, everyone suddenly silent and staring at her. She retrieved the rings scattered around the floor and painfully climbed to her feet. She could barely put any weight on the leg he'd kicked, blinking back tears at the pain and her failure. Maybe it wasn't too late. Maybe Cliff would catch him.

But she knew what the odds were. It was pitch black on the streets and Ellison didn't know his way around Leeds. Lottie limped outside, standing by the door with no idea where to go. In the cold, out where no one could see, the tears began to fall.

Somewhere in the distance she heard the crack of a gun.

CHAPTER NINETEEN

THEY were sitting in her office at Millgarth when McMillan arrived. Lottie had asked the desk sergeant to ring him when they stumbled into the station. She was hanging on to Ellison, barely able to walk; her knee had ballooned after the kick. And Cliff was bleeding, his cheek sliced open.

'Christ,' McMillan said when he walked in, standing with a hand still on the doorknob. 'What happened to the pair of you?'

'We found Hilliard,' Lottie replied. McMillan's mouth opened and she knew what he was about to ask; but he stopped himself. Instead he said, 'There's a report of a weapon being discharged.'

'I chased him,' Ellison explained. 'He took a shot at me. Hit a building. A piece of brick came off and hit me.' He pulled the handkerchief away from his face to show the wound.

She went through it all for him. The rings lay on her desk, seven of them, gold and gems glittering under the light.

'I'm sorry,' she finished. 'I really thought we had him.'

'He's a slippery son of a bitch,' Ellison said. 'I couldn't keep hold of him. Once he was outside he just took off. About all I could do was make out his footsteps and run after him.'

McMillan listened carefully, chewing on his top lip. 'Do you know where you were when he fired?'

Ellison shook his head. 'Haven't a clue. I know there must have been a few people around. Someone started screaming.'

'From the reports it was behind the Corn Exchange. You hadn't gone too far.'

The American shrugged. 'I don't know. I was just following. I couldn't even see where I was going. I'll tell you something: that guy's either lucky or one hell of a shot.'

Lottie could see everything in McMillan's face: the frustration, the anger, the pain. She'd let him down.

'I'm sorry,' was all she could say.

He shook his head. 'You did your best.'

But she couldn't help hearing a judgement in his words. Their best hadn't been good enough. Maybe she was just imagining it. But it was how she felt: her best really hadn't been enough. 'You might as well go home,' he continued, then to Ellison, 'And that cheek looks like it needs stitching.'

'I'll have one of the medics look at it when I'm back on base.'

Ellison drove the Jeep slowly, crawling along so the sliver of headlight could pick out the white bands on the poles to guide him on the road. Finally, he parked in front of the house and Lottie winced and gave a small moan as she climbed out.

'Come here, I'll help you.'

He had an arm around her, taking her weight as she hobbled. Inside, the blackouts drawn, she switched on the light and caught a glimpse of herself in the mirror. God, she looked a sight. Her make-up had run, mascara trailing down her cheeks. Like a clown.

Ahead, the stairs loomed like a mountain. The way her knee felt, it would take an hour to climb to the bedroom.

'How about a hand?' Ellison asked. As she stared at him, he raised his hands, palms out. 'Strictly to get upstairs. That's all I meant.'

Lottie smiled. He must have read her mind. 'Then yes. Thank you.'

It was awkward and painful, even with his arms to help her.

'You should really get some ice on that.'

He was right, it would stop the swelling. But who had ice in this country?

Up on the landing she clutched the bannister. 'I appreciate it, Cliff.'

'It's nothing.' He smiled, showing those large, even teeth. 'About tonight…'

'We did what we could. John understands that.'

'That doesn't matter. I'm a cop. I shouldn't have let him get away. And shooting like that? I meant it; he's crazy.'

'No, he's not. He's scared.'

'If you say so.' He dabbed his cheek with the handkerchief again. 'Felt more crazy and dangerous to me.'

Of course he was. Hilliard was deadly. And he knew exactly what would be waiting for him when he was caught. Hanged by the neck for the murders of Kate Patterson, Anne Goodman, Pamela Dixon, and Lily Kemp. She felt as if the names would stay with her forever.

Her knee began to throb hard, bringing her back to the present.

'I'll be fine now,' she told him with a gentle smile. 'I appreciate this, Cliff.'

'I'm just sorry we didn't catch him. I should have—'

'Should and would don't really matter, do they?' Lottie could hear the sadness in her voice. The regret.

'No.' He leaned forward, giving her a small hug, then went down the stairs, not looking back. As she heard the Yale lock click into place, she breathed deeply.

Her left knee was huge the next morning. An ugly purple flower of a bruise blossomed just below the cap. Lottie tried to bend the leg but it was too painful. Even moving around the house was going to be difficult.

No work today. She wouldn't be able to drive like this. Dressing herself seemed to take hours, then the slow, painful descent of the stairs, holding on for dear life.

She pottered. It was all she could do. She took everything slowly. Sat with her leg up on the pouffe. At least it didn't look any worse, she decided by dinnertime. But no better either. The knee still hurt when she put weight on it.

A little after one o'clock she heard a knock on the door and shuffled out of the dining room to answer it.

'I'll be there in a minute,' she shouted.

McMillan, holding a bunch of early daffs and looking stupid. She grinned at the sight, looking beyond him to the Humber. A man driving him, one of the Specials to judge by his uniform. At least he hadn't picked another woman for the job; that was heartening.

'Come on in. Don't just stand there.'

He shook his head. 'I can't stop.' He glanced at her leg. 'How is it?'

She raised her hem to show him, watching as he winced.

'A day or two and it'll be a lot better.'

'I'd say don't rush but I need you back.' He seemed suddenly aware of the flowers, thrusting them on her. 'That lollop they've given me is useless. I'd be better off driving myself.'

'Nothing new on Hilliard?'

'Gone to ground. I've had men on the railway station and bus station since last night. We'll just have to smoke him out somehow. There's a reward, everything.'

'Maybe you'll have him by tonight.'

'And pigs might fly.' He looked weary, the stubble showing on his face; he probably hadn't been home after being called out last night. But she could see there was something more. Something he wanted to say but didn't know how.

'Come on,' Lottie told him. 'Spit it out. We've known each other too long.'

He breathed in, uncomfortable at being put on the spot.

'It's… I don't know, it's been bothering me since you told me what happened with Hilliard.'

'Go on.'

He kept his eyes on her as he spoke.

'Do you think Ellison could have deliberately let him go? I know, he's your friend and all that. But he's lied to us before, don't forget.'

For a long minute she didn't say a word, replaying every moment of the evening in her mind. No, it was impossible. Hilliard had dodged and squirmed. He'd shot at Cliff, almost hit him. But the more she thought, the more questions came. Ellison was a policeman, used to keeping hold of suspects. He was big, strong. He shouldn't have let the man get away. And yes, she'd heard a shot, but she only had his word for what happened. She'd simply never doubted it.

Had he recognised Hilliard? At the time she didn't think so. She hadn't noticed anything between them when the man came close; she'd swear to that. And Ellison seemed to relish the idea of catching the man.

No, it was all above board. It had to be.

'I don't think so.' She answered slowly. 'Everything happened so quickly. It was like Hilliard was greased. And my knee was killing me,' she added.

'I just wondered, that's all.' He sounded forlorn. Overwhelmed. 'Come back when you can drive again.'

'You can catch Hilliard as a get well present for me.' She smiled but it didn't cheer him.

'Let's hope, eh?'

She'd barely put the flowers in water and set them on the table when there was another knock on the door. Had he forgotten to tell her something? Muttering to herself she hobbled back down the hall and pulled the front door open.

'Hi.' Ellison stood, cap under his arm, smiling bashfully. 'I hope you don't mind. I just wanted to see how you were doing.'

'Muddling through.' It was the best answer she could offer. And for once, the words were completely truthful. 'Do you want to come in?'

He shook his head. 'I'm supposed to be on my way to a meeting.' It seemed like it was her day for gentlemen callers who didn't get past the door. He brought his hand from behind his back and held out a box wrapped in colourful paper.

'Candy,' he told her. 'I thought it might make you feel better.'

Lottie took it, looking into his face, trying to see if something was hidden behind his eyes. Until McMillan's question she'd never doubted a thing about the night before. She'd seen it happen. She'd been part of it. Now just a tiny bit of her was left wondering.

'Honestly,' she said, warmth in her voice, 'you shouldn't have.'

She didn't like him bringing her gifts; it made her feel beholden. A few flowers from John McMillan was one thing; they'd known each other for donkey's years. This, well, it was kind and generous. But...

'I appreciate it,' Lottie said.

'It's nothing much.' He made it seem like an apology. 'From the PX.'

'It's a lovely thought. You know, I can't remember the last time anyone brought me chocolates.' She chuckled. 'I can't even remember the last time I saw anything like this in the shops. Feels likes centuries.'

'How's your knee?'

'Big. Colourful. Stiff. It'll mend.'

'If there's anything I can do...'

'You helped me last night and now you've brought me these,' Lottie told him. 'I'd say that's ample.'

'I feel guilty about it all. I didn't expect him to start moving like that. It took me by surprise.'

She wanted to believe him. Part of her *did* believe him. But out on the edges a few small doubts niggled at her.

'You did your best. Did the medic look after your cheek?'

'Butterfly bandage. I took it off when I shaved this morning. Made me look too much like a soldier.'

'You took off after him like a policeman.'

'I didn't feel like one when I came back empty-handed.' He shifted uneasily from one foot to the other. 'Look, I need to get going for that meeting. Would you like me to check on you later?'

'Would you mind if I said not tonight? I don't think I really feel up to entertaining.'

'You bet.' He smiled. 'Once you're fighting fit I'll take you dancing and give that knee a workout.'

She laughed. The ridiculous things he said. 'I'll look forward to that.'

Then he was gone, walking with that open, easy stride.

Chocolates: a whole box of them. She'd meant it; he really shouldn't have bought them. But he had, and she couldn't refuse them; that would have been rude. And after four years of rationing, no one in England would turn down chocolates. Eating one would feel like an indulgence, a little sin. She'd make them last, just one or two a day to eke out the box.

She found a walking stick hidden away in the cupboard under the stairs. Geoff had used it back in '36 when he twisted his ankle. It made moving around a little easier. Still, she knew it was going to be few days of frustration.

By the third morning most of the swelling had gone. Lottie eased out of bed, cautious about putting weight on her left leg. She winced, but it held, and she could walk around the bedroom without much pain. Tentatively, one hand resting on the dressing table, she flexed the knee. Not too bad, she decided. As long as she was careful she should be able to work.

People gave her second glances as she crossed from the bus station to Millgarth, in full uniform, leaning on the walking stick. She could almost hear the questions in their minds and smiled to herself. It was still slow going up the stairs to McMillan's office, and she was sweating by the time she reached the landing. But she was here. She'd made it and she wasn't going home again.

The routine felt comforting. Rattling around the house, her days had felt empty. In spite of her resolution, she'd finished the chocolates that first evening as she listened to the Billy Cotton band on the radio. So what if she'd been a pig? They were delicious. And Cliff had been right; in a curious way they did make her feel better.

'Well, well.' McMillan stood in the doorway and grinned. 'Ready for the hundred-yard dash?'

Lottie picked up the stick. 'I'm ready to take this to you if you don't behave. Do we have him yet?'

The Chief Superintendent gave a long, deep sigh. 'Do you know that brick wall downstairs, at the back of the yard?'

'Yes,' she answered hesitantly. 'Why?'

'Next time you pass it, take a look. You'll see the indentations where I've been banging my head against it. Does that tell you anything?'

'Somebody will shop him sooner or later.'

'I wish they'd do it bloody quick, then.' His voice rose and his nostrils flared slightly. 'I'm pulling men from every division to search. Inspectors are complaining because they don't have enough bobbies to walk the beat properly. And I still don't feel as if we're any closer to catching him.' McMillan shook his head. 'How are you on stairs?'

'Slow and careful,' she replied. 'Why?'

'I was hoping you could go down to the canteen and fetch us a cup of tea.'

'It'd be stewed by the time I got back.'

He sighed. 'Story of my life. I'll get them and we can have a confab.'

'I've been thinking,' Lottie said. They were in his office, smoke from his cigarette curling up to the ceiling. 'What you said about Cliff Ellison.' McMillan cocked his head. She took a sip of the tea before continuing. 'I've gone through it again and again.'

'And?'

THE YEAR OF THE GUN

'He's genuine. I'm sure of it.' She turned to look at him. 'He visited me the other day. Just after you left, in fact. He apologised. I believe him.'

'You believe him or you want to believe him?'

She raised an eyebrow. 'I believe him. I had a couple of doubts after you came to see me. But I don't think it was a put-up job.'

'That's good enough for me.' He stubbed out the Four Square and lit another. 'How do we catch Hilliard? None of my ideas seem to work.'

'You were right about the pubs,' Lottie said.

'And now Hilliard won't dare go back into any of them.'

'Have you gone to see the people he knows again?'

'Every single one of them. If you want the truth, I'm at my wits' end.' He ran his palms down his cheeks and exhaled slowly.

She didn't know what to say. There was one thought, but she didn't know how well he'd take it.

'Have you thought about bringing in a fresh pair of eyes?' She paused, glancing at his face. 'Someone who's not so close to it all?'

'The Yard?' She could hear the loathing in his voice.

'No.' She knew the only way he'd accept that would be over his dead body.

'Who, then? Our American friend?'

'Why not? He's a copper on Civvy Street. He knows how things work.'

McMillan sat back, smoking and staring up at the ceiling.

'Are you absolutely certain we can trust him?' he asked eventually.

'Yes,' Lottie said. But there was just a glimmer of a hesitation before she answered: enough to make him jerk his head.

'Well?'

'Yes, I think we can.' She slammed the mug down on the desk. 'For God's sake, stop putting me on the spot. We're on the same side – don't try and trap me.'

'I'm sorry. But if you're not absolutely positive that he's with us, I don't want him.' McMillan stared at her.

Ellison hadn't been acting the other night. She was sure of that. But he'd lied to them once, maybe more. He could do it again.

So much for the idea, she thought.

'Fine. No Ellison.' Gingerly, Lottie pushed herself to her feet and reached for the stick.

'There is something he can do for us, though,' McMillan said.

'Make up your mind. You either want his help or you don't.'

'I want to catch Hilliard.' His voice was hard. 'That's what I want. Ring Ellison and ask if any bullets were packed with those guns.'

She didn't understand. 'Don't they all come with bullets?'

He shook his head. 'No, and none of the ones we recovered had any. Hilliard's getting them from somewhere.' He thought for a second. 'While you're at it, better ask him if any ammo's gone missing, too.'

CHAPTER TWENTY

W HY was she reluctant to pick up the telephone and ring him? She didn't even have to look up the number, it was right there, at the front of her mind.

He'd been kind. She was sure he'd really gone after Hilliard and almost been shot for it. Why the hesitation?

Lottie didn't know. And for now she didn't have the time to examine it. She'd be like Scarlett O'Hara; she could think about that tomorrow.

'How are you feeling? Back at work now?' Ellison's voice was warm and cheerful.

'I'm on the mend. Thanks again for the chocolates. They were delicious.'

'It's nothing.' From the way he said it, she believed him. 'Is this social or business?'

'Business.' Her tone became crisper. 'I need to ask you about bullets.'

'What about them?' He sounded amused.

'Those pistols that were stolen; were they shipped with ammunition?'

'Never. They're always separate.'

'That's what the boss thought. But Hilliard has ammunition. We know he's fired at least six shots.'

'Ammo goes missing,' he said cautiously.

She caught his tone. 'Is that a general statement or something specific?'

'Specific,' he answered after a second. 'At least according to the quartermaster's figures.'

'How much?'

'If he's right, we were lucky. On the .45s it was just a box.' He phrased that carefully, she noticed. What other calibres had vanished? And how much? 'It's hard to be sure, with all the training and exercises. People are supposed to sign for things, but they sometimes slip by.'

'I see,' Lottie said. 'How many in a box?'

'There were a hundred in this one. Like I said, we try to keep a tight control on things, that's how he noticed.'

But not tight enough, she thought.

'Is the same man who sold the guns responsible?'

'Probably.' Ellison sighed. 'I was more concerned with the weapons. A box of ammo didn't seem like much.'

Maybe it wasn't, until the bullet killed you.

'It means Hilliard could have ninety-four more bullets,' she told him.

'Yeah.'

'So he hadn't bothered to tell us that, either.' McMillan's face was grim. 'Is there anything else he hasn't mentioned? Does Hilliard have a bazooka hidden away somewhere that fell off a US Army lorry?' He tossed his fountain pen on to the blotter, leaving a spatter of ink. 'What next?'

There was nothing she could say. Inside she was furious at Cliff for keeping quiet. What would he have done if McMillan hadn't started wondering? Would they ever have known?

'You know, there are times I wonder if the Yanks really are on our side.' For a moment he sat and stared into space, then he exhaled slowly. 'I suppose we'd better go and pay a call.' She heard the reluctance in his voice.

'Who are we going to see?'

He eyed her, chewing on his lip, then said, 'I think you'll want to stay in the car.'

'Who?' Lottie asked again. 'It's not a state secret, is it?'

'Chief Superintendent Carter,' he told her after a moment. 'I believe he was still Inspector Carter when you knew him.'

Lottie felt a chill rise up her spine. Yes, he'd been an inspector then, and she was a WPC, right at the bottom of the ladder. Carter had made it clear that he didn't approve of policewomen. He was unhappy when an investigation needed her help. And he seemed to relish his position on the board that dismissed her from the force. McMillan was right; she'd want to remain in the Humber. She didn't ever wish to see the man again.

'He must be retired by now,' she said.

'Left in 1937.'

Good riddance to bad rubbish, she thought.

'Then why do you want to see him?'

'I know you never cared for him—'

'That's putting it mildly.' She snorted her disgust.

'—but he was one of the best coppers I've ever known. Not a particularly nice person,' he added before she could open her mouth, 'and we didn't always see eye to eye, but he understood the job. He got results.'

'You think he might see something we haven't?'

'I don't know. But right now I'm willing to try anything.' He offered her a weak smile. 'Even him. Do you have a good book?'

She patted the pocket of her uniform. She'd finished the novel she'd been reading. Now it was Agatha Christie, *The Moving Finger*. Pleasant enough, but absolutely no resemblance to reality, and Miss Marple annoyed her. Still, it would pass the time.

Lottie gasped as she first pressed down on the clutch and pain roared through her knee. The second time was a little easier, the third better still. Within two minutes she didn't even notice it any more, concentrating on the traffic and following the sketchy directions McMillan offered.

Carter lived at the near end of Armley, a quiet street of through terraces just a stone's throw from the library. It was a working man's neighbourhood, cobbled streets, no cars parked by the kerb. Not somewhere she expected to find a retired detective inspector.

'I'd have thought he'd have lived somewhere…' She struggled for the right word, something that wasn't offensive.

'Posher, you mean?' McMillan's lip curled in a smile. 'Not Tommy Carter. This was the place he bought as soon as he could afford somewhere. Always reminded everyone they raised six children here. Didn't see any reason to move.'

She could almost hear the man saying it, the strange pride shining in his voice. 'I'll leave him to you.'

She was grateful for her heavy greatcoat as she sat in the car. Her knee seemed to stiffen and she rubbed it gently, wincing at the pain. Finally, bored by the village tedium of the book, she grabbed the walking stick and eased herself out of the Humber.

The first few steps hurt so much that they almost made her cry. But she wasn't going to stop; by the time she reached the end of the street, moving was easier and smoother.

She rested against the low front wall of a house, staring across an open patch of land. The remains of a building, jagged chunks of masonry, a chimney that had been cut off ten feet above the ground. Small hills of rubble everywhere. It took her a minute to understand she was staring at a bombsite.

Everything was overgrown, weeds and ivy reclaiming the earth. On one open stretch a pair of grubby boys kicked a ball around, oblivious to the cold in their school shirts and shorts. Their blazers were bunched up to make goalposts. Part of her wanted to grab them by the ears and march them back to classes. But sense won out: let them be, let them enjoy them-selves. If this war stretched out another ten years they could be in uniform. And sometimes it felt as if it might never end, that the fighting would still be going on decades from now.

Lottie made her way back to the car slowly. The damage and rubble had given her pause for thought. It was so long since the last raid. Eighty-seven dead in Leeds from bombs. It was bad enough, but nothing compared to other cities. She just wished it could all be over.

McMillan was taking his time. Perhaps Carter had some good ideas after all, although it seemed hard to believe. He always seemed to run things by the book. But twenty years had passed since she'd seen him. People changed. Finally she heard a door close and turned the key in the ignition just as the Chief Superintendent settled on the creaking leather of the back seat.

'Worthwhile?' she asked, one eye on the mirror to catch his expression.

'Nothing we haven't already tried.' He lit a cigarette and seem to relish the plume of smoke he blew. 'I think he enjoyed the company more than anything. I got the impression he doesn't have many visitors.'

That didn't surprise her. But Lottie bit her tongue.

'Back to Millgarth?' she asked as they reached the end of the street.

'Might as well.' He sounded as old as the sky.

At the bottom of the hill they had to wait as a convoy of olive drab US Army lorries drove past. The canvas flaps were tied open at the back to show youthful, happy faces. People stopped to stare: women, children, even some men. Some of the soldiers threw chocolate bars whenever they spotted a child. Others waved. Where would they all be in six months, she thought. How many of them would be laughing then?

Without thinking, she counted the vehicles. Twenty-three of them, traffic backed up behind to leave her sitting in the idling Humber.

'Do you think the Americans are moving out?' she asked.

'I don't know,' McMillan said. 'Did Ellison say anything?'

Lottie shook her head. Would he even bother to tell her? Would he be allowed to?

She looked ahead, only half-watching the road. 'Did you see that?' she asked suddenly.

'What?'

'The Jeep that just went by. It's Del Vecchio. Driving himself, too.'

'Really?' She heard the soft sound as McMillan sat upright and craned his head. 'Do you think you can follow him?'

Lottie eyed him in the mirror. This was like a scene from a film. 'Are you serious?'

'Yes, go on. Let's see where he's going.'

She slipped the Humber into gear and nudged her way into the flow, of traffic then kept a steady speed. A van and two cars separated her from the Jeep. Del Vecchio didn't seem to have noticed her. Lottie removed her WAPC cap and tossed it on to the passenger seat. Now he'd never give the vehicle a second glance.

They were heading away from Leeds, towards Kirkstall Bridge. The abbey was out there, and a few miles away, Horsforth, Rawdon, then the countryside around Yeadon. Maybe all the troops were going on manoeuvres.

But del Vecchio wasn't following them. At the bridge he slowed, ready to turn right and go up the hill. She was lucky; the car in front of her was going the same way, a shield between the Humber and the Jeep.

It was tricky, especially after the car in front turned towards Headingley station. The Jeep was now right in front of them.

'Pull your hat down to shade your eyes,' Lottie advised. McMillan obeyed. Now he could be anybody.

She kept her distance, as far back as she dared, foot ready to push down on the accelerator. But at North Lane the traffic left her no choice. He was stuck, waiting to turn and she had to stop directly behind him.

Del Vecchio never seemed to glance in the mirror. Yet at the first chance he gunned the Jeep, leaving her standing. Had he noticed them? She honestly didn't know.

Her palms were sweating on the steering wheel as she forced her way between vehicles. He was a good fifty yards ahead.

She blinked and then he wasn't there at all.

A good try, she thought with a smile as she turned on to Shire Oak Road. Just not quite good enough.

'Do you want me to park here or go all the way to the end?'

McMillan considered the question. 'Let's go all the way,' he said. 'We might run into our friend there.'

A Jeep was parked in the drive of the empty house. Lottie angled the Humber to make it difficult for him to leave.

'Now let's see what he has to say for himself.'

The front door was ajar, no sign of the colonel downstairs or in the garden. She heard the creak of a floorboard and raised her head. McMillan put a finger to his lips and stood facing the stairs, hands in the pockets of his overcoat.

Another minute as the man moved around upstairs, every noise amplified by the empty building. Finally he came striding back, halting suddenly as he faced McMillan.

'Fancy seeing you here, Colonel.'

She had to give him credit: del Vecchio recovered his composure in a flash. The surprise vanished from his face, replaced by an easy, lazy smile.

'Chief Superintendent. What brings you out this way?'

'Murder. I told you the last time we met. We've come for another look around. A coincidence, isn't it? Running into you like this.'

The colonel shrugged. 'We've got more men arriving so we're going to need more billets. We've already got too many with local families. You reminded me about this place when we talked. I thought it might be worth another inspection.'

'And?' McMillan asked.

'I'm not sure. I could probably put twenty guys in here, no problem. But it'll take money to get it in shape.' He tapped his head. 'Now I have to figure out if it's worth the cost.'

'I can't imagine any troops would be staying that long.'

'I wouldn't know about that. All I'm told is we have men coming, find them somewhere to live. Billeting officer, remember.'

'Among other things.'

Lottie watched the two of them. She'd once seen a pair of boxers sparring; it reminded her of that, little jabs, darting forward and away. As she remembered, by the end of the round, neither one of them had landed a proper punch.

'Welfare officer, too,' del Vecchio added. 'Organising entertainment for the men.'

'I was thinking more of other duties.'

It was only there for a moment, but a shadow passed across the man's face.

'That's all I do, Chief Superintendent. Good Time Charlie – I know what they call me.'

'Then may your good times continue.' The way McMillan phrased it, the words came out like a warning.

'Is that supposed to mean something?'

'Just what it says, Colonel.' An ingenuous smile. 'We're all on the same side. That's what's on those printed sheets you give all your troops arriving in England, isn't it?'

De Vecchio came down the rest of the steps until the two men stood no more than three feet apart.

'Anything else?'

'There's always something else,' McMillan told him. 'That's what being a policeman means.'

'And being a good policeman means knowing when to back off, Chief Superintendent. So you think you know something about me? Great. Even if it's true, there's nothing you can do with it. I told you why I'm here, and that's the truth. Check at HQ if you want, they'll tell you. Now I'll ask you again: anything else?'

'I still believe you had something to do with the young woman who was here.'

Del Vecchio gave a shark's smile, all teeth and no warmth. 'Like they say, prove it, copper.'

He began to walk. As he passed Lottie his eyes narrowed, as if he was making sure he'd remember her face. The front door banged behind him.

'Well,' McMillan said after a while, 'what did you make of that?'

'I know there's something about him that gives me the creeps,' she said. 'The question is, do you believe his reason for being here?'

'Unfortunately, I do,' he admitted. 'But I still think he's involved somewhere in all this.' McMillan gave another glance around. 'We're not going to learn anything more here.'

Her leg ached. The knee felt a little swollen as she limped back down the drive to the car.

'The rotten devil.'

'What?' McMillan asked.

Lottie ran a hand along the front wing of the Humber. The metal had been scratched and dented. Flakes of dull green paint clung to the damage.

'He scraped us. I left him just enough room, he must have done it deliberately.'

'It won't stop you driving, will it?' Lottie shook her head in reply. 'Then we can send the United States Army the bill.'

CHAPTER TWENTY-ONE

M ILLGARTH felt hot, as if someone had turned all the steam radiators on full. She could see the sweat on men's faces as they worked, smell it as she walked past them.

'The boiler's on the blink,' McMillan explained after a word with the desk sergeant. 'Someone's supposed to be mending it.'

Office windows were open wide, the frigid air welcome in the stuffy rooms. The canteen felt like a Turkish bath. Helen from the switchboard was sitting at a table close to the door, constantly dabbing the perspiration from her face with a handkerchief.

'I don't know how they can expect us to work in this,' she said as Lottie settled across from her with a plate of homity pie. 'What is that, anyway?'

'I'm not sure.' She prodded it with a fork. 'The woman said they make it in Sheffield. Doesn't seem to be any meat.' Lottie shrugged. She was starving; as long as it was filling and tasty, she didn't care. She was used to doing without. They'd all become experts at it.

'Do you know they won't let us take off our jackets while we're working?' Helen asked. 'Even in this. It's all right for you; half the time you're out and about.'

They'd been through this so many times since Lottie joined the WAPC. It wasn't her fault that McMillan wanted her as his driver. But she understood Helen's resentment: she wouldn't want to spend her working days answering the telephone and connecting people. It would drive her barmy. Especially when the station was as hot as this.

'Do you fancy the pictures this weekend?' she asked. It was a change of subject. Touch wood, her knee would be fine tomorrow.

'We could.' Helen lived for the cinema. She knew every film that was playing, everywhere in town, and spent hours reading *Picturegoer* each week until she could quote chapter and verse. '*Going My Way* is on at the Empire. That's supposed to be quite good. Bing Crosby. Or *Casablanca*'s playing again.'

'*Casablanca*,' Lottie answered without any hesitation. It was an easy choice, Bogart over Crosby. She'd seen the film twice before, but that didn't matter. It would take her away from here for a couple of hours. A little escape from England to somewhere exotic.

On the tram home she glanced through a copy of *Woman's Weekly* someone had left on the seat. Their patterns might save coupons, but she wouldn't have wanted to make any of them. Unflattering. Worse, they looked dowdy. Old lady clothes. Something to wear when you were pushed around in a bath chair. Still, a couple of the recipes had possibilities. She had plenty of potatoes, carrots, and parsnips from the crop she'd grown in the garden. More than enough for her own needs.

Her mind wandered. Del Vecchio. There was something about him. A coldness he tried to hide. She could imagine him killing without a second thought. But perhaps that was what he needed if he really was a spy. He didn't seem to have much respect for morality or law. She couldn't see any link between him and Hilliard, though. What would he see in a deserter and a coward? What use could he have for a man like that?

None, she decided.

Yet that didn't square with everything else they knew. Del Vecchio had been in the house on Shire Oak Road. So had Pamela Dixon; she'd left her knickers behind. And the neighbour had spotted a woman being carried out of the place to a Jeep with a US Army insignia. The local air-raid warden had heard it leaving the area.

But Pamela's body had been found in a furrier's cold storage, dead from a bullet that had been fired by Hilliard.

Add to that, she'd been in Leeds for what appeared to be a dirty weekend with a man who was still unidentified.

Make sense of all that, Lottie told herself.

By the time she reached her stop, she still hadn't managed to connect any of those dots. The only theories that came to mind were all too wild and fanciful.

Rummaging through the larder she found a tin of snoek. Lottie had bought it when the fish first went on sale, curious, but after all the reports she'd never tried it. Now she had no choice; the shelves were bare. She'd need to go shopping tomorrow. Trying it with some boiled potatoes, she could easily believe the rumours that all the unsold tins had been re-labelled as cat food. After three mouthfuls she gave up. She hated wasting food – even peelings went into a bucket for the compost heap – but this was vile.

She appeared in the doorway of McMillan's office the following morning holding two mugs of canteen tea. Her knee felt better; most of the swelling had gone down. She'd been able to manage without a walking stick and only the trace of a limp.

'You're a lifesaver.'

'All part of the service.' Lottie sat in the visitor's chair and waited as he took out a Four Square and lit it. 'There's one thing we haven't pursued properly.'

'What's that?' Cigarette in his mouth, he gave her a quizzical stare.

'This man Pamela Dixon was meeting at the hotel. Her lover. He might be able to help us.'

'Why? Do you think he killed her?' McMillan asked sharply.

'No, not that.' She struggled to put the idea into words. 'But everything seems to start with her. She was the first victim. If we can find this chap, we can at least get the beginning of the story. He might know something that could help us.'

McMillan steepled his fingers in front of his face and looked at them.

'We haven't been able to trace him. He left a false name in the register, remember. We have fingerprints from the room, but we don't know which ones are his. Anyway, I've got them to check everything they found down at the Criminal Records Office the Met has. Nothing on file that could be our man.' He gave a wan smile. 'It's a dead end. We know we're after Hilliard, let's focus on that. We'll worry about everything else later.'

'Nothing more overnight?'

'Not a peep.'

'Hilliard hasn't tried anything since that Johnson girl,' Lottie said slowly.

'That we know about, anyway.'

'OK,' she acknowledged. 'No one's mentioned it, and nobody reported missing. What would make him stop, just like that? He had four of them in about as many nights.'

'That's easy,' McMillan said. 'Right now he's probably more concerned with saving his own skin. I'm not one of those trick cyclists, but that seems rather self-evident.'

Maybe that really was the reason, Lottie thought, back behind her own desk. As simple as that. Survival. Stronger than the compulsion to murder. The phone began to ring and she picked it up without thinking.

'Hi.' There was no mistaking the accent.

'Hello,' she said.

'How's your knee?'

'It's much better, thanks.' She swung her leg a little. Definitely on the mend.

'That's great.' Ellison sounded as though he genuinely meant it, not simply a question for form's sake. 'Listen, I was wondering if you were doing anything tomorrow afternoon.'

'Tomorrow?' The question puzzled her. What was there to do on Sunday? Everything was closed. He must have learnt that about England by now. 'Nothing. Why?'

'The USO has organised a dance. One of the service bands is coming through. Since your knee's improving I thought you might like to go. You don't have to dance or anything if you're not up to it,' he added quickly.

'I don't know.' She felt dumbstruck by the invitation. It caught her by surprise, scrambling for an answer. For a second she almost said no. She'd never been much of a dancer. The foxtrot and the waltz were her limit. And she daren't even try those at the moment.

But she was curious, too. What would an American dance be like? She'd heard rumours about the events they put on: plenty of food and drink, even better than England in peacetime. She'd never have another chance to find out how the other half enjoyed themselves. She couldn't turn that down, could she?

'It'll be fun.' He dangled the words like a promise.

Still Lottie hesitated. Would it be fair to accept? After all, she'd doubted him, if only for a little while. He knew their agreement, but what would he think if she said yes? Would he read too much into it? She took a deep breath.

'Thank you, I'd love to,' she told him. Curiosity had won out. Then a thought came: 'Did del Vecchio organise the dance?'

'Yeah, he's the entertainments officer; it's his job. Don't worry, he's not going to be there. I wouldn't have invited you if he was. I heard John talked to him yesterday.' He gave a short laugh. 'The whole base must have heard, he was yelling so loud. Anyway, he left for London last night.'

That was something. She wouldn't need to look over her shoulder the whole time.

'I'll pick you up at home about one. OK?'

'Fine, yes.' What else was she supposed to say? She'd need new stockings. The kick and the fall the other night had ruined her only good pair. At noon, once her working week was done, she'd go shopping. And perhaps the Co-op salon could fit her in for a quick shampoo and set. She was making a list in her mind when she realised McMillan was standing in the doorway, watching her.

'It must be something good,' he said.

'Sorry. I was miles away.' Lottie felt herself starting to blush.

He placed a bundle of files on her desk. 'Could you file those? Unless something comes up on Hilliard, I need to look at some of the other cases.'

She went down to the Records room, gossiping with Margaret as she worked. Boring work, but chat helped the time pass quickly.

'What's going on with that American of yours?'

'He's not mine,' Lottie said. She was straining to keep her tone light. 'Honestly, I don't know why everyone thinks he is.'

'You were out with him the other night.'

'Come on, that was work and you know it.' She put her hands on her hips. 'We were trying to catch Hilliard. The boss wanted people who didn't look like coppers.'

Margaret arched an eyebrow. 'If you say so. I wouldn't mind having an American. Money to spend, free nylons, all those things from their commissaries. And they always smell so nice, have you noticed?'

She had. It was impossible not to. But everything in England was in such short supply here. Even soap was impossible to find sometimes. No wonder people smelt bad and looked grubby. It had become one of those facts of life. Most of the time she never even thought about it.

'There are plenty of Yanks around,' Lottie told her.

'I know.' Margaret sighed. 'But my Peter would kill me if he came home and found out I'd been messing around.' A quick shrug. 'A girl can dream. They can't hang you for that.'

Back upstairs there was no sign of McMillan. His coat and hat were missing. Nothing urgent, she decided, or he'd have come looking for her. She passed the rest of the morning with the Agatha Christie novel, one eye on the clock, willing the small hand to twelve.

He reappeared just as she was tying her scarf around her neck.

'Come in here a sec,' he said. She followed him into his office. 'Close the door.'

Mystified, she obeyed.

'I've just been to see the Assistant Chief Constable.' She stood, waiting for more. Very slowly, he brought his right hand out of the overcoat pocket, his fingers around the grip of a Webley revolver. Lottie said nothing. She just stared at the weapon. 'He's authorised it. Four dead, an officer wounded, a shot at Ellison.'

'How many of you are armed?'

'Only Andrews and myself.' He paused and looked away. 'For now, anyway.'

'I see.' She didn't have a proper response. She hated guns. But Hilliard would kill again if he had the chance, she was certain of that. She adjusted the cap on her head. 'I'm off. Don't work too hard, please. And make sure you go home and see Sarah.'

He pushed the gun back out of sight. 'I will. I might even take tomorrow off.'

Lottie woke refreshed. She and Helen had enjoyed the evening, a drink and then *Casablanca*. But she'd adored the film from the first time she'd seen it; by now she even knew some of the lines by heart. It was a perfect weepie, exactly what the doctor ordered. She pulled back the blackouts. Outside, the day looked clear and cold, frost heavy on the grass and the windows.

It was a good morning for turning the rest of the soil. By noon she'd worked up a fair sweat, digging up heavy clods of earth then breaking them apart with the fork. Once the weather warmed a little she'd get some manure on there, work it in, and she'd be ready for spring planting. The winter cabbage and leeks hadn't done too well this year. But it was too late to worry about that now.

In the bathroom she scrubbed the dirt off her hands, rubbing with a pumice stone where it was ingrained into the skin, before giving herself a thorough wash. She slipped into the Utility dress she'd worn the other night, the CC41 label prickly against the back of her neck. Stockings straight from the packet, another two coupons gone. She rolled them up very carefully and attached them to her suspenders, finishing the outfit with a pair of brown Seltona shoes that she'd purchased in 1940; she'd only worn them twice and they still looked smart. A touch of powder, eye shadow and lipstick, then she ran the brush through her hair and looked at herself in the dressing table mirror.

Quite presentable.

Lottie took her coat out of the wardrobe and removed the mothballs.

Deep red wool with a pale fox fur collar. Her luxury coat. Geoff had bought it for her birthday the year before he died. She hadn't worn it since she'd been alone, but maybe this was a good occasion. He'd approve. A small hat, red and black, decorated with three feathers, set everything off perfectly. She checked her watch: five minutes to one.

CHAPTER TWENTY-TWO

'YOU look a million dollars.'

Ellison was in uniform, dark olive wool jacket, tan shirt and beige tie, fawn trousers. He'd had his hair cut, and now it shone with oil.

'Thank you.' How long was it since anyone had complimented her appearance? 'You don't look half bad yourself.'

'Ready?'

Sitting in the passenger seat of the Jeep she felt like Cinderella on her way to the ball. It was a change simply to take in all the scenery, to enjoy a journey without thinking of directions or traffic.

He headed out of Leeds, driving along the road towards York.

'Where are we going?' she asked eventually. A cold draught whistled through the doors; her legs were freezing.

'RAF base,' he answered. 'Church Fenton. A bunch of our guys are training there.'

By the time they arrived she was glad just to be out of the vehicle and walking around, working some life and warmth back into her knee. The ride had been bumpy and uncomfortable; it made her appreciate the smoothness of the Humber. Jeeps and US Army lorries were parked everywhere. Music blared from a large Nissen hut, the sound of a big band.

As Ellison opened the door for her, the noise surrounded her in a roar. The musicians were crammed together on a platform, a blare of brass and the hard kick of drums. Tables had been packed around the edges of the hut, leaving a large dance floor.

Plenty of couples were moving around. American servicemen, all ranks, and with them, young women dressed to the nines or in their best uniforms. And all of them smiling, happy, glad to be here, now, not even thinking what the future might hold.

It was hot, the air heavy with tobacco and sweat, hair oil, perfume, and the smell of food. Lottie glanced around. A buffet of some kind had been set up, and next to it a bar, in front of a group of pin-up pictures on the wall. The rumours were right, she thought; the Yanks did their troops proud, everything was laid on.

Ellison commandeered a table, pulling rank on a corporal with a face full of freckles, and held the chair while she sat.

'Do you want a drink?' His mouth was close enough to her ear to feel the warmth of his breath.

'Would they have a G and T?' Lottie asked. He looked at her, not understanding. 'Gin and tonic.'

'I'll find out.'

While he was gone she gazed at the dancers. They were mostly couples holding each other and shuffling round in time to the music. But a few had style; they'd had lessons, felt the rhythm naturally and relished the chance to show it.

He returned balancing two glasses. She lifted hers in a toast, hearing a tinkle.

'Ice?'

He grinned. 'You're in America now. We use ice. And there's pizza if you're hungry.'

Pizza? She had no idea what that was; at the moment she didn't care. The band was playing up a storm and the air crackled with pleasure and a sense of wildness. It was nothing like the dances she used to go to with Geoff. Here there was a thrilling sense that anything might happen.

The musicians and singers all wore army uniforms, even the young woman with pale skin and black hair who waited for her turn at the microphone.

'Do you want to dance?' Ellison almost had to shout over the music. Lottie shook her head. She'd sit, look after her knee and leave all the jitterbugging and jiving to the young. But she couldn't help tapping her feet.

A few officers came up to Ellison, saying hello and shaking his hand. He was enjoying himself, sipping on his beer and smoking, nodding in time with the music, then he joined every other voice in the place, yelling out 'Pennsylvania 6-5000' during the pause in the melody.

For once, he looked relaxed. Carefree. She could imagine him like this, off-duty in Seattle, maybe at one of the baseball games he enjoyed in the summer. He applauded loudly at the end of every song, smiling as the female singer made *Don't Sit Under The Apple Tree* into a warning for the man duetting with her.

A moment's hush, then the drums started to beat a kind of rhythm she'd never heard before. It felt primal, exciting. Without even realising, she drew in a breath. The horns started, a raw, dirty roar she felt in her stomach.

Out on the dance floor, couples had formed a circle. In the middle a GI and his blonde WAAF date were already lost in the music, dancing so their hands barely touched. She had her jacket off, tie tucked into her shirt, eyes closed and a look of bliss on her face. She moved, just carried by the sound, no pattern. He leapt and jumped, curly hair bouncing. It was as if the music was pumping directly into their bodies.

The relentless drumming continued, the instrumentalists taking solos – trumpet, trombone, clarinet, saxophone – and the dancers kept moving, never slowing, not even aware of the rest of the world around them.

Then finally it ended. Without a word, the pair of them collapsed into each other's arms, faces flushed, hair soaked with sweat. The crowd clapped, as much for them as the band, and she joined in.

A quick pause for breath as the drummer took a bow.

'What on earth was that?' Lottie asked.

'It's called *Sing Sing Sing*,' Ellison told her. His eyes were shining. 'Always sends the dancers wild. I got to say, though, that was really something.'

The reeds struck up a slow, sweet melody. She knew it immediately: *Imagination*. The introduction built, and as the vocalist started the first line, she couldn't help singing softly along.

Ellison must have seen her. He reached out, took her hand and gestured to the dance floor. Lottie allowed herself to be led, feeling his arms lightly around her, looking up into his face as they muddled their way around, trying not to stand on each other's feet. She was smiling, wrapped in the song, enjoying these few moments. But life wasn't going to be like the lyric: no gentle touch, she told herself. No kissing, and no going round willy-nilly.

The final verse was beginning when she became aware of someone standing there. Ellison halted, letting go of her. A private, leaning forward and talking quietly into the captain's ear, receiving a nod. The last notes of the song were hanging in the air as he said, 'I'm really sorry, something's happened. I'm going to have to go. I'll take you home.'

He helped her into her coat and hurriedly drained the last of his beer. Going through the door, she was astonished to still see daylight, all the noise and the music suddenly muffled behind them. Surely she'd been in there for hours?

Climbing into the Jeep she looked back over her shoulder. By the corner of the hut a couple held each other, lost in a kiss. The tip of a cigarette glowed somewhere in the shadows.

A bitter wind whistled across the wide space of the aerodrome. By the control tower, the windsock was at full stretch. No aircraft; they must all be in the hangars.

'I really am sorry,' Ellison said. He glanced across at her. 'You were just starting to have fun, too.'

'It was all wonderful,' she told him honestly. 'I loved it. But the war comes first.'

'Uh-huh.' But he didn't say why he needed to return so urgently and she knew better than to ask.

'Del Vecchio must be a good entertainments officer,' she said.

'One of the best I've seen. He takes care of all the details. Band, drinks, food, getting the place set up. The whole shebang.'

Cold air brought her back to reality. The roads were empty and he made good time. The closer they came to Leeds, the city's chimneys rising like fingers, the more the dance seemed like a strange dream, an interlude from life.

Dusk was deepening when he parked outside her house. He left the motor idling.

'Thank you.' She smiled at him, pleasure in her eyes. 'I can't remember when I enjoyed something so much.' She meant it; it had been an experience, bold, brash, overwhelming and joyful.

From the look on his face she could tell what was coming. Lottie didn't turn as she felt his lips lightly on hers. But she didn't surrender to the kiss, either. Her body tensed. He seemed to understand, pulling back after a moment.

'I do like you, Cliff,' she said. 'But…'

'I know. You made it clear enough from the beginning. Honestly, it's fine. Sorry. I guess I got a little carried away.'

She stood on the verge, watching as he drove off.

'You look happy,' McMillan said as she walked into the office on Monday morning.

She still felt the wave of indulgence from the dance. A luxury. The band played on in her head; she could see the joy of the dancers if she closed her eyes. The only nagging reality was a twinge in her knee.

Lottie had spent the evening quietly, eating spam and chips in front of the fire, the American Forces' Network on the radio, big bands crackling out of the speaker to keep the mood of the afternoon alive.

Even putting on her uniform this morning, the starched white shirt and black tie, then walking to the bus stop, couldn't dampen her spirits.

'Good,' she answered. 'Did you manage a day off yesterday?'

'Part of one.' He gave a rueful smile. 'There was a possible sighting of Hilliard, so I had to come in. Turned out to be nothing.'

'There's still no word?'

'Not since his escape at the Star and Garter.' He didn't mean it as a reproach but Lottie felt herself blush; that still seemed like her fault. 'He's keeping his head down. Someone must be helping him.' McMillan raised his eyes to look at her. 'Time to look at all his friends and family and all the places he's lived again. Do you have the list?'

It was impossible to tell how exhaustive it was, but everyone on the list had been visited at least once.

'And we won't use the Specials this time,' he added.

It took time to arrange, checking with Andrews and co-ordinating the plain clothes officers. Then with the division inspector in charge of the uniforms at Millgarth. He'd need to ring the other divisions and arrange for men from there.

They'd manage to settle on a time – noon. Police officers would visit all the people on the list then. No opportunity for word to pass from one to the other. For the next half hour Lottie was busy making telephone calls to ensure everyone had the proper information. Finally, when she rang through for the umpteenth outside line of the morning, Helen at the switchboard said, 'You must have some big op going on. Is CID going to win the war?'

'That's tomorrow,' Lottie told her. 'Just a small push today.'

'*Casablanca* was good on Saturday, wasn't it?' Without waiting for an answer, she continued, 'Did you do much yesterday?'

'Not really. Some digging in the vegetable patch.' It was the truth. Just not all of it. But she didn't need everyone knowing her business.

Half-past eleven. She brought two cups of tea from the canteen. Not a biscuit to be found.

'Are you going out on any of the visits?'

McMillan sat back in his chair, pulling out a cigarette packet. 'I'd love to. But I'd better stay here and be ready.' He eyed her curiously. 'Why, were you hoping for some action? That knee of yours must be better.'

'I did some gardening yesterday. Good exercise.'

'If you say so,' he said doubtfully.

The phone rang just as she sat down at her desk. Someone who'd lost the information, probably, or checking details.

'Hi.'

No need to ask who it was. Lottie gently closed the door to her office.

'Thank you again for yesterday,' she said. 'It was absolutely marvellous.'

'Really?' He sounded surprised. 'Good, I wanted you to enjoy it. I just wish it could have gone on longer.' She waited but he said no more about why he'd been called away. 'Listen, I have to see someone in town and I wondered if I could buy you lunch.'

'I'm sorry, Cliff. We've got a bit of flap going on.'

'Anything important?' She could hear the disappointment in his voice.

'A big sweep for Hilliard.'

'Yeah, I guess that takes precedence. Another time?'

'Of course.'

The phone calls started in earnest at five past twelve. She'd made a chart and as the men gave their quick reports, ticked off each address. Nothing, no one at home. House empty, all the furniture gone. The list went on. One place had apparently been destroyed by an air raid in 1940. That was odd; she queried the address and discovered the constable had gone to Rathbone Terrace instead of Road.

By half past she'd heard from almost everyone. Only three left. Her ear felt hot from keeping the receiver jammed against it.

'Well?' McMillan stood in the doorway. She pushed her chart across the desk.

'No luck so far.' She pointed at the three spaces. 'We're still waiting on those.'

The telephone rang again. Lottie listened for a moment.

'Right. Thank you. No, just carry on.'

She crossed off one more address. The last two were taking their time. Did that mean they'd found something? She looked up at McMillan's face. Lost in thought. They waited, not speaking; there didn't seem to be anything worth saying at the moment.

The telephone bell made her jump.

'Yes, I see. No, thank you.'

Another ticked off. Just one remaining. They'd had thirty-five minutes to search. It was out past Headingley, not too far from the Castle Grove HQ where the Americans worked.

'Do you want to go out there?' Lottie asked.

He shook his head and lit a Four Square. 'We'll give them a little longer,' he answered through the smoke. 'Maybe they can't find a police box.'

By one o'clock he was pacing so hard he was wearing grooves in the lino.

'Come on,' she said finally, standing and reaching for her greatcoat. 'Let's go and take a look.'

As she drove she could feel the tension. What were they going to find? There had to be something after all this time. It was a respectable address, in shouting distance of the Cottage Road cinema. A stone through-terrace, the roses in the tiny front garden neatly pruned back.

No sign of the constables who'd been sent out here. McMillan knocked on the front door. The sound of feet moving slowly along the hall inside. The drawing back of a chain and a bolt. Lottie stood back. A lock clicked and a woman stood there, blinking in the daylight. She was short, barely five feet tall, grey hair neat, peering up at them through a pair of glasses.

The cut of her woollen dress was dated, but on someone older that hardly mattered. It was good quality, Lottie could see that, elegant but not quite top drawer; it must have come from Schofield's or Matthias Robinson, she decided, not Marshall and Snelgrove. But the tattered slippers on the woman's feet ruined the elegant effect.

McMillan raised his hat and the woman softened at the gesture. She was the type to value politeness; he'd judged that well.

'I'm sorry to bother you. I'm Detective Chief Superintendent McMillan with Leeds Police.' He produced his warrant card and gave her time to study it. 'Have any constables been here?'

'No,' she answered, confusion on her face. 'Why would they have come here?'

'We're looking for a man named Hilliard. According to our records, he used to live here.'

'If he did, it's not been since 1938,' she told him tartly. 'We bought the house then.'

Old information. It happened. A waste of their time.

'I'm sorry,' Lottie said with a gentle smile. 'I hope you understand.'

'Of course.' The woman gazed at McMillan. 'I'm sorry I can't help you.'

'Just a mistake.' Another tip of his hat and they left, the wooden gate clattering behind them.

'Still doesn't answer the question, does it?' he asked as she unlocked the Humber.

'No,' she agreed. Why hadn't any coppers called to ask about Hilliard? Everything had been clear enough.

'If they decided to ignore the order, I'll give them a rocket that'll send them into the next century.'

'Where now?'

McMillan thought for a second. 'Go down to Meanwood.'

When he came back from the shop he placed a brown paper parcel on the passenger seat and gave her a wink. Lottie raised an eyebrow.

'My friend the butcher was feeling generous,' McMillan said. 'I thought you might like some.'

'I won't say no. Thank you.'

'Millgarth,' he decided. 'Let's see if we can find these bobbies.'

The constables had been called to an accident on the Ring Road. No one dead, but three taken to hospital, all the witness statements to take and wait until the damaged vehicles were hauled away. They'd simply been doing their duty.

Lottie looked at the list on her desk and put a tick beside the final address. They'd come away with nothing from the operation. Hilliard was still out there, still armed, still deadly.

She raised the window and placed the package of meat on the ledge outside. Definitely cold enough to keep it fresh until she went home. She'd grown to enjoy the little extras McMillan passed on to her. Perks, he called them. Sweeteners. Always a surprise, and completely illegal. But Lottie knew she'd ignore that when she sat down to eat. No guilt.

Across the hall she could hear McMillan on the phone, snapping out questions, then the harsh jangle as he dropped the receiver back on to the instrument.

'We're going back out,' he shouted.

Lottie didn't know Swinnow well; it was a part of Leeds she'd rarely visited. But she followed the Stanningley Road until she came to a cluster of vehicles parked by a railway embankment. She recognised the pathologist's car and the coroner's unmarked black van. This had to be the place.

All McMillan had told her was they had a dead body.

'Not a woman,' he added when she stared at him.

A uniformed copper stood guard, coming smartly to attention and saluting as he recognised the Chief Superintendent. A few yards away, Inspector Andrews stood and gazed down the steep bank towards the tracks. DC Smith was making notes as he talked to an old man walking a mongrel. The animal kept glancing up impatiently at its owner and pulling gently at its lead.

A long rope had been tied to a tree, the only way for men to make their way to the bottom on the cut. The doctor was already there, bent over a corpse. Ten yards away, the coroner's men waited and smoked, the canvas stretcher rolled up tightly. Ted from Police Evidence was taking photographs.

Lottie watched as McMillan finished his conversation with the inspector then began his slow descent to the body, hand over hand down the rope. She could see the strain on his face, the veins bulging on his neck. For God's sake, she thought, he was too old to be doing that; but saying it would have been a waste of breath. She knew how he worked; he needed to see for himself. And in his mind he probably still believed he was twenty.

The pathologist stood, dusting off his knees, and Lottie drew in her breath as she saw the face of the man lying by the railway tracks.

George Hilliard. She stared, hardly daring to believe he could be dead.

It was a quarter of an hour before McMillan returned, hauled up the hillside by a pair of burly coppers. He was red-faced and sweating, leaning against the Humber to catch his breath then lighting a cigarette before he spoke.

'You saw?'

She nodded. It still didn't seem quite real, that he was down there, dead. After they'd searched so frantically for him, come so close to arresting him, an ending like this seemed so mundane, so ordinary, that it was shocking. She felt cheated. How could there be a sense of victory about this? They hadn't won. They hadn't caught him.

'How did he die? What did the doctor say?'

'Broken neck.' He blew out a long plume of smoke. 'And the fall didn't cause it. He's certain of that.'

'Murdered?' She was surprised; the idea didn't astonish her. A phrase came into her head: live by the sword, die by the sword.

'He'll know more once he has Hilliard on the slab, but yes. Someone killed him.'

Lottie looked around. The nearest house was a couple of hundred yards down the road. Another a little farther the other way. A nice empty spot for getting rid of a body.

Hilliard was dead. She had to keep repeating it in her head. He was dead. No more killing of young women.

'What about the gun?'

'Still in his pocket,' McMillan told her. 'It looks like someone took him by surprise.'

'It could have been someone he trusted.'

'True.' He nodded. 'Or the killer put it back there.' McMillan ran a hand through his hair. 'I don't know. Andrews is organising a team to go door-to-door and see if anyone noticed anything.' He stared at the deserted road. 'I'm not going to hold my breath.'

'Who found the body?'

'A goods train driver. Stopped at the next station and rang in. It was in some bushes, just good luck he even noticed it. The doctor had to move Hilliard to examine him.'

'At least someone's stopped him,' she said. He was dead. She should have felt relief. Instead there was emptiness; another killer was still out there. Lottie shuddered, as if someone was walking over her grave.

'Who did it, though? And why?'

She dropped McMillan close to the mortuary. He'd be there, ready when they brought in Hilliard's body. The first post-mortem he'd attended in years, but he wanted to be there for this one.

'The sooner we know, the sooner we can get moving.'

'You don't need me, do you?' she asked.

'You go back to Millgarth,' he said with a smile. 'Have a cuppa and a gossip.'

'I never gossip.' Without thinking, she began to bristle.

'A natter,' he corrected himself. She snorted, pulling away as he closed the door. Cheek.

By four o'clock he still hadn't returned. The newspapers had rung, local and national. Helen had put through a constant stream of calls. All Lottie could tell them was that the Chief Superintendent would make a statement in due course. Even the BBC had been on the blower; they'd have to wait like everyone else.

She wasn't sorry that Hilliard was dead. Women in Leeds were safer now. Any jury would have convicted him; this just saved on a trial and a hanging. Killing him like that was justice of a sort.

But it wasn't the law.

Now they needed to find his murderer. The job was only half done.

She heard McMillan trudge up the stairs. When he appeared in her doorway he looked wrung out, battered, as if he'd been pulled through a mangle.

'I'd forgotten how gruesome those things can be.'

'Did you learn anything?'

He managed a wan smile. 'Apart from the fact that retirement can't come too soon? The break came from a sudden, sharp increase of pressure on the head until his neck snapped.' Lottie shuddered as she thought of it. 'Done from behind. Not gentle. Not kind. And *very* professional.'

They had a nation full of trained killers. Men who'd been taught unarmed combat.

'What now?'

'I don't know. I've been trying to puzzle it out on the way back. Has anyone rung?'

Lottie held up a fistful of notes. 'Press, radio. They all want to know what we're doing.'

'I'll cobble something together,' he said with a sigh. 'You might as well go home. I'm settling in for a long night.'

'Are you sure?'

'Yes. We're not going to solve this one in a couple of hours.'

She was halfway down the stairs before she remembered the package waiting on the windowsill. Meat and potato pie for dinner.

CHAPTER TWENTY-THREE

M CMILLAN didn't wake as she opened the office door. Head back, he snored gently, large, dark circles under his eyes.

Down in the canteen Lottie persuaded the cook to make a bacon sandwich, and carried it back upstairs with a mug of strong tea. She placed them in front of him and gently shook his shoulder.

'Breakfast,' she told him.

He blinked, passing a hand across his mouth. 'I must have dropped off. Forty winks.'

He needed a shave, and the collar of his white shirt was ringed with dirt. Lottie picked the papers off his desk.

'You get yourself ready and I'll put these in order. Nothing overnight?'

He shook his head. 'No.'

The pathologist's report had been hastily typed, full of spelling mistakes. But it confirmed what he'd said at the scene. The neck broken, snapped. Efficient, brutal. Whoever murdered Hilliard knew exactly what he was doing.

He'd died somewhere between midnight and four. The abrasions on his hands and face had happened after death, almost certainly when he was tipped down the embankment.

The evidence bods had been thorough, but they had little to tell. Hilliard carried a counterfeit ration book and National Identity card in the name of John Graham. A wallet with two pounds, another five shillings and threepence in change in a trouser pocket. Handkerchief, wristwatch. It didn't seem as if anything had been stolen. The Colt pistol was in his pocket. Two sets of fingerprints on the weapon. One set belonged to Hilliard, the other from someone unknown, without a record.

DS Lawton in ballistics must have worked late, too. He'd tested the Colt, comparing a spent bullet to those that killed the four young women. The same. That confirmed it, if there'd ever been a shadow of doubt. Hilliard was guilty of all four murders.

Canvassing the area hadn't brought anything. But the bobbies had found many people out when they called during the day. They'd had more luck in the evening, but still no joy. No one remembered anything. Three places left where there'd been no reply. She noted the addresses for later.

By the time she'd collated it all, McMillan had washed, shaved, combed his hair and put a fresh collar on his shirt; he looked awake and alert. The empty plate and mug stood at the corner of the desk and he was smoking a cigarette.

'Thank you for breakfast.'

'Payment for that lovely stewing steak you gave me yesterday,' she said. 'But you'd do well to grovel next time you're in the canteen. I had to beg for that bacon.'

His smile only lasted a second.

'You've read it all. What do you think?'

'We know someone dumped him there.' It echoed what Hilliard had done to Anne Goodman at Kirkstall Abbey, she thought. Just tossing the body away. The killer must have brought the body in a car. 'The house-to-house need to ask if anyone heard any vehicles. It was the middle of the night. It might have woken someone.'

McMillan scribbled a note. 'Smith can go back and check.'

'What about this other set of fingerprints on the gun?'

'Nothing in Records.' He shrugged.

'What can we do?'

'I've spent half the night trying to work that out,' he said with a sigh. 'And I still don't have an answer.'

'There's one thing that baffles me. Why would they leave the gun? Surely whoever killed him could sell it on the black market. Or use it himself.'

'Hilliard's murderer probably knows what he did with that Colt,' he said. 'He doesn't want to risk being caught with it.'

That made sense. Anyone arrested with the weapon would be looking at a hanging.

'The way he was killed—'

'Doesn't mean much. You know that. How many troops are wandering around Leeds? How many who've served? Last time around, too. Every one of them knows how to do that.' He paused. 'I telephoned the Ministry of War last night.'

'Why?' She didn't follow his thinking.

'Hilliard must have had friends in his platoon. I wanted some names. You never know, he might have stayed in touch after he deserted.'

'How does that help us find his killer?' Lottie still didn't understand.

'Maybe we can learn what he'd been up to. It could point us in the right direction.'

'That sounds like a very long shot,' Lottie said.

'It is,' he agreed with a long sigh. 'It is. That's how desperate I am.'

A little after ten o'clock. Lottie had brought another cuppa from the canteen and finished it. She'd gone back over the reports, making a note of every detail and trying to connect them, to see if anything popped out. All in vain. The only thing she had were some scribbles on a piece of paper.

McMillan's door opened. He was already wearing his over-coat, trilby in his hands. His eyes looked hopeful.

'The Ministry rang back. We have someone to see.'

He was eager, already disappearing down the stairs as Lottie buttoned her greatcoat, slipped on a pair of gloves and jammed the WAPC cap on her head. By the time she reached the car he was tapping his foot impatiently.

Lottie played with the choke, adjusting the mixture before turning the ignition. The engine fired immediately.

'Where are we going?'

'Chapel Allerton. The hospital.'

Lottie glanced in the mirror as she eased out into traffic. She'd passed the place but always been thankful she never needed to visit. The prosthetic hospital, that was what people called it. Full of troops who'd had their arms and legs blown off, being fitted with new limbs and prepared for Civvy Street.

An easy drive, up Harrogate Road then turn on to Harehills Lane. A brief stop at the gates while a guard checked their identification.

The hospital itself was a big old house, sandstone blackened by the years. In spite of the cold, a few men wandered outside. Some with crutches, others in wheelchairs. In battledress and dressing gowns. One of two limped cautiously, growing used to the false legs. At least they had some freedom, she thought; it was probably better than being cooped up inside all day.

The place was heartening and depressing at the same time. She parked the Humber and followed McMillan into the building. Voices echoed. The medical smell of antiseptic filled the air. A harried nurse directed them, pointing down a long corridor.

In the ward, the sister looked them over carefully before nodding and leading them to a bed where a man in flannel pyjamas was propped up, reading *Weekly Illustrated*.

'William, this gentleman is from the police. He'd like to ask a few questions about someone you might know.' The way she spoke, it was a demand that brooked no objection.

He looked up and Lottie could see the burns that covered the left side of his face. He'd had surgery but the scars would remain for the rest of his life. As bad as anything she'd seen after the last war.

'Hello.' The man extended a hand and smiled. 'Have a pew if you can find one.' He turned his head towards Lottie. 'Sorry, miss, we're a bit short on chairs around here.' A sly wink. 'I think the nurses must be nicking them.'

McMillan introduced himself, perching on the edge of the bed.

'Bill Broadhurst. Corporal. For the moment, anyway.' The man grinned. 'Let me guess. You're here about George Hilliard.' He had a London accent, just like the cockneys she'd seen in the films, cheerful, devil-may-care.

'What makes you think that?' McMillan brought out his cigarettes and offered one to Broadhurst.

'Ta. Well, he was the only one in our lot likely to be in trouble with the rozzers. If it wasn't nailed down, it would disappear when George was around. He made sure he kept his hands off our personal gear, though. Just as well.'

'You were friends?'

'Not close or anything. But you know how it is, you get to know everyone in the platoon. He was light-fingered but he was pleasant enough. Always good for a laugh. We had fun. I was sorry when he took off, really. I think the brass was glad, though.' He grinned. 'Not as many things vanishing. What's he done now?'

'I'm sorry to have to tell you. He's dead.'

Broadhurst looked from one of them to the other, waiting to be told it was a joke.

'George?' he said finally.

'We found the body yesterday,' McMillan said. 'Someone killed him.'

'Christ.' He looked at Lottie and tightened his lips as an apology. 'I know he was a bit of a lad and all that, but why? What had he been up to?'

'He'd killed four young women.'

Broadhurst stayed silent for a long time.

'I see,' he said finally.

'You don't sound too surprised.'

'I don't know what to say. I heard things. You know, that George could be a bit rough with a woman. Didn't like to hear them say no, that was the rumour. But no one brought charges. And killing them?' He shook his head doubtfully. 'George was always a bit of a coward. I reckon that's why he deserted.' The man paused. 'You're sure it's him?'

'There's no doubt,' McMillan said. 'No doubt about any of it. He shot a policeman, too.'

'It just… I don't know…'

A slight pause and McMillan asked the important question. 'After he deserted, did you ever hear from him?'

'No. I liked him, but he knew I'd have turned him in. Deserting, it isn't fair on your mates, is it?'

It was the type of question that didn't need an answer. Lottie cleared her throat and Broadhurst turned his head to look at her.

'Was there anyone from the platoon who might have kept in touch with him?' she asked.

'I don't know. Honest truth, miss, I don't. I suppose it's possible, but...'

'The rest of you couldn't trust Hilliard after he deserted.' McMillan finished the sentence and Broadhurst nodded.

'That's it. He was always a bit... and you've got to trust the lads with you.' He cocked his head. 'Were you in the last one?'

'Yes.'

Lottie knew he wouldn't say more than that; McMillan never talked about his time in the army.

'You know, then.' The man stared at Lottie again. 'You see, miss, didn't matter that George was a laugh. It's a matter of loyalty. I couldn't see any of the boys wanting to know him. Still a shock that he's dead, mind.'

McMillan left the packet of Four Squares and a box of matches on the table beside the bed. Outside, in the corridor, the ward sister caught up with them.

'You're the first visitors he's had.'

'It was hardly a social call,' he told her.

'That doesn't matter. It's something. His family was bombed out in the Blitz. They can't get up here.'

'What happened to him?' Lottie asked.

'Those burns to his face. More on his chest. And he lost his right leg above the knee.' She said it matter-of-factly; no doubt it was the kind of injury she saw every day. 'Italy. Monte Cassino. From what William says, we'll be seeing quite a few more from there.' She gave a tight smile, turned away and returned to the ward.

Outside, away from the smell of carbolic and medicine, McMillan breathed deeply.

'Maybe that explains a few things about Hilliard,' he said. There was a sense of finality in his voice. He glanced back over his shoulder at the building. 'Let's get out of here. Places like this always scare me.'

After she parked at Millgarth, he disappeared, returning half an hour later with a sombre face.

'I went over to the war memorial for a few minutes.'

She didn't need to ask why. All those thoughts of old comrades among the dead. And the knowledge that one of his sons could so easily join them, another body somewhere in the Far East.

'You didn't miss anything.'

He frowned, took a new packet of cigarettes from his pocket and lit one.

'More's the pity. Can you bring me everything on Hilliard and the girls he killed?'

It took three trips. There were piles of paper, two box files, and a score of reports. Lottie mounded them on his desk and stood back.

'I'm going through everything again,' McMillan said. 'Maybe I'll see something different after what Broadhurst told us.'

'Do you really believe we missed anything?' It felt as if they'd followed every path, no matter how hopeless.

'I hope we have,' he answered and sighed. 'We're stuffed otherwise. I don't suppose you fancy nipping down to the canteen for a couple of cups of tea, do you?'

Lottie shook her head. But she was grinning, already reaching for the doorknob. Her knee was close to normal again. Still bruised and tender if she poked it, but the swelling had gone and she could move easily.

She placed the mug on his desk and closed the door on the way out. In her own office she took a book from her uniform jacket. *Double Indemnity*. After seeing the film she'd wanted to read the book. Ten pages in and she was already intrigued. The style was so different, very American.

Her telephone rang several times, reporters hoping for some fresh news on the Hilliard killing. All she could tell them was the official line: McMillan would make a statement in due course. Two of the calls brought tips, but neither sounded credible. She passed them to CID.

A little after four she took McMillan another cuppa. He scarcely noticed, lost in paper, reading his way through a document. Quietly, she retreated again.

The twenty-ninth of February, she saw on the calendar. Leap year. Tomorrow it would be March. Soon enough spring would arrive. She already had seeds growing in trays in the back bedroom. As soon as the danger of frosts had passed she'd get them in the ground, a cloche over the top for the first few weeks to keep them warm. Maybe they'd have a fine summer; it was about time. The last one she could remember was '39, so many warm, cloudless days. The good weather had remained well into September, after the declaration of war, after Geoff died so suddenly, the sun staying to mock her.

At least he'd gone home, Lottie thought when she checked McMillan's office in the morning. The new month had dawned chilly, frost on the grass, her breath blooming in the air as she walked to the tram stop. But the sky was clear and the sun was shining. She'd arrived early at Millgarth and sat down in the warm fug of the canteen, eating scrambled powdered eggs and baked beans.

Helen and Margaret came in together, waving, then joining her.

'I don't know how you can stomach that,' Helen said.

'I suppose I'm used to it by now.' But even as she said it she pushed the plate away, remembering the taste of a real egg. The black market might be busy but there weren't too many of those around.

'Has your boss cracked that murder yet?' Margaret asked. 'I was reading about it in the *Express* on the way in.'

'We're getting closer.' Maybe it was true; he might have found something. Lottie leaned forward and the others imitated her, desperate for gossip. 'He had a gun in his pocket when we found him.' It was hardly a secret, even though the press hadn't printed it. And it put them in the know. She stood and winked. 'Work calls.'

McMillan arrived at half past eight on the dot, looking fresh, as if he'd slept well for once. He was wearing his good suit and the West Yorkshire Regiment tie.

'Very dapper.'

'I have to see the Chief Constable this morning. Tell him how we're getting along on this.' He gestured at the files.

'Any progress?'

He shook his head. 'We were thorough the first time.' He glanced at his wrist watch. 'I suppose I'd better walk over to the Civic Hall. Unless you fancy driving me.'

'By the time I scraped the windscreen you'd be halfway there.' She eyed the bulge of his belly under the overcoat. 'Besides, a little exercise might do you good.'

Close to eleven and she'd almost finished the novel, reading fast. She didn't even know anyone was standing there until knuckles rapped softly on the jamb.

'Do you know where the boss is?' Detective Constable Smith. He always looked diffident, not quite sure of himself, as if he was happiest existing in the shadow of Inspector Andrews.

'He's at a meeting,' she told him. 'Is it something important?'

'I was talking to a bookie's runner this morning,' he began, hesitating as if he was unsure whether to give her the information.

'Does it have something to do with Hilliard?' Most gambling was illegal. But there were so many worse crimes; the police usually ignored it.

He nodded, Adam's apple bobbing. She waited.

'Russ Templeton,' he said. 'That's his name. He fancies himself a bit of a spiv but he's nothing, really. Asked if there was a reward for information about Hilliard's death.'

'What did you tell him?' So far the city hadn't put up any money.

'I said I might be able to bung him a quid. But he wants to speak to the boss.'

'Where is he now?' When he didn't answer immediately, she said, 'Oh, come on. Spit it out.'

'He said he'd be on Leeds Bridge at noon.' Smith shrugged. 'I told him he's been watching too many spy films. But that's what he wants.'

'I'll make sure the Chief Super's there,' she promised, giving the poor lad a smile. 'Thank you.'

It was twenty past eleven when she parked in front on the Civic Hall and hurried up the steps. The stone of the building was brilliant white, sparkling in the sun. Inside, everything was as hushed as a church.

'Is DCS McMillan still here?' she asked the chief constable's secretary, a prim woman in her early sixties with dark, intelligent eyes.

'They should be finished in a minute, love.' It was a warm, Leeds voice. 'Is it urgent?'

'Yes,' Lottie said. 'It is a bit.'

Two minutes and they were in the car.

'Tell me again,' he said, and she repeated all the information Smith had given her.

'On the bridge?' McMillan asked. 'What does he think he is? A spy?'

'Don't ask me, I'm just the messenger. And the one making sure you arrive on time.'

She parked on Dock Street, no more than a hundred yards from the bridge but around the corner and out of sight. Better if he went alone; if Templeton really did have information, they didn't want to scare him. And it gave her a chance to finish the book.

Lottie slapped the cover closed, satisfied. There was justice in the ending; it completed the circle. She sat back and closed her eyes.

The solid clunk of the car door as it shut woke her.

'Sleeping on the job,' McMillan said. 'I ought to report you.'

Lottie stretched her back and looked at her watch. He'd only been gone a quarter of an hour.

'What did he have to say?' she asked, stifling a yawn.

'Chummy claims he knows the man who was sheltering Hilliard the last few days he was alive.' Someone named Johnson.

'Really?' Quickly, she turned in the seat and stared. 'Do you believe him?'

'He'd better be telling the truth – I gave him two pounds for the name. Didn't even make fun of all his cloak and dagger stuff.' It was a tidy sum. McMillan gave a dark smile. 'Told him if he was lying I'd take it out of his hide. He swore up and down it was right.'

'Is it someone you know?'

'No.' He grimaced. 'That's what worries me. Someone working the black market, he says. I thought I'd heard of all the criminals in Leeds by now.'

'Did he have an address?' She started the Humber.

'He claimed he didn't know it. Let's go back to Millgarth, see if any of the others have heard of this man.'

They hadn't. It brought blank looks and shrugs. Jimmy Johnson. No record. If he really existed, he was making his home deep in the shadows.

'Talk to your narks,' McMillan ordered the men. 'Offer them a few bob, make them a deal, whatever it takes. I want to know where this Johnson is. If this lad's been playing clever clogs and I've been conned, God help him.'

There was no word by the time she left for the night. Nothing first thing the next morning, either. Then she saw Andrews tap on the Chief Superintendent's door and enter. Less than a minute later McMillan appeared, hat already on his head, coat in his hand.

'We're on our way.'

She dashed after him. In the car she pulled on the choke and turned the key in the ignition. 'Where?'

'Meanwood Road. Near the public baths.'

The building had been a factory once, but it had been empty and dilapidated for years. Even the need for war work hadn't brought back the machines and labourers here. It was too far gone, only fit for demolition. Lottie parked down the road, tucking the Humber behind a black van.

She stood, feeling useless as McMillan talked to the vehicle's driver. A few seconds later the back doors opened and four large coppers emerged, pulling on their helmets, truncheons drawn. This time they'd come prepared.

'Andrews pushed one of his snouts. Finally got him to cough up that this Johnson lives out at the factory,' McMillan had explained as they drove from town. He shook his head. 'Sounds like something in Dickens if you ask me. Evidently he's only been around a few months. It might explain why there's been so much on the black market lately. Maybe why we haven't heard about him, too. Built himself quite a little empire in that time, though.'

The Chief Super gathered the men around and gave his instructions, watching as they dispersed.

'Time to see what Mr Johnson has to say.' He stared into her face. 'It would probably be better if you stayed here.'

CHAPTER TWENTY-FOUR

'WHY?' Lottie asked. Her voice was like flint.

'It could be dangerous,' McMillan said. He waved a hand at the crumbling stonework. 'For God's sake, look at the place. A hard gust and it could all fall down.'

'Then it could just as easily collapse on you.'

He sighed. 'Lottie, it's an order. I don't know what's in there. We're all trained to look after ourselves. You're not.'

She looked back at him, not saying a word. Finally he turned away and strode towards the factory. Lottie waited until he turned a corner, hidden by a stone wall as tall as a man, and then followed slowly. What was the worst he could do – sack her?

Thin tufts of grass grew between the cobbles in the yard. All the windows in the building were smashed; the fragments of glass that remained were covered in years of grime. A doorway without a door led inside.

She stood there for a few seconds. Light tumbled in through a gap in the roof. Large, deep pools of shade filled the corners.

McMillan was easy enough to follow. He was trying to be quiet, but that was impossible when rubble and debris were scattered across the floor. Lottie carefully picked her way through it all.

Then through another doorway into a cavernous space: the factory proper, she guessed. The slates fallen and most of the roof beams were gone, leaving it empty and haunted. Beyond that, she edged into a dark corridor, close enough to hear everything but still keeping her distance. She intended to be there when they found Johnson. Not an adjunct, left behind when it suited.

She'd earned it. She'd seen the bodies of the young women who were murdered. She'd touched them, felt their stillness. If this was where it all ended, this was where she needed to be.

A heavy creak somewhere and she paused for a moment. Not even breathing. She could hear McMillan ahead of her, following the path as it turned left. Very quietly, she moved closer until she could see the closed door ahead of him, and the slight hesitation before he barged it open with his shoulder.

Lottie kept to the shadows, treading very lightly, closer still until she was enough to peer over the chief super's shoulder. Three oil lamps burned bright in the room. No windows, but a grate with a fire burning, a camp bed in one corner. All very snug, she thought. And, sitting on the chair, pen in his hand, a man with the blackest skin she could imagine.

'You must be Mr Johnson.' The man looked around as if he was ready to bolt. There was a door in the far wall. Perfectly on cue, it opened, filled by a copper.

Johnson began to move, his arm reaching for something. McMillan brought the Webley from his pocket.

'That would be a very bad idea,' he said. He waved the gun. 'Up.'

Johnson stood. He was tall, easily six feet two, eyes full of hatred as the cuffs locked around his wrists. He was wearing a ragamuffin's uniform – a scarred brown leather jacket, woollen battledress trousers, army boots, and a khaki jumper. Deserter, she decided. He had to be.

McMillan pushed him back down on to the chair. The man hadn't said a word yet.

'Search the place,' he ordered the constables. 'Odds are you'll find a few things. If this is the right bloke, the black market here might never be the same again.' Once the men had disappeared, he turned back to Johnson. 'I wonder how many authorities will be interested in you?'

He picked up the pistol that had been beyond Johnson's grasp. A Colt M1911. The same model that Hilliard had used. One had remained unrecovered from the stolen case.

Fascinated, Lottie could hardly take her eyes off Johnson. His skin was so dark that light seemed to vanish in it. She'd only ever seen anything like it in newsreels about Africa.

'Sir,' she said. McMillan turned sharply, then his eyes followed to where she was pointing. An American soldier's forage cap sitting on top of a battered wooden filing cabinet.

'Well, well, well,' he said, looking at Johnson again. 'The Yanks aren't satisfied with going after our women; now they want our crime, too.'

The uniforms took Johnson away. He'd be waiting at Millgarth when they returned. Soon enough the evidence men would be out here to dig through everything thoroughly. But even the quick search had already turned up more than a hundred jerrycans filled with petrol, cases of canned food, a carton of women's stockings and a dozen bottles of rye whiskey.

'He must have good contacts at the base,' Lottie said.

'I'm sure we'll find a lot more here, too. It like Aladdin's cave. And all of it nicked.' He picked up a pair of nylons. 'You might as well take some of these. No one's going to count them.'

Lottie shook her head; it didn't seem right.

'I told you to stay outside,' McMillan continued.

'I know.'

'He was armed.'

'I kept back.'

He sighed. 'Twenty years and you still don't learn. I should probably discipline you but I just don't have the energy.' A final glance around and he started towards the fresh air. 'Let's go and see what he has to say for himself.'

'We should tell Ellison,' she said. 'After all, he's one of theirs.'

McMillan grinned. 'When I'm good and ready. After all, he hasn't always been forthcoming.'

They left Johnson to stew in the cells for the rest of the day. It wouldn't have any effect on him, she was certain, but it gave the evidence bods time to go over the factory. Late in the afternoon she put the list on McMillan's desk. He glanced through the two tightly spaced sheets and raised an eyebrow, impressed.

'He had a warehouse out there.'

'All from the American commissaries, by the look of things,' Lottie said.

'God, from the look of this he must have been supplying half the black market in Leeds. I'm amazed we hadn't come across him before.'

'I wonder how he's tied to Hilliard?'

'Don't worry, I'll find out.' It sounded somewhere between a promise and a threat. And it probably was. 'Isn't it time you were off?'

Quarter past five. Close enough. She knew why he was dropping the hint. He was ready to question Johnson and didn't want her around for that. It was going to be rough. No matter; she'd expected that. McMillan wanted answers and he'd do everything he needed to get them.

She'd been home for more than an hour, the last of the meat and potato pie eaten, pots washed, sitting in front of the fire with the Home Service playing softly on the radio, when she heard the knock on the door.

'Hi.' She smelled his clean scent.

'Come in,' Lottie said. She could hardly leave him on the doorstep. Not after he'd taken her to the dance on Sunday. She closed the door behind him, tugged the blackouts back into place, and switched on the light. 'Would you like a cup of tea?'

'No, thanks.' He smiled, but she could see the worry in his eyes.

'It's warm in the dining room.'

He sat but he didn't relax, playing with his cap, eyes wandering around, glancing at the ornaments and pictures.

'You look like you have something to say.'

'Yeah,' he admitted then stopped. 'I'm sorry about that kiss—'

'Don't worry about it,' she told him. 'All forgotten.'

He managed a weak, shy smile. 'It's been a crazy start to the week,' he said. 'Too much going on.'

'Plenty of crime?'

'Not really.' He looked into her eyes. 'It feels like we might be getting ready to move.'

'Oh?' The words took her by surprise. It had to come, of course, that was the only way they'd win this war; she just hadn't expected it yet.

'No one's saying anything but everyone knows.' He cocked his head. 'Do you understand what I mean?'

It happened everywhere. Ideas carried on the air. By the time the announcement came it was nothing more than a confirmation.

'Any idea when?'

'Not yet. But they never give us much notice for a move. I wanted to come and see you, let you know. I might not have a chance later.'

'I'm glad.' She meant it.

'I was wondering…' He leaned forward, elbows resting on his knees, awkward as a schoolboy. 'Would you mind if I wrote to you?'

Lottie almost laughed. It seemed so ridiculous, so old-fashioned and formal to be asking permission to send her letters. She smiled.

'I'd be very glad if you did.' As long as he understood that nothing would happen, that he'd never be able to persuade her to anything more than friendship, then it would all be fine.

'Good.' Some of the tension seemed to vanish and he sat back. 'Is that tea still on offer?'

'I'll only be a minute.'

When she returned with two cups he was staring thought-fully into the fire.

'Penny for them.'

'Nothing, really. Wondering where I'll be in a few months, that's all.'

'You miss Seattle, don't you?'

'Yeah.' He lit a cigarette. 'I do. It'll be good to get home. To have everything normal again.'

What was normal, she wondered? She wasn't certain she could remember. Normal had been when Geoff was alive and the country was at peace. That seemed a long, long time ago, and it could never return. Not in the same way.

'Pardon me?' she said. He'd been talking, but she'd strayed into her thoughts.

'I was asking how your work has been. Have you caught the guy who killed Hilliard?'

He must have read about it in the newspaper.

'No, not yet. Still all sorts of tests.'

'Are you getting anywhere?'

She was suddenly wary. Was it purely professional interest, one policeman asking about another's case, or was there something else behind the question?

'You'd have to talk to John about that. Sometimes he plays his cards close to his chest, even with me.' She tried to keep her voice light, to make it all seem ordinary, as if she knew nothing.

'I hope he finds his murderer.'

'I'm sure he will.'

Another ten minutes of idle talk. She steered the subject back to Seattle and saw how his eyes lit up as he talked about the mountains and the water near his home.

'You know, I promised myself, when I make police captain, I'd buy a house right down on the shore. Then I'll be able to sit on the porch every night and listen to the waves.'

'It sounds like heaven.'

'You could come and visit.'

Lottie smiled and shook her head. 'That's a lovely thought. But I can't see myself going all the way to Seattle for a holiday.'

The farthest she'd ever been was to Torquay for a week in 1936. That had seemed a real distance; America was the ends of the earth.

'Never say never.' He shrugged. 'Del Vecchio was back at HQ this afternoon.'

'Oh?'

'I've never seen him so mad. He had two of the girls in tears.'

'Why?'

'No idea.' He chuckled. 'John hasn't been after him again, has he?'

If he was trying to be subtle, it wasn't working. 'Not this time.'

'I guess I'll find out sooner or later.' He smiled and stood. 'Or maybe I won't. I'd better get going.'

At the door he kissed her lightly on the cheek. A kiss of friend-ship. She listened to the snick of the catch on the front gate, then the sound of the Jeep's engine as he disappeared down the road.

In the kitchen she washed the cups, wondering. Later, settled in bed, she was still thinking.

McMillan was dressed in his sober court suit, dark grey, with a maroon tie.

'Johnson's up before the magistrate this morning,' he explained. 'We'll get him into Armley. The case is serious enough to warrant a crown court hearing. It'll give us time to question him properly.'

'What's he told you?'

'Not enough. He's tough.' Absently, he rubbed his knuckles; they were scraped and grazed.

'Anything about Hilliard?'

'He did admit that Hilliard had stayed for a few nights. Then he went out and never came back. The next thing Johnson knew was the story in the papers.'

'Do you think that's the truth?'

'I don't know.' The frustration was right there in his eyes. 'I'm not even sure what the truth is any more.'

'Do the Americans know we have him?'

'I haven't said a word.' He turned to look at her. 'Why?'

'I had a visitor last night.'

By the time she finished the tale he was pacing around the office.

'Did it seem like he was fishing?' he asked.

'Yes.' She'd spent hours thinking about it, awake until two, going over every single word Ellison said, examining it for meaning. 'It did. He was trying to be casual with his questions.'

'What he said about del Vecchio is interesting.'

'If it's true.'

McMillan dipped his head in acknowledgement. If. He glanced at the clock on the wall.

'I need to go. Keep thinking about it.'

She heard him stamping up the stairs. Standing in her doorway, he had a face like thunder.

'You're positive you never said a word to Ellison about Johnson?'

'Of course I am.' Lottie started to rise from her chair. 'Why? What's happened?'

'The bloody Yanks turned up mob-handed. A bunch of army lawyers. They're claiming jurisdiction because he's one of theirs. Brought boxes of paperwork to back it all up. They must have had their clerks working all night.'

'But how—?'

'I don't know. What's worse is the bloody magistrate let them take him. Some guff about co-operation and precedent.' He slammed his fist against the door jamb. 'You should have seen Johnson's face when the Yank MPs led him out. Smirking to beat the band.'

'What now?' she asked.

'There isn't anything.' His voice rose. 'The Americans just took him. That's it. All done.' He started towards his own office. 'Get Ellison on the phone, will you? I want to see him as soon as possible.'

'Yes, sir.'

'Captain Ellison's out.' The American voice at the other end of the line was polite but firm.

'When will he be back?'

'No idea, ma'am. Do you want to leave a message for him?'

He'd be more likely to ring back if he thought it was something personal.

'Yes please, if you don't mind. Can you tell him Mrs Armstrong would like to speak to him?'

'I'll see the Captain gets this when he comes in, ma'am.'

Lottie replaced the receiver gently. 'He's out,' she told McMillan. 'I left a message asking him to ring me.'

'We could just go out there.' He was prowling restlessly, still fuelled by all the anger inside.

'What good will that do?' she asked. 'We can't just barge our way through to his office and see if he's around.'

McMillan pursed his lips, took another Four Square from the packet and lit it. 'What are we supposed to do, then? Sit here and twiddle our thumbs and hope he deigns to pick up the phone? How in God's name did they even know we had Johnson? Why would they care that much about a deserter? Something's going on.'

'And you think it's connected to Hilliard?'

'I'm bloody certain it is.'

She went through the list once more, all the items they'd found at Johnson's hideaway. McMillan had been right about one thing: taking this off the street would put a real crimp in the black market in Leeds. These weren't small backstreet bargains or whispers in the pub. The sheer amount and variety of items meant it was carefully organised. It was a business, and someone was making very good money off it. Someone who was powerful enough to know what was happening and to pull plenty of strings.

There were two possibilities. And either one could fit the bill.

The harsh ring of the phone pulled her out of her thoughts.
'WAPC Armstrong.'

'You left a message for me to call you.' He sounded worried.
'Is something wrong?'

'No, it's nothing like that.' Hearing his voice, she wanted to
believe he was a good man. But wanting was one thing; reality
was another. And she didn't know which was the truth.

'Good.' She heard him chuckle. 'You know, it took me a
minute to figure out who Mrs Armstrong was.'

'I think you know why I wanted to speak to you,' Lottie said.
It needed to come into the open; better now than later.

He was silent, long enough for her to hear the faint crackles
of the line.

'Yeah.'

'Is that all you've got to say?'

'For now. Can you meet me in an hour?'

'All right,' she agreed.

'Just you. Please.'

'No,' Lottie told him.

He sighed. 'OK.'

'Ellison rang me back.'

'Really?' He couldn't hide his astonishment.

'We're meeting in an hour.'

'Who's "we"?'

'The three of us,' Lottie said.

McMillan nodded his approval. 'Where?'

'I suggested by Thwaite's mill in Hunslet. It's quiet there, out
of the way.'

'It has to be him or del Vecchio,' McMillan said quietly. 'You
know that, don't you?'

'Yes.'

They arrived early, the Humber bumping down the unpaved lane and over a bridge built for horses and carts, not cars and lorries. She could see people moving around between the buildings of the mill, hefting sacks or standing and talking.

'I don't even know what they make out here,' Lottie said.

'Putty,' he answered. 'Plenty of need for it, all those windows broken by German bombs.'

She parked with two wheels on the grass, looking out over the canal. To the other side, the River Aire crashed over a small weir to turn a pair of water wheels. 1944 and they were still using water power for machines.

For some reason the song popped into her mind again. *Imagination.* Dancing to it on Sunday, smelling him so close, feeling his arms around her.

It was history now. The past.

McMillan sat and smoked. Lottie looked at the time. Five minutes to one. Without thinking she wound her watch, then sat back with a sigh. They didn't try to talk – what was there to say?

Maybe in a few minutes they'd learn what was happening. Or perhaps they'd hear another pack of lies. How would they even know if he told them the truth? Maybe Ellison had made up all the parts of his life he'd told her. But even as she thought it, Lottie knew he'd been honest about Seattle. That was obvious from his face.

She heard a sound and looked in the mirror. A Jeep was approaching, the white stencilled star of the US Army on the bonnet.

'I think it's time.'

CHAPTER TWENTY-FIVE

H IS brown shoes hardly seemed to make a sound as the three of them walked to stand beside the canal. Although the water hardly seemed to move, the surface smooth and even, Lottie could feel the cold and the wind blowing along the valley. She pulled up the collar of her greatcoat and glanced at Ellison.

'Jimmy Johnson,' McMillan began.

'I knew about him.' His voice was hoarse and dry.

'I see.'

'I was under orders not to do anything.' He stared at the ground, as if he couldn't bring himself to look at them. 'He wasn't my man,' he said, as if that explained it all.

'Were you under orders not to do anything about the stolen guns, too?'

'Not orders,' he said. 'Pressure. Until one was used for murder.'

'Whose orders? Who applied the pressure?'

Ellison gave a long, sad sigh. 'People at the top. Plenty of them are making money off the black market.'

'Who?' McMillan pressed.

'One-star generals. Majors.' He paused for a fraction of a second. 'Colonels.'

'You mean del Vecchio?' Lottie asked.

He turned to face her. 'Yes. He's the one who organised it all.'

The sharp scratch of a match and she smelled tobacco as McMillan lit a cigarette.

'But you went along with everything,' he said.

'I didn't have a choice. Not when they outrank me. What would you do?'

McMillan ignored the question. 'Hilliard? Who killed him?'

'I don't know. Not for sure, anyway,' he added. 'But I'd guess it was del Vecchio.'

'How much do you really know?' Lottie asked. When he didn't answer, she repeated, 'How much, Cliff?'

'Not a lot. I tried to keep my distance.'

'Tried to ignore it?' There was acid in the chief super's voice.

'If that's what you want to think.' He was silent for a moment. 'I was a good cop in Seattle. I enjoyed it. I like keeping order. But this is different. When the people who are giving you orders every day are the bad guys, what can you do?'

'Hobson's choice,' McMillan said.

'Yeah. A rock and a hard place.' He turned towards Lottie. 'Just because I'm a captain doesn't mean I have any power. I'd been told to keep my nose out of things.'

'Told?' she asked.

'Told.'

'I want del Vecchio,' McMillan said. 'I want to question him properly, down at the station.'

Ellison shook his head. 'It won't happen. They won't allow it. The people right at the top, I mean. He really is a spy and he's good. We'll all be heading over to France pretty soon; they need him. The way I hear it, he already has a network in place over there. It doesn't matter how greedy he is, they're not going to sacrifice him.'

'So he walks away from everything? Scot free?'

'Pretty much.'

'Last night…' Lottie began. Ellison looked at her, confused.
'What about it?'

'You were asking me what we'd been doing.'

'I was making conversation. You know why I came over.'

'I thought I did.'

'Look, the first I heard about Johnson being arrested was this
morning. The colonel had guys working all night.'

She wanted to believe him. It should have made her feel
better to know he wasn't behind it all. Yet somehow it seemed
to make no difference at all. Truth, lies; they were all a tangle.
A pair of swans glided by, regal and aloof, not even noticing
the people.

'So he'll go home richer and not a stain on his character?'
McMillan asked.

'Just like the general and the major.'

'Couldn't you report them?' Lottie asked.

'Who to? They're my senior officers. Even if I found someone who'd listen, it's my word against theirs. I'm the one with
the lowest rank.' He shrugged. 'Who do you think people are
going to believe?'

'Then what do we do now?' McMillan wondered. He took a
last drag from his cigarette and tossed it into the canal.

'We all walk away,' Ellison told him. 'I know,' he continued
before the super could object. 'It's not right. But your murderer's dead. You've broken up their little ring. They won't be
starting another one here – we won't be around long enough.
Isn't that something?'

'No. It's not enough. I still have too many questions.'

'Then you'd better ask them while you have the chance.'

They all turned. He was ten yards away, hands pushed into the pockets of his greatcoat. None of them had heard him approach.

Lottie's mouth felt dry. She stared at del Vecchio, seeing the arrogant smile on his lips, the mole dark on his cheek. He was cocky, he was the winner. Nothing could touch him.

'Well?' he said.

'How did you know we'd be here?' she asked. She was the one who'd chosen the place.

'Your boyfriend needs to check his mirror when he's driving.' He shook his head. 'I thought you were better than that, Captain.'

'Hilliard,' McMillan said. Over at the mill an engine started with a grinding of gears, then a deep, repetitive thrum like a muffled drumbeat.

'I met him at Johnson's place. He was small-time.' He made the man sound like nothing. 'But he knew Leeds, I figured I could use him here and there.'

'And Pamela Dixon?' Lottie asked. Hers was the death that didn't make any sense at all.

'The lady speaks.' He gave her a small, mocking bow and she had the urge to slap his face. 'I met her in a pub. She'd come up here with her boyfriend, they had a row and she stormed out.'

'Shire Oak Road?' she continued.

'I told you, I'd been looking at it as a billet. We went up there, fooled around a bit and had a couple of drinks. She passed out. Johnson's place was pretty close. Hilliard was there. He said he'd see she got back to her hotel.' For a short moment his voice became fragile. 'I didn't know he was planning to kill her. Or the others.'

'And how easy was it to kill him, Colonel?' McMillan said.

'Simple enough.' He shrugged. 'He was a murderer. You'd have caught him sooner or later.'

'And you didn't want to risk the house of cards falling down?'

She caught a movement from the corner of her eye. A blur. By the time she focused, McMillan had the Webley in his hand, pointing at del Vecchio.

'I'm arresting you for the murder of George Hilliard. You've admitted it in front of witnesses.'

The Colonel didn't move. His expression didn't even change.

'No,' he said. 'You're not. You've had your explanation. Now the party's over and your case is closed. It's time to go. Do you understand, Chief Superintendent?'

McMillan pulled back the hammer. The sharp click seemed very loud.

'Don't,' del Vecchio said. His voice was still calm, no sign of fear in his eyes. 'No arrests. Nothing.'

'Put your hands out for the cuffs.' The gun was steady in his hand.

For a second the men stared at each other. Then, very slowly, the colonel started to bring his hands from his coat pockets. She couldn't believe it. Was he giving up?

The shot exploded. It made her ears ring. Beside her, McMillan seemed to fall in slow motion. The revolver tumbled out of his hand.

She was screaming, already on her knees beside him when the second bullet came.

CHAPTER TWENTY-SIX

B LACK for the funeral. Skirt, coat, hat, shoes. She sat near the back of the church. Sarah McMillan was in the front pew, with her daughter in her Wrens uniform, a son in Air Force blue on the other side. Other friends and relatives scattered around. And policemen, dozens of them. All ranks, from bobbies to brass. The Chief Constable, his voice grave, gave the eulogy.

Lottie didn't listen. She didn't need to. She'd known the man.

CID officers from across Leeds made up the pall bearers. Andrews, Smith, some faces she didn't recognise took the weight and carried the coffin. The others filed out. Sarah spotted her, a glance and a nod from under the black veil.

She sat after they'd all gone, gave them time to leave for Lawnswood cemetery. This had been enough; she didn't want to be there for the burial.

He must have died instantly, she learned later; that was what the post-mortem report said. The bullet had pierced his heart.

But she stayed on her knees next to the canal, cradling his head, trying to talk to him through her tears, to keep him here, willing him to stay alive.

'You're not going to die on me now, John McMillan. What will Sarah say?'

Someone from the mill must have rung for an ambulance. She could hear the bell, then a man's hands were pulling her gently away.

'We'll take care of him now, love.'

Lottie daren't look away as they put him on the stretcher. If she did, he might die.

A different hand on her shoulder. This one smelt of cordite.

'I'm sorry.' The words broke the spell. They let the truth in. McMillan was dead. She'd lost the power to keep him alive.

There was blood on her hands, on the skirt of her uniform. But it really didn't matter any more.

Lottie turned her head. Del Vecchio was sprawled on the ground. Half his face was gone, a dark pool soaking into the dirt by his head. His right arm was angled away from his body, still holding the pistol.

Ellison put his arm around her shoulders. He felt warm. Human. Alive. But Lottie pulled away. She closed her eyes, wishing the world would just go away, that she'd blink and vanish.

But it could never be so easy. Life wouldn't let that happen. It needed cruelty. It demanded blood sacrifices. She heard the ambulance men load the second body and close the back doors of the van.

When she looked again, some of the workers had gathered near the factory gates, smoking and watching them.

'I guess your guys will be out here pretty soon,' Ellison said.

'Yes.' They'd gather their evidence and take their statements. But words wouldn't bring John McMillan back. They wouldn't make his death reasonable.

'I had to do it,' Ellison said. The words seemed to rush out of him. 'He'd have gotten away with it otherwise. They'd have shipped him out, the brass would have avoided a political incident and they'd have put it all behind them.' He turned to look at her, pain in his eyes.

Inspector Andrews questioned her. Smith was with Ellison. One of the women from the mill brought out mugs of tea, hot and strong and sweet. As she held it she realised how cold her hands were.

She talked, living through it all again, seeing everything and feeling the wrench in her heart. She saw Ellison walk away and start the Jeep. A quick wave of his hand and he was gone.

When it was over she sat in the Humber. The car felt empty without him. Everything seemed pointless. She turned the key and the engine caught.

Lottie didn't drive straight back to Millgarth. McMillan's house first. Sarah would have had the news. But she deserved the whole story.

She typed up the final report. Two days since he'd died. All the paperwork, the endless questioning. And her letter. Her resignation.

She couldn't be a part of this any more. She'd only joined up because he asked her. A few more minutes and she'd be a civilian again.

That morning a rumour had buzzed around the station. Helen had rung from the switchboard, eager to pass on the gossip.

'Have you heard?' Her voice bubbled with excitement.

'Heard what?' She knew her voice was dull and uninterested. She didn't care. Whatever this news was, it couldn't touch her.

'The Yanks are moving out. Going south. Lorries full of them.'

'I see.'

She hadn't heard from him since it happened. Perhaps he'd write sometime. A new base, a new town. Or perhaps there was nothing more to say.

Lottie gathered her things and put them in her handbag. Outside, the evening sun was shining.

She'd be fine.

ABOUT THE AUTHOR

CHRIS NICKSON is a popular music journalist and crime novelist whose fiction has been named best of the year in 2011 by *Library Journal* and in 2017 by Booklist. Specialising in historical crime, Chris is the author of three series for The Mystery Press: a medieval mystery series set in fourteenth-century Chesterfield; the private investigator Dan Markham series set in 1950s Leeds, and, of course, the Lottie Armstrong series.

Also by the Author

The Crooked Spire
The Saltergate Psalter
The Holywell Dead

*

Dark Briggate Blues: A Dan Markham Mystery
The New Eastgate Swing: A Dan Markham Mystery

*

Modern Crimes: A WPC Lottie Armstrong Mystery

www.chrisnickson.co.uk

PRAISE FOR

Dark Briggate Blues: A Dan Markham Mystery

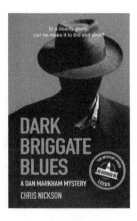

'This is a tense thriller, all the more disturbing for the ordinariness of its setting among the smoky, rain-slicked streets of a northern industrial city. Nickson has captured the minutiae of the mid-20th century perfectly.'
Historical Novel Society

'The book is a pacy, atmospheric and entertaining page-turner with a whole host of well-rounded characters.'
Yorkshire Post

'[*Dark Briggate Blues* is] written with an obvious affection for the private investigator genre; this is a skilful tale in an unusual setting. It has real depth which will keep you turning the pages.'
Hull Daily Mail

PRAISE FOR

The New Eastgate Swing: A Dan Markham Mystery

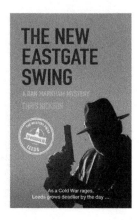

'[*The New Eastgate Swing*] provides a fast-paced and unpredictable insight into the dark underbelly of 1950s Leeds.'
Leeds City Magazine

'Chris's enormous affection for his home city shines through the books.'
Mystery People

'Chris writes with such gusto, pouring his immense knowledge and passion for Leeds into every story he brings to life, and I love his clever fusion of history with fiction.'
theculturevulture.co.uk

 The destination for history
www.thehistorypress.co.uk